WHISPERS OF FIRE AND SHADOW

Kristine Starling

STARLING HOUSE
BOOKS

Printed in the United States of America.

Author email : author.kristinestarling@gmail.com
Author website : kristinestarling.com

Cover design by Kristine Starling.

ISBN - Paperback: 979-8-9989282-0-8

First Edition : August 2025

STARLING HOUSE
BOOKS

Author's Note

Writing is an incredibly rewarding experience, but it's not without its challenges. It requires patience, dedication, and an openness to growth. I wish I had started this journey earlier in life, but I'm grateful for what it has taught me about resilience, creativity, and the art of storytelling.

While none of the characters are based on one specific person, I've sprinkled pieces of myself throughout the story, especially in Autumn's struggles with feeling out of place. Her journey reflects some of my own, and writing this book has been a way of reconnecting with parts of myself I didn't realize were there.

My greatest hope for this book is that it resonates with those who feel like outsiders, just as Autumn does. I want readers to know that they're not alone in their struggles and that there is beauty in discovering who you truly are.

Whispering Pines, with all its magic and mystery, is a reminder that everyone has a story, and every story has its own magic. I hope you find a piece of yours in these pages.

For my sisters.

"I am out with lanterns, looking for myself."
- Emily Dickinson

PROLOGUE:
THE WATCHER ON THE EAVES

They say there's a cat in Whispering Pines who remembers more than any creature ought. He drifts through the alleys and rafters like smoke from an old hearth-fire, lingering in places even ghosts have abandoned.

Some say he was born in the roots of the first tree felled to build the town. Others, that he will pad its rooftops long after the last stone sinks into moss. But all agree on this: when his eyes are upon you, something beneath the earth begins to wake.

He watched now from his perch atop a sagging rooftop. The night air bit with a cruel sharpness, the kind that slid beneath fur like fleas, itching with old memory.

Below, the square lay still. The inn's hearth was dark. No tavern songs stumbled into the street. No children shrieked past with careless joy. Only the statue remained, ancient and rain-slick, arms outstretched as if offering to a god long silent.

The cat sat unmoving, tail tucked close, a gargoyle carved from onyx. His eyes burned like embers, low and steady.

She had touched it again, the girl who belonged to no one, as if carved from the same sorrow that built the ruins. Foolhardy. Or brave. He no longer bothered to tell the difference. Both tasted the same when ruin came.

He remembered another. A girl with eyes like sapphires. She too had reached for what should have been left to crumble.

The cat rose. His bones spoke softly of the years, each step a whisper from a life too long lived. He stretched, arched like a bowstring drawn, and flowed down the roofline.

Along the gutter, across the beam, down to the cobbles. Silent, always. Silence was his birthright. The vines had returned, creeping like old lies, coiling between the stones. He paused, sniffed. Blood. Still warm in the memory of the ground.

He hissed, a low, curling sound like steam from a cracked kettle, and the vines recoiled. They knew him. He had burned them once, and they bore the scar.

He circled the statue. Once, she had known him; called him not by name, but by truth. In the old tongue. In the old days. Now she stood blind and empty-handed, waiting for a girl who had not yet chosen whether to flee or to fight.

But the fire was in her. He had felt it stir beneath her skin, as if her bones remembered what her mind had not yet dared to dream. The fire was older than kings. Older than the stones.

A footstep. A shift in the wind.

A man passed. Cloak spotless. Boots that did not know mud. He smelled of roses and soil, of caskets sealed too tightly. Of magic that had been bled dry.

The cat's ears flicked back. His tail twitched once. Watching was enough.

When the man had vanished into the dark, the cat sprang into the crook of the statue's arms. It welcomed him like it always had, a shrine forgotten but not abandoned. He rubbed against the cold stone with a low, contented purr, as if greeting an old friend.

He sat there a moment, nestled where lost things belonged. Then he was gone as cats go. Without sound. As if he had never been there at all.

CHAPTER 1:

A MAN OF ICE AND SHADOW

Time had not been kind to the old house, and kindness was never its due. Tonight, the town would gather, not to remember, but to decide whether to bury it deeper…or unearth what should have stayed in the ground.

As dusk pressed its fingers against the windows of the town hall, the council took their seats; seven souls, chosen not by blood, but by the trust of their neighbors. No single leader held sway here. Even under the distant shadow of the Sylvancrest monarchy, Whispering Pines remained a place apart, its fate guarded by the Illumine Mountains.

Autumn Ashwood sat in the back row, where shadows softened the hard edges of the room. Her fingers fidgeted with the edge of her sleeve, tugging at a loose thread as if it might anchor her thoughts.

Would people even listen to me if I were up there?

The seat beside her remained empty. She'd come to observe, not to speak. Yet part of her wished Evelyn would glance her way, offer the smallest nod, some unspoken assurance that her thoughts mattered, and that her presence meant something more than a silent witness.

Beside Evelyn sat Henry, the elderly bookstore owner. He was a man who had seen much and bore the weight of it with dignity.

Clara and Thomas, the farmers, who had spent their lives coaxing life from the ground, brought the earth's voice to the table. Rosemary, the schoolteacher, spoke for the future with a deep passion for the children and their learning. Samuel, the blacksmith, was a man of iron and fire, his booming voice and unyielding will a shield for the town's safety and prosperity.

And then there was Birdie, who tended the Willow's Rest Inn alongside her brother, Callum; its cozy hearth and rustic charm were a refuge for travelers and locals alike.

Samuel's voice broke through, steady, deep, and much too close. Autumn inhaled sharply, her fingers curling into her lap.

How long have I been gone from the conversation?

"We need to discuss the old abandoned house on the edge of town," he said, looking at the other council members. "It's been a safety hazard for so many years."

Clara sat forward, a line forming between her eyebrows. "I've learned from some of the neighbors that it's still attracting unwanted attention from nosy children. We need to decide whether to demolish it or renovate it."

Thomas nodded. "Renovating it would be a huge project, and costly. However, demolishing it and recycling what materials we can would be more feasible. We could let the space grow into nature again."

"It's important we make a decision soon before it becomes more of a problem," Rosemary added.

Evelyn spoke softly. "I think it's best to demolish it. The safety of our town comes first. We can make sure to preserve any historical artifacts we find and let the rest return to nature."

A chair scraped against the wooden floor. The candle flames trembled, though no wind stirred, flickering once, twice, then steady again, as if the room itself had taken notice as a man rose to speak.

Maxwell Wolfsbane.

He did not rush. He never did. Instead, he took a moment, adjusting the cuffs of his dark coat, surveying the room as though counting pieces on a board only he could see. When he spoke, his voice was smooth, a thing carved and polished from stone.

"The house has stood for generations; it has endured the rise and fall of time, standing when lesser things have crumbled. Some see decay, but I see something else…opportunity." His fingers traced slow, thoughtful patterns against the wooden table.

"You call it ruin. I call it a foundation. Restore it, and you do more than save a building; you reclaim a piece of Whispering Pines itself."

A slow, measured breath. "Yes, it will be costly. But what of worth is ever won without sacrifice?" His lips curled at the edges, and something flickered behind his eyes. "A place like that deserves more than dust and neglect. It deserves to be remembered."

The room murmured; some nodded, others frowned. Maxwell Wolfsbane had always taken an interest in the house. Too much interest. Not like the others, who saw it as a relic of another time, a crumbling ruin to be debated over and forgotten again.

He watched it the way a wolf watches wounded prey: quietly, patiently, waiting for the right moment to move.

Autumn shifted in her chair, the wood creaking like old bones beneath her. Her fingers were now laced together in her lap, her knuckles white as midwinter snow, and memories rose like the tide in a storm-wracked bay.

The first time she had laid eyes upon him, the skies had wept, and the smell of wet stone and moldering books had saturated the air of the Whispering Pines Bookstore and Library, like the crypts beneath an ancient castle after the spring thaw. He had come without herald or announcement, as silent as poison taking its victim, his presence consuming the candlelight as surely as night swallows day.

And then he looked at her.

For the space of a single heartbeat, the careful mask he wore—polished as rare steel and twice as unyielding—fractured, and she glimpsed what lurked beneath. Surprise, sharp as a dagger's point. Recognition, cold as a northern wind. And something else, something that reminded her of the tales old folk used to tell of the great darkness, when winter fell and did not lift for a generation.

Her breath had frozen in her throat, her heart fluttering like a wounded sparrow. *He knows me*, she thought. *Or rather, he knows something about me.*

His gaze probed as a scholar examining an ancient text, as if her jade-green eyes concealed some secret even she had not discovered. It had not been the idle curiosity of a man encountering a stranger in a public house.

No, it ran deeper. As if looking upon her face, he had seen a ghost from times long past, and had not expected that ghost to be watching him in return.

Maxwell was handsome and stood tall as any royal guardsman in Sylvancrest City. His voice never rose above that which a lord might use when addressing his sworn men, his courtesy as practiced as any courtier in the high halls of Greenhaven Keep.

But beneath his chiseled face and his dark, neatly styled hair lay something else, a coldness in his eyes, an emptiness that reminded her of the waters of the seas in her books, where sailors claimed great sea monsters slumbered in the depths. She had offered him a smile, but her insides had twisted like snakes in a pit from the moment his eyes touched hers.

Even now, as he spoke of ordinary things, that feeling returned to her, urging her to hear not just the words that passed his lips but the silence that lingered between them, where truth often hid like a cutpurse in the shadows.

Autumn had also been fascinated by the old house and wandered there in her youth, led by the restless stirrings of curiosity, the same reckless yearning that had pulled many before her toward places best left undisturbed. But her fascination was not like Maxwell's.

The other children at the orphanage had whispered, weaving stories of ghosts and curses, of witches who never truly died and doors that led to places no one should go.

It loomed at the edge of Whispering Pines, where the wild pressed in, ever hungry, past the violets, their delicate petals a soft spill of color against the green. Past the hydrangeas, with dreamy blues and passionate pinks. Past the peonies, full of secrets and old-world romance.

A lonely husk of stone and timber, it stood half-sunken into the earth, its grandeur gnawed away by time and neglect.

Ivy clung to its walls like grasping fingers, twisting through the fractures in the weathered masonry. The roof sagged, its bones exposed to the sky where the wind wailed through broken slats.

The front door, crooked on rusted hinges, swayed with the breath of the wind, groaning as though protesting its fate. Windows, long shattered, glared out like empty eyes, their jagged edges clouded with the filth of long years.

The silence within was broken only by the soft complaint of rotting floorboards beneath an intruder's step. Yet even in decay, the past refused to be forgotten. A tarnished candelabra still stood upon the mantle, its filigree dulled but untouched by ruin.

In the darkest corner, a tattered tapestry hung limp, its once-vivid portrayal of sorcery now faded. A half-toppled bookcase cradled books with spines that cracked and flaked at the touch, their titles lost to dust and time.

On a small table, a mirror, its glass marred with age, reflected only the ghosts of memory. Beside it, an ornate box lay open, its treasures spilled carelessly upon the wood: a dragon's-head pendant and a ring, its emblem of thorns and roses barely visible beneath the layers of dust.

"The house is beyond saving." Samuel's words brought Autumn back. She blinked, her fingers tightening around the hem of her sleeve.

"The cost is too great. The structure is failing. It serves no purpose but to waste away. It will be torn down before winter, its remnants repurposed, its bones returned to the earth."

Agreement rippled through the chamber. Maxwell Wolfsbane did not move at first. His expression remained composed—his shoulders loose. A man unaffected. A man above it all.

But Autumn saw the way his fingers curled ever so slightly, slow and deliberate, against the polished wood of the table. The way his jaw tensed for just a fraction of a second before he exhaled, measured and even, as if forcing himself to release the breath at all.

"A shame," he said, eyes narrowing. "Whispering Pines is so quick to erase its own past. But I suppose practicality must always win over sentiment." He turned his eyes toward the assembly. And for the briefest moment, Autumn swore she saw something in them—something calculating, as if he were already shaping a new plan in the ruins of the old one.

He adjusted the cuffs of his coat as if the conversation had already left his mind. But she knew better. He was not a man who lost easily.

***

Autumn began the familiar walk home. The evening should have been no different from countless others, save that the world had changed somehow. No wind stirred the dead leaves; no spring peepers dared break the silence.

Her foot caught on something unseen, and the ground betrayed her. She fell forward onto the old cobblestones. Pain flared sharp and sudden as thorns pierced the flesh of her palms and caught at her sleeve and the hem of her dress. Blood welled between her fingers, bright as rubies against her fair skin.

A curse escaped her lips, one she'd learned from the traders who frequented the dockside taverns. She dropped her eyes at the stone to see what had ensnared her.

Roses. Vines, dark and twisted, with thorns like tiny daggers.

She knew every crack in this road, every loose stone and bit of broken paving. The vines had not been there yesterday, nor any day before in her memory.

Yet now they crept like something summoned, black-veined and blooming from earth that had lived here since the founding days of Eiryndor, long before Sylvancrest had a name of its own.

The air changed then, stirring with sudden vigor. It carried scents both familiar and wrong, roses from a garden long abandoned, soil from a freshly dug grave, leather from the skin of some strange creature.

"The ground has tasted your blood now," came a voice from above. "Few give the cobbles such a gift."

For a moment, she forgot the sting of scraped skin and the throbbing in her palms.

Who would say such a thing?

Maxwell Wolfsbane stood above her, a dark silhouette against the moonlight. His clothes were fine, and his boots were polished to a mirror shine. No dust clung to his cloak.

While she bled upon the street, his eyes held the cold detachment of a man who had watched others fall a thousand times and found each one amusing. There was something in his gaze that spoke of secrets kept and pleasures taken in the dark.

Her pulse quickened, sharp and erratic, a bird trapped in a cage of bone.

"What...what did you say?"

Maxwell blinked. "I said, 'Are you hurt?'"

He stretched out his hand, sheathed in black leather. She hesitated, and a warning crawled through her belly like a serpent.

Yet, what reason did she have to refuse him? She swallowed her fear and placed her bloodied hand in his. His fingers closed around hers with a grip as cold as the harshest winter and he pulled her upright with the ease a man might lift a child or a butcher might hoist a slaughtered lamb.

But she withdrew her hand quickly and brushed the dirt from her dress, her eyes drawn back to the vines that had now claimed the path.

"Strange," she said.

"What troubles you?" Maxwell asked, his head canting to one side like a crow eyeing a corpse.

"These vines," she replied, brow furrowing beneath her ginger hair. "They've never grown here before. Not...not in all my years."

Maxwell reached down and plucked a rose from the vine. Its crimson petals were fresh with dew. He turned it between his fingers, considering, before offering it to her.

"A gift," he murmured. "A reminder that even from the cruelest roots, beauty may rise."

The bloom was flawless, the color rich, as if it had been waiting for this moment—for his hands, for hers. Slowly, cautiously, she accepted it as he pressed it into her palm.

His fingers then extended to the golden pendant hanging from her neck, the barest touch against the delicate chain. Pleasure danced in his eyes as he toyed with the locket.

A pause stretched between them, thin as a thread, waiting to snap.

"What sleeps beneath the earth need not stay buried forever... May I escort you to your door?" he asked, his tone courteous as any knight's, though no true knight stood before her.

She pulled away from him, his fingers slipping away from the locket.

Then, with the ease of a gentleman, he extended his arm.

"No." The word left her lips before she could soften it. Too quick, too sharp. Though his smile did not falter, something in his posture shifted, a subtle withdrawal, like a blade slipping back into its sheath.

"Another evening, perhaps," he said with a shallow bow of his head. He turned away without awaiting her response and walked down the empty street.

Autumn watched him go, the unease still coiling in her belly. She waited in the square until she was certain Maxwell had disappeared into the shadows.

She approached the ancient statue that had stood in the Whispering Pines square since before the oldest grandmother's grandmother had drawn breath. Her steps were light, as if afraid to disturb the silence. The figure was carved from pale marble that had grown mottled with age, gray and white like the beard of a wise man who had seen too many winters.

The woman's face was peaceful, her lips parted as though she had been stilled mid-utterance, some secret counsel now lost to the cruel passage of time.

Her arms reached outward in an eternal gesture, but her hands cupped nothing but air, a void where once some treasure had rested, something precious that had been claimed by thieves or time or treachery.

What had those stone fingers once cradled?

A book of ancient wisdom, some claimed, its pages now dust and its knowledge forgotten. A lantern to guide lost souls through darkness, others whispered. A bird with wings unfurled, ready to carry messages to distant shores.

But the truth of it, if any had ever truly known, had been ground away like wheat beneath a millstone, leaving only chaff and mystery.

The folk of the town had made their peace with not knowing. They filled the hollow spaces in their histories with comforting lies, with harmless fantasies and sweet impossibilities. But Autumn had never been one to accept the soothing balm of ignorance.

She stretched forth her hand, her flesh meeting cold stone. The marble had been worn smooth by countless seasons of wind and rain, by the touch of curious fingers much like her own.

"Who were you?" she asked, though she expected no answer.

The breeze stirred then, lifting strands of her hair—nothing more than the natural movement of air, they would say.

The stone fingers seemed to shift, stretching toward the sky as if grasping for something just beyond reach. Autumn blinked hard, and the illusion vanished.

She withdrew her hand as though the stone had suddenly burned hot. The statue had heard her, but the hands were still again, lifeless, as they had always been, a riddle with no key to unlock its meaning.

Foolish girl, they would say.

Now certain that Maxwell had taken his leave, she ran for home. Her feet struck the cobbles quick and sure, skirts clutched tightly in her fists.

The last desire in her heart was for that man of ice and shadow to appear at her cottage door, with his pleasant words that tasted of lies and his eyes that saw too much.

CHAPTER 2:
THE WHISPERING WOOD

The air smelled of snapped pine, and branches clawed at her face, thin, sharp fingers scraping skin, snagging in the tangle of her hair. Each captured strand sent a jolt of pain through her scalp.

Get through. Just get through!

She tore at the grasping wood, felt splinters bite into her palms. A final, ragged heave, and something gave way with a brittle crack.

She plunged, tumbling into white. Snowdrifts swallowed her past the knee, a sudden, shocking cold that stole her breath and bit deep into her flesh through the thin nightgown she wore in this dream place. It packed around her legs, heavy as wet sand, making each movement a trial.

Where was she? A wilderness of white stretched away under a bleak, sunless sky. She forced one leg forward, then the other, sinking deep with every step. The effort burned in her thighs, spreading upwards. Each breath was a plume of white vapor snatched away by the wind, a wind that carried the taste of ice and iron.

Cold seeped into her bones, and tiny crystals of ice clung to her lashes. Her nose and cheeks grew numb, the skin stretched tight, a frozen, rosy mask.

Ahead, the endless white yielded to a vast expanse of ice, flat and grey. The surface was crazed with dark lines, like veins in old stone—a lake, frozen solid.

Some unseen current pulled her toward it. The air grew colder still, raising the hairs on her arms beneath the useless cloth. She stumbled to the edge and peered down. The ice was thick and opaque, showing only distorted, grey reflections. Nothing else.

Then came the sound. It started not in her ears but in her teeth, a low vibration that resonated deep in her jaw. It grew, swelling from beneath the ice, a beating that became a vast and unearthly shriek. It clawed up from the black, unseen depths, the sound of something immense and ancient and utterly wrong, trapped and raging against its prison. It was the sound of a world breaking or a monster waking. Fear, colder and sharper than the wind, lanced through her gut.

Autumn's eyes snapped open. Blackness pressed close. The only sound was the frantic thunder of her own heart against her ribs and the ragged rasp of her breath. Sweat, cold as meltwater, slicked her skin beneath the covers. The awful scream still echoed in the hollows of her mind. A violent shiver wracked her frame. She fumbled for the edge of the blankets, pulling them up to her chin. A flimsy shield. It did little to banish the chill that had seeped out of the dream or the memory of the ice and the thing screaming beneath it.

***

Autumn had always seen and heard things others did not. As a child, she had spoken of such things. Magic ran through the world, she had told them, not the sort found in tavern songs or whispered over flickering hearths, but something wilder, woven into the roots of the earth and the marrow of the mountains.

The old pines leaned in her passing, their roots twisted deep in the earth, as if clinging to something lost beneath the soil. When the night stretched long and the air grew still, she swore she could hear them creaking, as if murmuring to one another in voices too slow for men to understand.

But it wasn't just the trees. The animals knew her too. They did not scatter when she drew near. They watched her with understanding, of something older than speech. Birds cocked their heads when she passed. Hares paused in their tracks, unafraid. Cats followed her like sentries. She had long since stopped questioning it. Some spoke with no words at all, with glances and gestures. Others spoke plainly, when the world had gone quiet enough to let the old magic slip through the seams.

She was ten when the lizard spoke. It was a hot day, the kind where moisture clung to the skin and every leaf drooped in protest. She had wandered to the stone wall behind the Ashwood home, where moss grew in patches and beetles skittered through the cracks. The lizard lay there, sun-drunk and still, until it turned its tiny head and blinked up at her with lidless eyes.

"You're not meant to stay here," it said.

She had stared, wide-eyed, thinking herself mad, or dreaming. But the lizard only turned away, its tail flicking once before it crawled back into the stones.

After that day, the world never felt quite silent again. The language of beasts had found her, and though she did not always understand it, she knew it came from a place older than names, older than kingdoms.

And always, there were the dreams. Vivid, unrelenting things. She saw places she had never been and heard voices that spoke her name. But no meaning ever came. They slipped from her grasp upon waking, like mist through cupped hands, haunting her more for their refusal to be known.

Even though Whispering Pines held to their legends like beggars hoarding scraps, spinning their tales of haunted glades and slumbering beasts, the villagers dismissed Autumn's claims of real magic. A harmless fancy, they called it, the nonsense of a girl with her head too deep in books.

Each year, on Legends Night, they gathered in the square beneath lantern light, raising cups to ancient heroes, retelling fables that had been told a hundred times before. Witches and kings, lost princes and vengeful gods, their names changed with each telling, shaped to fit the whims of the storyteller.

Children grew up with these stories, learned them by heart, passed them down like heirlooms. But that was all they were— stories.

No one truly believed. Not anymore. Perhaps once, long ago, there had been something real at the heart of it all, some sliver of truth buried beneath the dust of forgotten years. But if there was, it had long since faded into myth.

Now the people of Whispering Pines wove their fictions to fill the void where history should have been. But magic, they said, was for fools and children.

Foolish girl, they'd say. By the time she had seen thirteen summers, the laughter had faded. Whispers followed her instead, not cruel but cautious, as if she were a girl out of step with the world.

Even Auntie Mae at the Ashwood Home, warm as she was, had told her, "Best to keep those thoughts quiet, love." But the thoughts did not keep.

The town had cradled Autumn since she was small, yet she had never shaken the feeling that it was waiting. Watching. Biding its time. Whispering Pines was no mere town. It breathed, it watched, it remembered. The stone paths, worn smooth by generations of weary feet, wound through streets older than Sylvancrest Kingdom itself.

She had spent her childhood beneath the shadows of the forest, The Whispering Wood, she called it, running where others feared to tread. Like the other orphans, she played in the Emerald Glade, that patch of earth neither wholly of the town nor entirely of the wilds.

While the others kept to the open space, their laughter ringing beneath the sun-dappled canopy, Autumn remained at the edges, where the trees grew thick, and the air turned cool.

But she wandered deeper than the rest, drawn by the unseen things that rustled just beyond sight. She never strayed too far, never beyond where she could still glimpse the glade through the tangled branches.

The glade was beautiful, but beauty could be a cruel thing. Autumn knew what the others did not, that the glade was no mere clearing. It was a threshold. A place where one might step too far and find the world had shifted beneath their feet. The trees stood too close, their roots twisting together, their tangled branches blotting out the sun like the fingers of unseen giants. Moss crept thick over stone, and the earth smelled damp, rich, alive.

The others might laugh and shriek as they ran through the tall grass, but they did not hear the forest as she did. They did not feel its pulse beneath their skin, nor the weight of unseen eyes waiting in the hollows between the trees.

The forest had always been watching her. That much, she knew. But whether it meant to guard her or claim her, she had yet to learn.

At the orphanage, she tried to be like them. She spoke when spoken to, worked when work was given, played when play was expected. She mimicked their smiles, their laughter, but the mask never quite fit. There was always a distance, an invisible wall between her and the others, as if she were watching the world through a pane of clouded glass.

Her differences were not loud, not glaring. No, they were quieter, deeper; woven into the way she moved, the way she listened, the way she knew things she could not explain.

And so, when the real world failed to make space for her, she found refuge in another.

In books, magic was real. Forests were alive, ancient things with voices of their own, and those who wandered too deep did not always return the same. The pages held truths the world refused to see, and in their ink-stained depths, she was not strange, not misplaced.

She was right.

She sat curled in shadowed corners, losing herself in stories of forgotten creatures and vanished kingdoms. The books did not laugh at her. They did not tell her she was wrong. They did not ask her to explain what she had always known in her bones.

But from those corners, she could still hear them, the shouts, the laughter, the sound of footfalls against stone. A life that was near enough to touch, yet always just beyond her grasp. They were not unkind to her, but kindness did not make her one of them.

Perhaps it was better this way. She belonged to a different path. And though she did not yet know where it would lead, she always knew she would walk it alone.

She let herself sink into the pages, let the words carry her to lands where magic still lived, where girls like her were not outcasts but heroines. In her stories, she was bold. She was strong. She was meant for more.

One day, perhaps, she would find that world beyond the pages. But for now, she had her books.

As she grew from a curious child into a young woman, she found comfort in the town's constancy; the way the seasons turned without fail, the scent of rain-soaked earth after a storm, the hush of snowfall blanketing the rooftops. It was in the creak of old wooden signs swaying in the wind, the murmur of the Starlit Run, the flicker of lantern light against stone.

The winding streets, the towering pines—these were the things that held her, that anchored her to the real world.

And most of all, she found it in the Whispering Pines Bookstore. When personal connections failed her, the books did not. They waited, patient and unchanging.

For the last five of her twenty-five years, Autumn had been more than a fixture within the bookstore's walls—she had become its lifeblood. Her duties stretched far beyond ledgers and sales; she was a caretaker of stories, a guardian of the written word. The shelves thrived beneath her touch, their contents as familiar to her as the lines of her own hands.

Every spine she straightened, every fragile page she turned, was a silent vow to preserve the stories that lived within those timeworn covers.

Chapter 3:
The Road to Familiar Places

Autumn clung to her rituals like a drowning woman to driftwood. Each morning, she woke before the sun, slipping from the tangled warmth of her blankets into the stillness of her cottage. The floorboards, worn smooth by time and habit, creaked beneath her bare feet as she crossed to the washbasin.

She bathed in silence, letting the warm water banish the weight of sleep, scrubbing away the half-remembered ghosts of dreams. Outside, the world stirred in quiet symphony: the distant trill of a morning bird, the gentle murmur of the Starlit Run. She soaked it in, let the sounds settle around her like a second skin, grounding her in the waking world.

The morning light slanted through her window, painting gold across the wooden walls, catching in the strands of her long ginger hair as she combed through them with careful fingers. There was a rhythm to it, a quiet order to be kept; each strand untangled, each motion deliberate. She had always found comfort in small things, in tasks that could be done with steady hands and an unburdened mind.

Last came the locket. She fastened the chain at her throat, letting the heart-shaped pendant settle against her skin. The amethyst inside gleamed like trapped twilight, its violet depths hinting at secrets she had never quite unraveled.

She had worn it for as long as she could remember. It belonged to her mother, or so she had been told, though no one had ever spoken her name. A relic of a life she had never known.

The town was just stirring when she stepped outside. The streets of Whispering Pines stretched before her, the air carrying the scent of damp earth and woodsmoke. She kept her gaze ahead, lost in thought, until a flash of color pulled her from her reverie.

There, nestled among a tangle of thorns, was a single rosebud, its petals just beginning to unfurl. A splash of crimson in a sea of green. Sharp. Unexpected.

She had walked this path a hundred times, traced these same cobbled streets through every season, yet the rose had never been there before. She frowned, tilting her head, as if the flower might answer the question forming in her mind.

What are you doing here?

It felt strange, out of place, as though it had no business blooming in this forgotten patch of bramble. The thorns should have choked it, the morning frost should have stifled it, but here it was, bold, unyielding.

Her fingers twitched at her side. She did not dare touch it. Was it meant for her? Had the world left her a message, wrapped in velvet petals and guarded by thorns?

A foolish thought, folks would say.

The streets twisted and turned like old riverbeds, their stones worn smooth by the passing of generations. How many footsteps had trod this path before her? How many lives had come and gone, leaving nothing behind but fading echoes and dust?

The cottages stood close, their timber frames bowed with age, their walls soaked with the scent of damp wood and memory. Chimneys jutted skyward, their plumes of smoke curling into the crisp morning air. The scent of burning cedar and fresh-baked bread drifted through the narrow lanes, warm and familiar.

The Spellbound Canvas stood just as it always had. Peonies burst beside its steps like drunken revelers, their petals flung wide in a reckless spill of blush and cream. Ivy framed the weathered door, and the windows were dulled with the scent of oil and varnish.

If magic had taken root anywhere in Whispering Pines, it was in the strokes of Iris Moonshade's brush. She ground her pigments from flowers, berries, and wild-growing things, many drawn from the forest itself, as though the woods had whispered their secrets into her paints.

Iris's paintings did not capture the Illumine Mountains as they were, but as they might have been before men carved roads through the valleys and named the peaks as if they owned them. Her brushstrokes breathed, whispered, and conjured, turning canvas into something alive.

Autumn had seen the mountains a hundred times in Iris's work, the silver-threaded waterfalls tumbling into unseen depths, the sky bruised with the coming of dusk, the great pine forests stretching beyond sight. But only in paintings.

She had never traveled that far, never stood beneath those towering peaks or felt the wind that rushed through their crags. To her, they were a dream, a place half-imagined, no more real than the stories bound between the pages of her books.

And yet, when she gazed upon Iris's work, she felt as though she had. The mountains in those paintings knew her, even if she did not yet know them.

Iris herself was as much a legend as the lands she painted. She carried her years like a cloak, moving with the grace of an old wolf that had outlived many winters. She had reached her golden years, but that had not diminished her.

Tall and statuesque, she seemed carved by the hands of some forgotten god. She walked among the townsfolk like a queen without a throne, her golden hair crowned with woven wildflowers, her deep violet robes a mirror of the twilight sky.

Autumn passed the shop without pause, though the scent of linseed oil clung to her as she went.

A turn of the street brought her before The Enchanted Bloom, Flora Hawthorne's domain. The apothecary crouched low between its neighbors, its sign groaning in the wind, its windows dark with old glass and shadowed shelves. The place had an air of something living, something ancient. Even from the street, Autumn could smell it, the sharp tang of crushed leaves, the ghostly sweetness of dried lavender, the faintest trace of something metallic, like old blood and rust.

Through the warped pane, she glimpsed Flora moving between the cluttered shelves, her hands busy, her face bent in concentration. The shop was more than an apothecary, more than walls and wares. It was a place where the line between remedy and hex blurred, where common folk came seeking cures and left with whispers of something older, something deeper.

On some mornings, Flora would glance up, her warm, brown eyes meeting Autumn's through the glass. Today was one such morning. She raised a hand in a brief greeting, fingers still dusted with some nameless powder.

A healer's hands, always at work, always shaping something unseen. Autumn wondered what remedies Flora was crafting today, what quiet secrets lay bottled behind that glass.

Autumn lifted her own hand in return before pressing on.

The town was waking now, the air alive with the songs of birds—sparrows and thrushes, wrens and robins, their melodies weaving through the stillness like threads of gold. Yet, beneath their chorus, there was a quieter music: the rustle of rabbits in the underbrush, the skitter of chipmunks across sun-dappled paths. These small creatures moved with caution, their eyes ever-watchful, a reminder that even in this tranquil place, life was a fragile thing.

Voices rose in lazy morning chatter; the world slouched into motion. But she felt apart from it, as she always had.

She pressed a hand against her locket, the metal cold beneath her fingers. There had to be more than this. There had to be more.

She paused to tighten the leather strap of her satchel. Her fingers moved from habit—bookstore keys, ledger notes, the string-wrapped parcel of repairs for the older bindings Evelyn had set aside. Everything in its place.

But then she turned the bend into the square.

And stopped.

There, at the base of the statue, sat Maxwell Wolfsbane. One leg crossed over the other, elbow resting on the back of the bench, as if he belonged to the place more than the marble did.

The bowl of his pipe glowed faintly, pulsing like a coal stirred to life. The smoke did not rise straight—it curled, coiled, moved as if it had thought. Autumn's heart did a small, unwelcome thing in her chest.

He looked at her, though his expression was unreadable, the tilt of his mouth too smooth to be careless, too polite to be kind.

Perhaps it was the smile of a man who knew he need not speak to be heard.

Autumn's hand tightened around the strap of her satchel. She did not wave. She did not nod.

But he did. Just once.

***

The soft chime above the bookstore door sang out as Autumn stepped inside. She closed the door behind her, the latch catching with a solid click. Her pulse had no business being as fast as it was. She stood still for a moment, fingers resting against the wood, listening to the silence of the shop. Only when she had drawn a breath, deep and slow, did she move past the counter and toward the teakettle. But even then, her thoughts lingered on the man outside.

He had smiled. And for reasons she couldn't name, she wished he hadn't.

But then came Papyrus, the resident feline of Whispering Pines Bookstore, acknowledging Autumn's presence with a flick of his tail. He was a sleek and contemplative cat with fur as dark as ink. He stretched lazily before blinking up at her with golden eyes that had seen more of this shop than she ever would. If the bookstore ever had a true master, it was him.

Autumn reached out, scratching behind his ears. "Still guarding the place, I see."

Papyrus let out a slow, rumbling purr, curling his tail around his paws as if to say, "As if there were any doubt."

The bookstore had stood longer than anyone could remember, its ivy-draped facade bowed under the weight of centuries. The threshold had been crossed by generations of weary travelers and quiet scholars, by poets, dreamers, and liars alike.

The shelves loomed high, their wooden frames groaning beneath the weight of a thousand untold stories. Shadows gathered in the corners, where the morning light dared not reach, and the air hung heavy with ink, leather, and the slow decay of time.

The community kettle whistled its familiar tune, a signal for Whispering Pines' early risers. Autumn poured herself a cup, the steam curling upward, warm against her face.

Clutching the steaming brew, she settled into the welcoming embrace of a faded burgundy armchair. The cushions had long since lost their firmness, their fabric softened by time and countless hours spent in their hold.

Papyrus wove between her legs, his fur brushing against her ankles before he leapt onto the armrest. He did not demand attention; he only settled there, a silent guardian, a constant in a life of unanswered questions.

She ran her fingers over his sleek coat, feeling the quiet rumble of his purr beneath her palm. "You're the only one who never expects anything from me," she said.

You never ask for more than I can give.

She couldn't recall a time when Papyrus was not part of the library; he had been there for as long as she could remember.

The tea cooled too quickly. She swallowed the last sip just as the soft chime of the door rang out. Autumn straightened, tucking a loose strand of hair behind her ear as a young man stepped inside.

"Hello," he said, his smile easy, his voice rich with the kind of confidence she had never quite mastered. "Is there a section you'd recommend? I'm looking for something captivating."

Autumn's fingers tightened around her mug. "Oh, um... Well, that depends on what you find captivating."

A slow ember of heat awakened beneath her skin.

His grin deepened. "Fair point. What about something with a bit of magic?"

Oh no. He noticed. Of course, he noticed.

"Oh, magic! Yes, that's...magical." Her tongue felt thick, the words slipping through her grasp before she could shape them properly. "The, um, fantasy section is over there. Wizards. Dragons. That sort of thing." Her skin tingled with a heat she couldn't ignore.

The young man chuckled. "Sounds perfect."

"You're welcome. Enjoy the...magic."

Enjoy the magic? If I ever needed a reason to run away and live in the forest, here it is.

She wanted to sink into the floor. Why did her tongue always betray her? Why did speech come so easily to others, while she stumbled through simple conversation like a traveler lost in fog?

She watched him go, disappearing between the shelves.

Books did not ask her to speak. They did not require small talk or easy smiles. They simply waited, patient and unchanging, offering their secrets as she turned their pages.

And yet, even in the sanctuary of ink and parchment, the questions remained—not of magic, nor dragons, nor far-off kingdoms, but of herself. Of where she had come from. Of who had left her at the orphanage all those years ago. Of the mother whose name she had never known.

She had been but a small child when the Ashwood Group Home took her in. The matrons there had provided for her needs, but no amount of bread, hot soup, or blankets could fill the hollow left by unspoken truths.

She had spent her life searching for answers in the stories of others. But buried somewhere within the corners of

Whispering Pines, she still hoped, one day, she might uncover the truth of her own tale.

Hours later, the shop lay quiet. The last of the customers had gone, their chatter fading into the old wood and flickering light. Floorboards creaked beneath Autumn's steps as she moved through the rows like a ghost.

Her fingers brushed the spines in passing; a silent goodnight to each.

Then—a sound. A soft thud. She froze, one hand resting on a shelf. Her eyes swept the dim rows.

"Papyrus?" she called. "Is that you?" No answer. Only a book on the floor. It had fallen from the topmost shelf, its spine split, pages fanned like wings caught mid-flight.

She crouched beside it, her hand brushing over the worn leather cover. The book was one of Henry's older volumes, tucked away in the corner where few bothered to look. Yet now, it lay open, the pages splayed against the wooden floor as if stirred by an unseen hand.

She tilted her head, examining the faded title. It was a book of dragon fairy tales. She had read it once or twice, long ago. Like nearly every book in this place. But why had it fallen? The air was still, the shop silent. No draft, no tremor, no hand but hers had touched the shelves.

Her fingers trembled as she lifted the book. The illustrations flickered in the low light. She closed the book slowly, her thumb tracing the embossed dragon on its cover. The shop felt colder now. The shadows longer. She looked behind her.

Nothing.

Only shelves. Only silence. Only the books.

She should have returned it. Nearly did. But that quiet summons stirred again. A whisper in her bones. The book was not finished with her.

She slipped it into her satchel and turned for home.

CHAPTER 4:

A GHOST IN THE TREES

It was neither day nor night but the uncertain hour between. Autumn traced her path homeward with careful steps, her eyes watchful for the treacherous thorns that had drawn her blood the evening prior. The memory of that fall was fresh as a new wound, and she had no desire to offer the ground a second taste of her flesh.

Ahead, where the path widened into the square, a trio of young women caught her eye.

Their laughter rang through the gathering dusk, bright and clear as silver bells on a feast day, while their smiles carried a warmth that almost lit the cobblestones beneath them. The bond between them flowed as easily as wine at a king's table, with bodies that leaned toward one another as naturally as saplings seek the sun.

They make it look as effortless as breathing, Autumn thought, a familiar hollow ache spreading beneath her ribs. *Perhaps I was never meant to share in such bonds. At least I have my books, my quiet hours, and Papyrus.*

Evelyn Meadows, the librarian, offered what companionship she could during Autumn's hours among the dust-laden shelves. Yet the winters that separated them and the different paths they had walked carved a gulf between them, one neither woman had found cause to cross.

Though they broke bread together in the silent company of leather-bound tomes, their words seldom ventured beyond discussions of old books and forgotten tales, leaving their connection as fragile as the brittle pages they both cherished.

Flora Hawthorne was the closest thing Autumn had to a friend. Where Evelyn sought knowledge in ink and paper, Flora found it in roots and petals, in the whisper of leaves stirring under the weight of a storm.

There was a thread, thin and frayed with time, that bound Autumn to Flora. It had been woven long ago, in the days when the world seemed simpler, though no less cruel. Their paths had first crossed in the days of their girlhood. It was Flora's tenth nameday, an occasion when the girls from the orphanage were invited to partake in the merriment.

Autumn remembered it still: the laughter that rang like bells, the tables laden with honeyed cakes and spiced cider, the way the firelight had danced in Flora's eyes as she opened her gifts. Even then, Flora had carried herself as though the earth itself had rocked her cradle.

Autumn had watched her from a distance, a girl with dirt on her hem and longing in her heart, wondering what it might be like to belong so completely to a place, to a family, to a life.

The thread between them had been spun that day, though neither had known it then. It was a fragile thing, easily forgotten—yet it had endured, like the roots of an ancient tree, hidden beneath the soil, waiting for the right moment to break the surface once more.

Their paths twisted and turned through the years, crossing and recrossing in the heart of Whispering Pines. Though their lives had taken different shapes, they found themselves drawn together by the town, its markets and festivals, its quiet mornings and bustling afternoons. They shared fleeting moments, brief as the flutter of a moth's wings. A nod here, a smile there, a word or two exchanged over baskets of herbs or bolts of cloth. Small things, insignificant to most, yet each one a stitch in the fabric of their shared history.

Flora had her own thoughts on magic, though they were nothing like Autumn's. To Flora, magic was the slow work of the earth, the pull of the moon over restless tides, the language of things that grew and withered and grew again. Not myths, not fairy tales, just nature's quiet inevitabilities.

Autumn had spent her life listening for something more. Flora had already made peace with what was.

The women's laughter faded behind her, and Autumn continued on her way until she was but a stone's throw from her cottage. That's when a sound reached her ears, a crack like a boot upon a fallen branch, too deliberate to be the wind's doing. Her heart seized within her chest, certain as winter's coming that Maxwell stalked her path like a cat tracking wounded prey.

She gathered her skirts and fled, swift as a hunted hare. Her cottage door, stout oak bound with iron, groaned as she thrust it open and sealed herself within, pressing her back against the weathered wood.

There she stood, still as a prey animal that senses the hunter's approach, listening for the dreaded rap of knuckles against wood, for the soft words that would doubtless follow, pleasant as summer wine yet sour beneath. Her pulse beat a frantic rhythm in her throat while sweat cooled between her shoulder blades despite the evening chill. A raven called in the distance. But no knock came to her door, no honeyed voice called her name.

When at last her breathing calmed, she moved about her small domain, hands still unsteady as she prepared her evening repast: venison left from yesterday's meal, accompanied by nuts and dried fruits. A humble feast.

As she chewed the tender meat, her gaze returned again and again to the door, to the shadows that gathered in the corners of her modest home.

She pushed her food around the plate, her appetite dwindling with each passing moment. She forced herself to take another bite, but the food turned to ash in her mouth. The silence outside pressed against her walls like a physical thing, somehow more disquieting than any sound would have been.

Autumn's fingers curled around the heart-shaped pendant, the metal familiar as her own breath. She traced its edges, grounding herself in the sensation, her other hand lingering on the doorframe. Beyond it, the night stretched vast and silent, waiting.

She hesitated. Just for a moment. Then, with a slow breath, she opened the door.

The evening kissed her skin, raising gooseflesh along her arms. The wind stirred her hair, tugging strands loose, while the hem of her nightgown rippled against her legs like the restless tide.

Twilight bled across the sky, gold and violet sinking into blue, shadows creeping long and lean over the earth. The leaves whispered as they danced on unseen currents.

She felt it then, a change in the air, subtle yet undeniable. Not quite a sound, nor a scent, but a presence—just there, just beyond reach, like a phantom in a half-forgotten dream.

The town's murmur faded behind her. Silence answered her unease. Nothing moved. Nothing breathed. Just wind. Just leaves.

Then, there it was again.

A crunch. Sharp. Deliberate. The weight of something pressing against the earth. A chill slid down her spine, every nerve on edge, waiting.

Autumn braced herself for whatever, or whoever, might be there.

Please don't be Maxwell.

A sigh of relief escaped her as her eyes fell upon a small group of deer standing quietly at the edge of her garden, their slender forms half-hidden in the shadows. She loved deer and their graceful silhouettes, and the way they belonged to the night.

They watched her, wary but unafraid. But something strange about one of them held her attention. A pale mark curved over its forehead, white as fresh snowfall, shaped like a crescent moon. Barely visible beneath the shadows, it shimmered ever so slightly, its shape catching the last remnants of dusk.

She took a cautious step forward and extended her hand. "You're safe here," she whispered. But the herd startled. A flurry of motion, bodies twisting, hooves kicking up dirt. They bolted, vanishing into the trees, all except the one with the moonlit mark.

It remained, its eyes wide and dark like pools of ink, locked on hers, unblinking. The deer tilted its head, the gesture unsettlingly human.

Just beyond the slight flicker of its ears, she could see them: translucent, ghostly antlers. Pale and spectral, flickering in and out of sight like light catching on water.

The deer tilted its head again. And in that moment, something passed between them. An understanding without words. A truth without language. Then, as if it had never been there at all, it turned and leapt into the trees, swallowed by the waiting dark.

The creature had not looked at her like an ordinary animal. There had been intent in those dark, endless eyes, something deliberate in the way it lingered while the others had fled.

No trick of the eye. No fancy of the mind.

It was the feeling she had known as a child, lying awake beneath the rafters of the bookshop, listening to the rain tap against the glass, certain the sound was forming words.

And somewhere beyond the trees, past the reach of firelight and familiar roads, something was watching still.

Each step she took toward the door was hesitant. Her fingers brushed the wooden doorframe, a fleeting touch, as if crossing the threshold meant leaving behind something sacred.

The deer had been trying to tell her something. She was sure of it, just as she had always been sure of the things others refused to see.

Weary, she climbed into bed, drawing the blanket tight around her like armor against the night. She turned onto her side, her gaze drifting, then stopping, on the rose atop her dresser. The gift from Maxwell. The petals remained untouched by time, too perfect, too red. She did not know why she kept it.

Sleep came, but it did not come gently. The forest called to her, its ancient breath stirring in the wind. Shadows danced at the edges of her vision. And the dream took her.

***

Autumn walked barefoot through the grass, cool and damp beneath her feet. The earth gave softly, as if remembering the weight of those who had passed before. Above, the stars burned cold and ancient, casting a pale silver across the land. Her path lay strewn with roses, red as spilled wine, bright against the creeping mist that crept low over the ground. Each bloom bristled with thorns, defiant and waiting.

The air grew warm until it pressed against her skin. The heat did not belong. It clung, smothering, and the world around her began to hum, as though something vast stirred beyond sight.

Then came the whispers.

They slithered through the mist like serpents in tall grass, soft, ceaseless, spoken in no tongue she knew. They circled her, shaping the air with unseen mouths. The fog thickened, climbing her legs like smoke, swallowing the stars, and drowning the path behind her.

A bird, small and pale as ash, settled on her outstretched hand. Its weight was nothing, its form barely there, yet the world paused to watch. It opened its beak, and no song came, only silence shaped like music, a melody she could feel but could not hear.

Then, a crack. Sharp and cruel. Like ice breaking beneath her feet.

The silence shattered. The bird fled, wings slicing through the mist. It vanished, and Autumn's hand remained outstretched, empty and cold. A hollow bloomed in her chest, sudden and aching, as though something vital had been taken before it could be named.

The roses began to move. They twisted, their stems writhing. The thorns lengthened, barbed and jagged. One coiled around her wrist, another curled around her arm. The thorns tightened. Blood welled, warm and real.

Her lungs fought for air as panic clawed up her throat. The more she struggled, the deeper they bit. Pain flared bright and sharp, blooming through her limbs like wildfire. She gasped, wrenched, tore herself from their grip, and stumbled to the earth.

Then…light.

It split the darkness without warning, searing through the fog with a brilliance that burned. It pulsed once, twice, in time with her racing heart, and she could not look away.

The mist surged around her, the stars flickered above, and the whispers rose into a crescendo of meaningless sound. Autumn raised her hand toward the light. It trembled, drawn by something she could not name. Her fingers reached—

She awoke with a gasp, limbs tangled in the bedsheets, breath ragged. The room around her was familiar, yet the line between dream and reality had thinned.

The moon-marked deer lingered in her memory, too, but she couldn't say if it belonged to the dream or if it had truly been there, watching her through the veil of night.

Autumn looked to the window, where the first light of dawn gently brushed the skyline. As she tried to steady her breath and calm her racing heart, her thoughts shifted from the surreal fragments of her dream to the comforting, familiar sights of her beloved town.

***

The steady song of Starlit Run filled the room. It was a quiet music, the kind that made the world feel smaller, safer…for a time. She brushed her hair in slow, thoughtful strokes. Her gaze drifted, as it often did, to the book resting on the dresser. Its cover was weathered, the edges softened by time and touch.

The book was titled *Enchanted Realms: Tales of Wonder and Whimsy*. Its cover was a deep forest green, adorned with intricate gold leaf patterns that intertwined around the edges, forming delicate vines and mythical creatures.

Its weight was a welcome thing in her hands, solid and familiar, like an old friend. Her fingers traced the worn edges of the cover, brushing over the delicate illustrations.

The sight stirred something deep within her, the world outside lost to the turning of pages. Hours slipping away as she wandered through realms spun from ink, where wonder and danger walked hand in hand.

She let the pages fall open at random, and at once, the world within beckoned. Trees rose like giants, their trunks gnarled with age. Creatures lurked in the shadows, their eyes twinkling like scattered stars. There was mischief in their gazes, secrets stitched into the darkness between leaves, as though they knew she was there, as though they dared her to cross the threshold between reader and story, to step beyond the page and into their world.

Her hands lingered for a moment, but the pull of the present called her back as a hidden photograph slipped from the book's pages, fluttering down like a forgotten leaf from an old diary. It landed softly, Philip's face smiling up at her from the worn paper.

Philip… How long has it been?

She revisited the photograph now and then. Memories, long nestled in the corners of her heart, began to stir, each one a thread pulling her back to the days when his presence was as natural as the rhythm of her own breath.

We were so young, so full of dreams. Do you ever think of me?

Her fingers hovered above it as one might above an ember, fearful of both the burn and the chill that would follow should it be extinguished.

His chestnut hair caught the light like freshly minted copper coins, the kind that traders from distant shores would press into a merchant's palm. His hazel eyes held the depth of the ancient forests, eyes that had once looked upon her as a starving man might gaze upon a feast.

Philip's passion for horses had run as deep and unwavering as the old rivers that carved their paths through her homeland. It was a devotion that had carried him from a boy who mucked stables with uncomplaining hands to a man who could read the ailments of those proud beasts as easily as she read the spines of her beloved books.

Their affection had flourished like a meadow in the first flush of spring, wild and ungoverned by the constraints that bound more cautious hearts.

Yet there had been one barrier that Autumn could not bring herself to cross: her fear of mounting those great beasts he so adored. The terror of falling from creatures that stood taller at the shoulder than some men kept her boots firmly pressed against solid earth. Philip had never demanded she overcome this fear, had never made her feel lesser for it, his patience as enduring as the ancient hills that had watched over their town since before the first hearth-fires were lit.

But the end comes for all things, she thought bitterly, even for loves that seem eternal in the heat of summer days. The moment had arrived when Philip's ambitions grew too vast to be contained within the boundaries of Whispering Pines.

He had spoken of roads that stretched beyond Heatherwood and Honeytown, of crossing the towering spines of the Illumine Mountains to wander the far reaches of Sylvancrest where, it was said, horses ran wild as the wind itself.

Autumn's throat tightened as she recalled the night before his departure. A thousand words had crowded her tongue, yet she had spoken none of consequence. A thousand chances to mount one of his beloved horses, to share that part of his soul. If she had tried, truly tried, might he have stayed? Or might she have found the courage to follow?

Philip had ridden toward the horizon on a dawn that promised adventure and discovery, while she had retreated to the familiar embrace of leather bindings and paper, seeking comfort in the one place that had never failed her. It was there, among the scent of old books, that Evelyn, the librarian, approached her with an offer. The opportunity to become a part of the bookstore and weave her own story into its legacy.

The memory of his parting smile haunted her still, in what might have been, had fear not carved a chasm too wide for even love to bridge. And even for all their wonder, books made for cold companions on winter nights.

CHAPTER 5:

THE WILLOW'S REST INN

Autumn had not set foot in The Willow's Rest Inn since the first frost. She came now at Callum's behest to examine an ancient map uncovered in the dust-choked corners of the inn's storage. Nothing urgent, he had told her, merely a curiosity he thought might interest a woman who dwelled more in the realm of parchment than people.

Her reputation as a lover of dusty books and forgotten histories had marked her for such discoveries. She abandoned her post at the bookstore earlier than custom allowed.

Now, she stood within the golden glow of the place, feeling the familiar stirring of wanderlust in her blood. The inn breathed deepest in the afternoon hours when men put down their tools and lifted their cups instead, when voices rose and fell over the music of clinking tankards and the heady scents of spiced cider and roasting meat hung in the air.

Several townsfolk nodded as she crossed the threshold.

"The lady arrives," Callum called from behind the scarred oak bar, a wooden mug in his grip.

Near the crackling hearth, old Edith Briarwood looked up from her drink. Her face was a map of countless winters. "Digging up ghosts again, dear?" The words carried a bite beneath their sweetness.

"Or buried treasure?" another crone added with a cackle.

"I'll believe in magic when it pays for my ale," growled a man slouched against the bar, conjuring laughter from the patrons nearby.

Here we go. Breathe. Just breathe. Autumn forced her lips into a courteous smile. They cared for her well enough, these townsfolk. Yet they would sooner drink seawater than believe in the truths she knew.

She turned away before their jests could continue.

Birdie descended the stairs, a basket of neatly folded linens balanced in her arms, a warm smile tugging at her lips.

"Pay them no mind, for they mean you no harm," Callum said. He led her to a table where the ancient map unfurled across wood polished by countless elbows and spilled drinks. Autumn bent low, her fingers tracing the serpentine paths of roads and rivers long changed since the ink had dried.

Her hand stilled upon a mark far beyond the lands she knew. Sylvancrest City. The ink had faded, but the name remained defiant against the slow death of memory.

Her breath escaped slowly between parted lips. Never had she walked the streets of the capital, yet she had dreamed of them a thousand times: the stone spires, great libraries hoarding knowledge like dragons with their gold, streets bustling with souls who had seen more than the same patch of earth season after season.

"That city lies a long journey from here, Miss Ashwood," Callum said, arms folded across his chest as he peered over her shoulder. "I saw it once as a green boy. The simplicity of our lives here..." He shook his head. "The city devours such innocence. Men there scheme before breakfast and lie before supper. Every coin passes through three hands before it buys a crust of bread." He sighed. "Life moves quicker there. Men walk faster, speak faster, and die faster. They know a thousand faces but not a single name."

His eyes softened then. "Yet the markets overflow with spices you've never smelled, and the libraries hold more knowledge than our little town will gather in a hundred years. Music plays on every corner, and the great theater shows sights that haunt your dreams for years to come. And don't get me started on the pastries and ale."

Oh...to lose myself in stories I've never touched, pages that don't already know me.

'Some day, perhaps," she murmured.

Callum's hand fell upon her shoulder before he retreated to tend the bar. Birdie sat down with the basket of fresh linens and began to fold, catching the tail end of the conversation, her ears always quicker than anyone gave her credit for.

"Oh, the city," she said, brushing lint from her blouse. "They may have their kings and queens, but I'll take Whispering Pines any day. Though I will say, King Alden has ruled Sylvancrest with a steady hand, even through shadows most never saw. And Queen Seraphina..." Birdie gave a small shake of her head. "Sharp as she is, everything she does is for the good of the realm. They've borne grief with grace. Losing Princess Nyssa left a wound they still carry."

Her voice softened. "Prince Dorian tries to fill that silence. He's no stranger to his people. You see him out there, listening more than he speaks. His sister's memory walks beside him every step of the way."

Autumn tucked a strand of stray hair behind her ear. So many lives tied to names she'd only ever heard in passing. And still, something about it stirred her, a thread brushing against her own story, just faint enough to make her wonder.

"Careful now," Birdie said. "Don't go spinning one of your tales and making poor Dorian out to be a long-lost dragon prince. Folks might start thinking you mean it."

Autumn gave a faint smile, but said nothing.

She sighed, one slender finger traveling the inked roads, as if by touch alone she might feel the dust, the stone, the ghosts of long-forgotten travelers.

But something had changed. Or perhaps had been erased. Then again, this map was old, older than the version she knew. Older than the laws that came after. Perhaps the difference was expected. Perhaps.

In every version she'd seen, the kingdom's northern border was marked by an impassable wall of thorns and bramble, unnatural growth that no blade could tame, that tore through armor and bone alike. The Northlands beyond were forbidden, deemed uninhabitable by decree. No roads led in. No names were given.

But here, there was no bramble barrier. No dark strokes to mark the cursed growth. The border lay open.

And stranger still, the land beyond was not labeled as The Northlands, not on this map. There was a mark, a settlement, maybe more than one. Small, forgotten.

She leaned closer. The letters blurred, worn thin with age, but one word teased at recognition.

Frost...something.

She felt it then, that soft stir at the back of her neck, as if the map itself remembered something the kingdom had chosen to forget.

The sharp clang of metal against wood snapped Autumn from her thoughts. Iris Moonshade now stood balanced upon a stool. A freshly completed canvas leaned against the wall, waiting for its place of honor.

Something like envy kindled in Autumn's blood when she looked at Iris. The woman lived as though the world had been shaped for her pleasure alone, bold and untethered by expectations. Her garments flowed in shades of violet and gold, and sun-blessed curls that had never known the discipline of a proper comb adorned her head.

And there, behind her ear, nestled within those locks—a red rose. Autumn's steps faltered as surely as if she'd struck a wall. The twin of the flower Maxwell had pressed into her palm.

No, it can't be.

"Hello, Iris. Another masterpiece, I see," Autumn said, the words catching in her throat like burrs.

Iris turned, a smile spreading across her face as she descended from her perch.

"The bookworm emerges!" She brushed at a smudge of paint on her cheek. "Come, tell me what truths you find in this one."

Autumn studied the canvas.

The forest at dusk unfurled before her: deep purples bleeding into greens, shadows stretching like clawed fingers across the leaf-strewn ground. The details spoke of patient mastery, each tree twisting skyward with gnarled limbs like the hands of drowning men.

"It's the forest," she said slowly. "Yet...different somehow."

Iris's smile sharpened.

"Good! What use are paintings that merely echo what eyes already see? I painted what was. Or perhaps what soon shall be."

Autumn's brows knitted together as she tilted her head, lips parting slightly but forming no words.

Iris laughed, not a mere chuckle, but rich and unrestrained, the sound spilling out of her like sunlight through open shutters. "History does not rest dead in the ground, my sweet. It breathes. The past shapes us all, whether we will it or not. Destiny is not a thing to fight—it is a tide that carries you to shores already written."

Autumn's gaze fixed on the crimson bloom. "Where did you get that rose?" she asked, the question a little sharper than intended.

Her clothes tightened around her, constricting like unseen hands, each breath a little shallower than the last as she waited for an answer.

Iris's fingers rose to touch the petals. "This? A gift," she said lightly. "From our brooding Mr. Wolfsbane."

Autumn's gut twisted. "Maxwell?"

"Say what you will of the man, but he knows the worth of a fine bloom."

Her gut twisted even harder. "But, um, why…why would he give such a thing to you?"

Iris shrugged her slender shoulders. "Who can say what stirs in that man's blood? He saw me painting in the square, and the next I knew, a rose appeared between my fingers." She twirled the bloom, utterly untroubled by its presence. "Quite the man of mystery, is he not?"

She gave a low, thoughtful laugh, then leaned closer as if confessing something wicked. "And so handsome. It's a shame, really. It only makes the strangeness worse. There's something about him that creeps straight under the skin, don't you think?"

Autumn said nothing but some part of her wanted to snatch the flower and crush it beneath her heel. To warn Iris of dangers she herself could not name.

Iris tilted her head, studying her own creation. A gust of wind swept through the open door then, and the flames in the hearth danced.

Autumn would have sworn a true oath that the trees in the painting swayed with that same wind.

Iris watched her. "See?" she whispered. "Art is magic of its own kind. Quieter, perhaps. But no less true."

The woman did not see what Autumn saw—only the wonder an artist sees in their own work. She did not feel the pull, the breath, the life that stirred behind the canvas.

Not the way Autumn did.

It called to mind another night, last winter, when Iris had painted a clearing veiled in snow beneath a sky laden with stars. The snow was soft, untouched, the trees silver with frost.

But Autumn had seen the fox.

Curled at the base of a pine, nearly hidden, its shape barely more than mist against the snow. Its fur was not red, nor white, nor any color born of this world. It rippled like the northern lights: green and violet and blue, shifting with every breath the wind did not take.

She had stared at it for a long time. Long enough to see its eyes open. They glowed like distant stars.

When she asked Iris about it, she only blinked. "There's no fox in that painting, love," she said. "Just snow and trees. Perhaps you saw the brushstrokes."

But Autumn had seen it. She was sure of that. And sometimes, when the wind rose and the sky turned green at the edges, she still felt its eyes staring into her soul.

Callum's return broke the moment, the innkeeper bearing two brimming tankards of golden mead. Iris seized hers with childlike delight.

"It's rather early," Autumn protested, yet she sipped all the same, the sweetness burning a path down her throat.

"I have the perfect frame for your map," she told Callum, reaching for the steadiness of ordinary things, grateful for the solid ground of practical talk beneath her feet. It was easier, she had learned, to be useful than to be believed.

***

The sun hung high over Starlit Run, its light spilling across the rippling waters and the wild meadow beyond. Autumn sat cross-legged on the grass at the riverbank, her simple meal laid out beside her. Coarse bread, sharp cheese, and an apple she had swiped from the counter at Willow's Rest.

She tore off a piece of bread, chewing slowly, willing it to settle the mead still sitting in her belly. She hadn't meant to drink so much. Or perhaps she had. Either way, food was necessary now.

She pulled her shawl tighter around her shoulders. Though summer had come, a stubborn chill sat in the air, like spring's dying breath refusing to yield. Even with the sun overhead, she struggled to feel its warmth when the breeze slipped through.

The river had always soothed her, its lullaby a comfort since childhood. Yet today, the unease coiled deep in her chest.

A delicate tear slipped quietly down her cheek. She brushed it away quickly, forcing a small smile as she watched Papyrus leap playfully through the tall grass, chasing a fleeing grasshopper. His joy eased her heart, if only briefly.

She caught sight of Sylas Finch then, standing beneath the great oak tree near the river's edge, half in shadow, half in light. Some called him a historian, others a madman. Perhaps he was both. His fingers traced the bark in slow, deliberate motions, lips moving soundlessly as though the tree itself might whisper back.

A dragonfly landed on the edge of Autumn's knee, its wings iridescent in the dappled sunlight, like shards of glass catching fire. It tilted its head, watching her with unblinking eyes far too ancient for such a fragile creature.

"Everyone carries a secret," it said. "But the river always finds a way to carry what's hidden into the light." The dragonfly took off without hurry, skimming the water once before vanishing into the reeds.

Sylas's eyes found hers across the distance. He paused. Then, he stepped toward her, his boots barely stirring the grass.

What could he want?

Her fingers curled around the apple core. Words tangled in her throat. She had never quite mastered speaking with Sylas. His cryptic wisdom always left her feeling like a child grasping at shadows, certain that the truth was there but never quite in reach. But he was a kind soul, and she showed him the respect he deserved.

"Autumn," he greeted, his voice as soft as the river's song. "The water speaks today. Do you hear it?"

She hesitated.

Sylas tilted his head, amusement flickering in his eyes. "It carries more than you realize. Secrets. Memories. If you listen carefully enough."

Her cheeks flushed, embarrassment curling hot in her belly. "I…I don't understand," she admitted.

A low chuckle rumbled from him, warm but distant, as though he stood in two places at once: here by the river, and somewhere far beyond.

"Some truths are too heavy for words alone," he murmured. "They must be borne gently, like water wearing down stone."

His expression shifted then, sorrow threading through the lines of his face. "Can't you feel it, love? The forest whispers your name. The river sings it softly. And when the night comes, even the stars will wait for you."

A shiver ran through her.

"Sylas, you're too kind," she murmured. She wondered, was it kindness? Or something else entirely? Beneath his graying hair and awkward gaze, he was a mystery. A good man, perhaps, but still a mystery.

He was already turning, his coat flaring like the wings of some strange bird. Over his shoulder, he called, "Trust the journey, love, even when the path ahead is veiled."

She watched him go, his form dissolving into the pines. Could Sylas hold answers, or would he offer only more riddles?

The river murmured on, steady and unbothered. Papyrus nosed at her hand, his whiskers tickling her fingers. With a faint smile, she tore off a small piece of cheese and offered it to him. He accepted with a soft, rumbling purr, curling up beside her as if to guard their quiet little feast.

Chapter 6:
The Woman in the Woods

The candle on Autumn's desk had burned to a stub, its flame guttering in a pool of melted wax. Golden light flickered across the carved wooden frame that rested beside her open book, the one she had promised to bring Callum for his weathered map. A simple errand, something to anchor her in the mundane world. But her thoughts scattered like ravens at a sudden noise, refusing to settle.

Her eyes moved across the yellowed pages, the collection of dragon tales that had tumbled from the highest shelf in the bookstore. Henry would forgive her for bringing it home, she was certain. He always did.

The book felt heavier in her hands now, as though it carried more than just stories. Her finger traced the faded ink, the words strange, as if they had shifted since she last read them:

"In the eldest days, when men still feared the dark, dragons ruled both sky and earth. Their fire was the only light, their will the only law. Men lived and died at their pleasure, for what are mortal lives to creatures who count their years in centuries? But the dragons kept their own secrets. It is said they came not from our world, but from a place beyond, where magic flows like water and time bends like a river…"

She turned the page, the parchment crackling softly. The ink smudged in places as though the writer's hand had trembled:

"The tales differ on how the dragons were bound. Some say they were tethered to the earth by blood magic and ancient words. Others claim they went willingly, their fire dimming as men's ambitions grew. But all agree that what is bound may be unbound. What sleeps may wake. And darkness always returns, no matter how long the summer."

Autumn frowned, her fingers wandering across the wooden frame's surface, following the intricate patterns carved by hands long dead. She looked at the rose from Maxwell, its crimson petals glowing in the candlelight. It was just a rose, wasn't it? A simple flower, nothing more.

Perhaps Maxwell was nothing more than an odd man with a flair for the dramatic, and she was a fool to lose sleep over such trifles.

My mind is making up phantoms. The trees in Iris's painting, shifting when no hand moved them. The red rose tucked behind Iris's ear, its petals too vibrant, too alive. Maxwell, his presence lingering beneath the surface of every conversation, his words smooth and calculated, like a blade hidden in silk.

And yet…

"It's nothing," she declared to the empty room, the words as unconvincing as a child's lie. She snatched the rose from the desk and threw it to the floor.

***

The bakery's door opened wide, spilling warmth and the aroma of rising loaves. The square now smelled of yeast and honey. Autumn wanted to lose herself in the sweetness, yet the cold stabbed through her shawl, seeking the hollow behind her ribs.

Why is it so cold? she wondered. *Where has summer gone?*

A cart rattled past, steel-shod hooves cracking against cobbles, sparks of sound that echoed like hammer blows in a forge. The driver tipped his cap, oblivious to the rose-vines now threading the wheel spokes.

She rubbed her arms, pretending the motion alone might kindle heat.

The roses are only flowers.

But the argument rang hollow, as if spoken through cracked glass. Once a wrong note is heard, the rest of the song will never sit quite right.

"Saw a woman standing at the edge of the woods last night," a boy of perhaps seven summers told his mother. "When I looked again, there was no one."

"Someone knocked half my wares to the ground, but there wasn't a soul nearby," grumbled an old spice merchant, his gnarled hands righting fallen jars.

A trail of crushed cinnamon and spilled anise dusted the stones like strange offerings. One broken bottle had left a smear of oil beneath the statue's outstretched hand.

The marble was stained. Dark streaks clung to the skirts of the stone woman, dried herbs and dirt caught in the folds of her robe. Someone had thrown more than spices—a wine bottle, perhaps. The base of the statue reeked faintly of sour drink and bruised fruit.

And then, the roses. They crept along fence posts, twisted through stone walls. Vines that had not existed when she had walked this path yesterday. At first, they were easy to overlook. Small. Inconsequential. But once seen, they could not be unseen.

Splashes of crimson where before had been only greens and pastels. The townsfolk paused to admire them, marveling at their unexpected beauty, seeing only the wonder and none of the wrongness.

Roses did not naturally bloom in this town. Perhaps someone had sprinkled seeds, but roses did not spread overnight like a fever.

The early morning trade was gone; in its place rose a busy hum, as though the roses themselves had coaxed every soul outdoors. A pair of children chased one another between the stalls, bright petals knotted into makeshift crowns. They giggled whenever a vine brushed their ankles, certain the creeping stems were playing along rather than seeking the warmth of blood beneath skin.

An old potter, fingers scarred by kiln-fire, straightened to admire a bloom that had burst through the mortar of his own storefront. "Blessings come when they will," he said to no one, eyes shining as if he had awakened in a tale told by hearthlight. Autumn managed a polite smile, but the sight chilled her more than the bite of dawn.

She rounded the next corner and nearly collided with Floren the butcher, beard still frosted from the cold room. He cradled half a dozen roses as carefully as he would a newborn lamb. "Fine day for beauty, Mistress Ashwood," he greeted. "If only every season offered gifts so sudden." She opened her mouth... *Warn him, beg him to notice the thorny roots drilling into the stone*, but the words sank beneath his good mood. When he moved on, a single petal fluttered to the ground, crimson as fresh blood on snow. She did not pick it up.

Near the public well a small crowd gathered, marveling at a vine that had climbed the pulley and braided itself round the bucket's rope. One by one they drew water, each sip proclaimed sweeter than any remembered. Autumn tasted none of it, yet their praise felt loud against her silence, like bells rung for the wrong feast.

A knot of seamstresses paused outside Lark's Haberdashery. Needles forgotten, they pressed palms to the glass, beholding their reflections framed by roses that had sprung across the lintel. "Imagine the velvet we could match to that red," one whispered. Autumn heard another speak of weddings, of festival garlands, of perfumes to rival those of the capital. They saw only promise, never the way the vines pulsed faintly, as though roots far below were drinking something other than simple water.

She tried once more. "Um…strange, isn't it, how…how quickly they grow?" she asked a passing broom-maker. The woman laughed, thinking it jest. "Stranger that you find it troubling, dear. The land remembers how to surprise us." Autumn watched her depart, broom bristles brushing petals that scattered like coins.

Heat flushed Autumn's cheeks—frustration, not warmth—and she understood at last that any caution she voiced would slide from their minds like rain from slate. She swallowed the lump and drew her shawl closer. Her boots struck the stones with newfound urgency, carrying her unease as privately as a secret sin.

The inn enveloped her, the aroma of spiced cider and woodsmoke a welcome shield against the morning's unease.

Callum acknowledged her with a brisk nod as she approached, setting aside a freshly polished tankard. "Right on time," he said, his voice rough from years of smoke and strong drink. "Brought that frame for me?"

Autumn placed it on the scarred wooden counter. Here was something real. Something that followed the proper order of things.

"Perfect," Callum declared, turning it in his hands. "I'll mount the map in my chambers before nightfall. See you at Legends Night, eh?"

She nodded, preparing to depart, when her eyes fell upon Iris's painting. She stopped as suddenly as if she'd struck a wall.

Something had changed. Autumn moved closer, the fire's dancing light casting shifting shadows across the canvas. The Whispering Wood remained, its ancient trees twisting toward a star-heavy sky.

But near the edge of the tree line, a figure stood watching. A woman's form, perhaps. Or something that wished to be seen as such.

It had not been there before. Had it?

A chill crept up her spine like frost climbing a windowpane, and she forced herself to turn away. Her mind was playing tricks. It had to be.

Foolish girl.

The unease followed Autumn like a faithful hound as she made her way toward the bookstore. The walk should have calmed her spirit, should have settled her racing thoughts. Instead, the air grew colder with each step, the kind of cold that seeps past flesh and settles in the marrow. The afternoon sun couldn't come quickly enough.

Papyrus was already waiting at the door, his tail curling like smoke as she approached. He greeted her with his crooked meow, the sound as familiar as her own name. She moved by long habit: struck flint to tinder for the kettle, reached for the tin of tea leaves she kept on the highest shelf.

And yet...the feeling persisted, clinging to her like a second skin. That the figure in the painting was no trick of light or shadow. That the roses were not simply growing—they were claiming.

She poured the steaming tea into her cup and her hands trembled as she drank and filled up on the warmth.

CHAPTER 7:

A MAN WHO PREPARES

From the perspective of Flora

Flora worked with the patience of one who knew that a single misstep could spell ruin. Her fingers, deft and practiced, moved like an old melody, each motion measured, each breath drawn in careful rhythm. Before her, a small kettle whispered its secrets in curling tendrils of steam, its contents shifting, catching the light in undulating waves.

The air smelled of the sharp tang of lemonglow herb, undercut by the cold, metallic bite of crushed moonstone. In her grasp, the vial of starlight dew performed an opalescent dance behind the glass. Her amber eyes did not waver.

"Too much, and the mind will drown in shadows," she murmured, more to herself than to any listener. "Too little, and the visions will slip away, nothing but mist and whispers."

She leaned in, her dark curls tumbling past her shoulders, her breath shallow, careful. The heat of the brew rose to meet her, damp against her skin. A bead of sweat carved its way down her temple, but she did not flinch. Her hand hovered over the kettle, poised and waiting.

Then she shook her head.

"No. The balance is wrong. The harmony…it lacks something."

Her fingers reached for the Silverthorn berries, trembling ever so slightly. Three dropped into the simmering brew, vanishing beneath the silvered surface. A moment passed, stretched thin as a blade's edge…

A sudden gust of wind rattled the shutters, and from the counter, a jar of dried herbs crashed to the floor, scattering their brittle remnants across the stone.

A soft cascade of leaves and petals drifted to the stone floor, yet their fall carried a weight beyond their measure, their rustling swelling into something greater, something unseen.

Flora exhaled a sharp breath through clenched teeth, her jaw tightening as she knelt to gather the scattered herbs.

Then the bell above the door rang. Flora looked up, her fingers still curled around a fallen sprig. A figure stood in the doorway, shadowed against the golden light spilling from the lanterns.

Maxwell Wolfsbane.

The door swung shut behind him, the brass bell overhead trembling.

He stepped inside, boots scuffing against the floor, the scent of the night clinging to him: damp earth, leather, and something wilder beneath.

Flora did not startle, though she felt the shift in the air as keenly as the wind that had sent her dried herbs tumbling moments before. Something had unsettled the shop before his arrival, but now, the unease had found a shape.

She straightened, brushing her hands against her apron, and shared the customary warmth she offered to all who entered. "Good morning, Maxwell." As she spoke his name, a shiver rippled through her.

His eyes scanned the myriad of crystals, herbs, and potions that lined the shelves. "A fine morning, indeed. Flora, is it? Your shop is quite welcoming," his voice smooth and unhurried. "Have I interrupted something?"

Flora smiled. Her connection to the natural world afforded her a sensitivity to the energies of others, and the man's presence was like a cold shadow passing over the sun.

She let out a small sigh, brushing a stray curl from her face. "It's nothing really. I'm just working on an improved batch of Elixir of Insight. What is it you seek today?"

"I have heard your knowledge of herbs is quite renowned. I wonder if you have anything that enhances one's...strength, vitality, vigor." He let the words settle, watching her with an expectant stillness.

"A curious request." Her gaze flicked to the shelves. There were many things that could restore the weary, awaken the senses, fortify the body, but the hands that wielded them mattered more than the herbs themselves.

She selected a small jar of powdered ginseng and a bundle of dried hawthorn berries. "Ginseng will wake the blood," she said, setting it on the counter.

Maxwell exhaled softly, as if amused. "A healer's approach."

Flora's fingers brushed the rough twine binding the bundle. "Would you rather a poisoner's?"

His laughter was quiet, nearly indulgent. "Now, Miss Hawthorne, do I strike you as a man who poisons?"

"No," she said, without flinching. "You strike me as a man who prepares."

"Miss Hawthorne, I find myself in need of something else today." Maxwell smiled. "A handful of crushed valerian root, dried belladonna, and...let's see, a few sprigs of nightshade. You do carry nightshade, don't you, Miss Hawthorne?"

Her hands were already moving, selecting jars from the shelves. "A peculiar list. Valerian for sleep, belladonna for shadowed intentions, and nightshade for something far less kind. Tell me, Mr. Wolfsbane, do you mean to soothe a troubled mind or silence it entirely?"

He chuckled. "You wound me, Miss Hawthorne. Such accusations from one who knows the language of roots and leaves. Surely, you understand that everything has its purpose. It is only the hand that wields it that determines its virtue."

The wind stirred again, rattling the windowpane. Flora measured out the valerian root without a word. The scent of crushed lavender and damp earth clung to the air, but beneath it was a note of iron, cold and metallic.

"You speak of virtue," she said at last, moving to the belladonna. "Yet I have seen the ivy that strangles, the frost that kills, the fruit that lures with sweetness before the poison takes hold."

Flora wrapped them in brown paper, hands steady. "Even nature warns before it strikes."

She handed him the wrapped bundles of herbs. Their fingers briefly touched, and a jolt struck her—a glimpse of the turmoil hidden beneath his facade. Flora quickly withdrew her hand.

Maxwell exhaled through his nose, a quiet hum of amusement. He traced a finger over the wooden counter, slow and deliberate, as if feeling for unseen cracks. "Warnings, yes. But warnings are often ignored, aren't they? How many walk into the forest, Flora, despite the whispers in the trees?"

She met his gaze, unflinching. "Some enter with reverence. Others with a torch."

His smile deepened, and for the first time, his amusement felt genuine. "Perhaps. But tell me, Miss Hawthorne... Do the trees care which it is?"

Flora studied him for a long moment. "The trees do not forget," she said. "And neither do I."

"And if I were in need of something stronger?"

Flora's fingers tightened slightly over the jar. "Then you would be asking the wrong person."

He held her attention a moment longer, then let the subject slip away like a leaf carried downriver. Effortless. As if it had never truly mattered.

"Everything in nature gives and takes, Maxwell. Strength comes at a cost."

He slipped a few coins onto the counter like a man placing a wager. "Then let us hope it is a price worth paying. Thank you, Flora. Your expertise is invaluable."

With a nod, he turned to leave. The bell above it gave a sharp, jarring ring, louder than it should have been, as if the shop itself protested his leaving.

Flora exhaled slowly, pressing a palm to the counter to steady herself, and whispered a small incantation for protection. Whatever shadows lingered in Whispering Pines, she hoped the light within her and her community would be enough to keep the darkness at bay.

CHAPTER 8:

THE BOOK OF SECRETS

Whispering Pines stirred as the town prepared for the celebration. Banners rippled from rooftops and voices rose and fell like waves against a rocky shore. Within the bookstore, stacks of books leaned against one another like weary travelers seeking rest after a long journey. Their spines bore the marks of countless hands, creased and worn as an old soldier's battle map.

The evening prior, Autumn had stayed up late stitching golden stars onto her costume. Her fingers still carried the memory of her labor, tingling from the delicate work. An owl had kept her company through the hours, hooting softly from the tree just beyond her window. She'd paused now and then to listen, the steady call a strange comfort, as if the night itself were keeping watch.

Legends Night. A tradition as ancient as the first stones laid in Whispering Pines, born from whispers and half-remembered truths, from myths passed through generations like cherished heirlooms more valuable than any gold.

They would don their silks and masks, gather beneath the early summer sky, and breathe life into stories that might otherwise crumble like old parchment—dancing with the shadows of what might have been.

This year carried a weight beyond ordinary remembrance. A full century had passed since these hallowed walls of the bookstore had first reopened, since they had once again offered sanctuary to dreamers and scholars, to those who understood that stories were the true currency of human experience.

Stories told, stories preserved, two legacies intertwined like lovers' hands, bound together by ink and time and the unbreakable spirit of human imagination.

No corner remained untouched by the festival's spirit, no surface without its carefully curated memory. Each artifact Autumn arranged was a fragment of narrative waiting to be discovered, to whisper its secrets to curious eyes.

A faded map found its place on the display table, its markings telling tales of explorers who had ventured beyond Sylvancrest. Beside it, an antique quill waited, its nib stained with the ink of a thousand untold stories, ready to bear witness once more.

Evelyn rounded the corner, her arms laden with baskets and bundles, the weight of them bowing her shoulders but not breaking her stride. A deep crease carved between her eyes, as if the weight of the celebration itself rested upon her. She muttered under her breath, her lips moving in a silent rehearsal of lists and instructions, her fingers twitching as though counting invisible items in the air.

Her steps were hurried, almost frantic, her gaze darting from one corner of the square to another as if expecting disaster to strike at any moment. The hem of her skirt brushed against the cobblestones, dusty and frayed from hours of relentless preparation. A strand of hair had escaped its pin, clinging to her damp forehead, and she blew it aside with an impatient huff.

Her hands tightened around the handles of the baskets, her knuckles whitening as she adjusted her grip, her mind clearly racing through a thousand details that no one else would notice, or care about.

Evelyn had walked the streets of Whispering Pines for fourteen years longer than Autumn. Her chestnut hair, forever pinned in a bun that straddled the line between elegance and careless charm, spoke of a mind too preoccupied to fret over appearances. Her garments, ever in shades of deep blue, cloaked her like twilight itself: calm, endless, steady. Behind her glasses, which she wore not as an accessory but as an extension of her being, her brown eyes gleamed with the fire of one who had spent a lifetime reading not just books, but people, their stories unraveling before her keen gaze.

Yet for all her wisdom and grace, Evelyn had the flaw of those who give too much. She bore the burdens of others with open arms, stretching herself thin, her own needs sacrificed upon the altar of duty. It was not a choice, but a compulsion, as ingrained as the ink upon her fingers.

She had been a wife for two decades, but the laughter of children had never echoed in the halls of her home. Some spoke of it in hushed voices, others never dared to ask. Evelyn had never offered an answer.

For a moment, Autumn considered stepping forward, offering to help, but something in Evelyn's expression gave her pause. There was a fierceness there, a determination to see everything perfect, even if it cost her every ounce of strength. It was a look Autumn recognized, one that spoke of pride and stubbornness in equal measure.

So she stayed where she was, watching as Evelyn disappeared into the throng of townsfolk, her voice rising as she began directing someone about the placement of the tables.

A lone figure now carved his path through the bustling streets, drawing the curious gazes of townsfolk as surely as a wolf draws the eyes of sheep. Sylas Finch, the town's most enigmatic gatherer of books, a man whom some called a hoarder of secrets and others a keeper of forgotten truths, strode forward with a wooden crate cradled in his arms as carefully as a mother might hold a newborn.

His coat, long and weathered as an old soldier's banner, flared with each step, carrying the scent of parchment and leather. His eyes, sharp as a falcon's and twice as keen, gleamed with a quiet satisfaction that spoke of knowledge few could comprehend. He understood that some mysteries were best kept close, like treasures too precious to be carelessly displayed.

The crate he bore was a marvel in its own right. Darkened by time, its wood spoke of journeys long past. Though small enough to be carried, it seemed to bear the weight of entire worlds within its modest frame.

"Ah, Miss Ashwood," he called, his voice threading through the noise like a silk ribbon. "I thought these might add a touch of mystery to our revelry." The words suggested he knew far more than he would ever reveal.

From the crate, he lifted artifacts and ancient tomes, some swathed in velvet, others bound with clasps that might have adorned a king's treasury.

"These relics carry the whispers of ages. In the grand dance of time, where shadows waltz with echoes of forgotten tales, the unraveling threads weave an intricate web of secrets. Each page turned is a step in the elaborate masquerade of destiny, revealing but a glimpse of the performance that ensnares us all."

The words were cryptic and compelling. A mysterious smile played across his lips. "Enjoy the revelry, my dear, for even the most bewitching tales have chapters yet to be written."

Autumn regarded Sylas as she might an unread book: leather-bound, spine cracked with age, pages promising secrets that only the most patient could unravel. There was something undeniably magnetic about him, an air of mystery draped across his every word and gesture.

Maybe he understands me in a way others don't, she thought, reflecting on her own struggles. *He seems to see the world through a different lens, just as I do.*

Beneath his peculiarities lay a warmth as genuine as hearth-fire, an unmistakable kindness woven into the very fabric of his being. The town knew him as he knew the town, in a way that suggested he saw deeper than most, understanding the weight of history that clung to every stone and shadow.

At times, Autumn wondered if his eccentricities were but a mask for a loneliness not unlike her own. A solitude navigated from a careful distance, never quite stepping into the easy rhythms of ordinary life. A different kind of solitude, perhaps, but solitude all the same.

But where she found such isolation a burden, Sylas carried it differently—like an old, well-worn coat. Comfortable. Familiar. A part of him rather than a weight to be shed.

Nearly finished with her careful arrangement, Autumn halted, her fingers hovering over the stack of books. A whisper brushed against her ears, so thin it might have been no more than the last breath of a dying wind. She straightened, brow furrowing, straining to hear.

Perhaps it was nothing. Just the murmur of patrons deep in conversation, their voices drifting through the labyrinth of shelves. But then it came again. Soft, insistent, like smoke from a distant fire.

Closer. Not the idle chatter of customers nor the creak of the old building settling into itself. This whisper carried intent, as if reaching for her, as if calling her name.

A slow chill traveled down her spine. The sound seemed to be coming from a door tucked away in the shadows: the entrance to the basement. For years, the door had been buried beneath stacks of books and forgotten crates, half-hidden as if the bookstore itself wished it to remain undisturbed. It was always more like a relic than a passageway, a thing meant to be ignored.

Yet now, there it stood, unobstructed.

The idea of stepping beyond that door alone made her pulse quicken. Her imagination painted the basement in shades of shadows stretching too far, silence thick with secrets. The basement represented everything unknown, everything that lurked just beyond the edges of understanding.

Leave it be, reason whispered. An echo, nothing more. Someone below, their words slipping through unseen cracks, twisting into something primordial and strange. A trick of sound, of ancient architecture. Nothing more.

The more she sought to dismiss it, the more insistent the whisper became. It tugged at her ears, teasing her curiosity with the delicate precision of a master manipulator.

Her feet moved of their own accord, defying reason, drawn forward by something she could not name.

The air around the door was colder. Not the biting chill of winter, but something deeper, older. She swallowed against the unease coiling in her chest as her trembling fingers wrapped around the iron doorknob. It was cool beneath her touch, cool as a tomb, smooth as polished bone, bearing the weight of years of stillness.

The door, long content to remain closed, now yielded beneath her hand.

A stairwell plunged downward into shadow, the light from above barely reaching past the first few steps.

A breath caught in her throat.

One step at a time, she told herself, her fingers tightening around the rail as she descended. The air pressed against her, warm and cloying.

Faint light slanted through narrow, grime-covered windows, barely enough to pierce the shadows pooling in the corners. Cobwebs hung like forgotten banners, swaying with her passage.

Shelves loomed on either side, burdened with books stacked high. Their bindings cracked, spines sagging under decades of weight. Dust lay thick and undisturbed. These books had not been touched in years, perhaps generations. A graveyard of knowledge, silent and forgotten.

She moved carefully, passing stacks of yellowed newspapers, their pages curling inward. Crates sat draped in cloth that had long surrendered to time's slow decay. A kingdom of relics, cast aside and left to wither.

And then she saw it—a door, half-hidden. Unlike the others, this one stood slightly ajar, as if left waiting for her alone.

She reached out, fingers pressing against the wood. The door creaked open.

The room was a trove of forgotten things. Boxes lay stacked in careless disarray, their contents hidden beneath time's patient hand.

Her fingers brushed across the brittle edges of old paintings. Faded faces peered back, their expressions frozen in a moment long past.

A faint glow, impossibly soft, flickered from between layers of dust and shadow. Her eyes followed the light to a single book, set apart from the others. A leather-bound book, its cover cracked and frayed, its title worn away. It had been left to slumber, but something about it felt…alive.

What's your story? Her fingertips grazed the spine before she carefully lifted the book from its resting place. Dust scattered as she cradled it, drifting lazily through golden shafts of light spilling through the narrow window.

She lowered herself to the floor, dust settling on her forest-green dress. The world around her faded. The murmur of the bookstore above, the hum of the town beyond these walls—none of it mattered now.

Here, in this forgotten place, only she and the book remained.

She wondered how long the book had waited, if ink and parchment could possess patience, if leather and thread could yearn for hands to turn their pages once more.

Chapter 9:
Some Things Do Not Stay Buried

The book sighed as she opened it, its spine creaking like the settling bones of an ancient keep, heavy with stories pressed between leather and time. Autumn turned a page. Then another. And another. She traced the ink with her eyes, her breath slowing, the world around her shrinking.

Beneath her fingertips, kingdoms emerged. Eiryndor, the text called this realm—a land once whole, now splintered by ambition and the slow grind of years. Starfell, where the rivers shimmered beneath banners of indigo and silver; Wyndamere, home to wind-scoured plains; Driftmoor, lost to fog and rumor, where marshes swallowed whole the careless and the bold. She read of Mystwood's high towers, Blackspire's haunted cliffs, Duskhollow's veiled woods.

And there, set like a jewel between sky and sea, stood Eiryndor's largest kingdom, Sylvancrest, its banners stretching farther than most dared to dream. Autumn knew these names.

They were as familiar as the contours of her own hand, woven into every legend and half-remembered tale.

Yet reading them here, written in old ink, preserved in words that outlasted flesh and memory, she felt the weight of it all. The kingdoms still endured, for now, though time gnawed at every border.

When she searched for the cold land she had glimpsed on Callum's old map—a place marked only with the ghost of a name beginning with Frost—she found nothing. The book spoke merely of "The Northlands," a single line drawn as a warning of the realm's edge, as if what lay beyond belonged more to legend than to any living king.

She turned another page, the candlelight flickering, and wondered what else the book would yield, what truths might lie between those storied lands and the quiet life she'd always known.

Unfamiliar names, events, and intricate drawings now danced across the pages in careful, faded strokes—runes, spells, and incantations in ink like dried blood.

She frowned, fingers tracing the torn pages, their edges frayed like the teeth of some long-dead thing. The story stuttered, gaps yawning wide, entire passages ripped from history. Lost to time, or torn by intent, she couldn't say.

She turned another page. Before her, dragons came alive on the parchment, more real than any living creature she had ever encountered. Not the simple beasts of children's tales, but creatures of terrible majesty that made her heart quicken.

The artist had rendered them with a hand as skilled as any master from Sylvancrest City. Their wings spread across the yellowed pages like great sails, each feathered edge defined with strokes so fine they might have been made with a blade rather than a quill. Scales armored their massive bodies, gleaming even in mere ink as if forged in the heart of a dying star.

Some soared over mountain peaks, elegant despite their terrible size. Others stood upon scorched earth, claws sinking into the soil as if claiming all they surveyed. The landscapes around them, castles, forests, entire towns, seemed no more significant than toys beneath a child's bed.

It was their eyes that made Autumn's fingers tremble as they hovered above the page. The artist had captured something ancient there, something that made her feel as though she gazed through windows into another time. Wisdom dwelled in those serpentine pupils, cold and deep as the waters of the South Sea.

One passage drew her eye like a raven to a battlefield. The script was different here, as if the writer feared interruption, and spoke of dragon's blood. Autumn leaned closer, candlelight casting shadows across her face as she devoured the words.

"The blood of the dragon carries power beyond mortal reckoning," she read. "A single drop contains the strength of armies, and the heat of a thousand forges. It can heal wounds that should prove fatal, bestow visions of things long past or yet to come, and, if the legends speak true, even grant…"

The final line was partially obscured, as if someone had tried to wipe it away before the ink had fully dried. Autumn traced the indentation with her fingertip. Such knowledge had not been meant for accidental discovery.

She had found something dangerous here, something that men would kill to possess…or destroy.

Another page. Beneath the lines of ink, a statue. Familiar in shape, yet altered in ways that made her breath still.

A woman, her arms outstretched, palms uplifted. But unlike the version that stood in the town square, this one was whole. In her hands rested a dragon.

Heat rose to Autumn's cheeks.

A dragon? No tale had ever spoken of that.

She turned deeper into the book and found a passage unmarred, untouched by time's hunger. Her breath shallowed as her eyes swept across the faded ink. The words struck, sharp and cold.

For a time, Whispering Pines had teetered on the edge of ruin. Blood had been spilled. Shadows had risen.

The book spoke of a conflict long past, a battle that had threatened to sever the town from the magic that once ran through its veins. A woman had stood against that darkness, wielding a power few could name, her ally a creature of fire and sky.

She had been a Fireborn. Dragonkin. A dragon whisperer. She had stood against a name written in even deeper ink, one that stretched beyond the page, reaching into something that had not yet let go of Whispering Pines.

Magnus Blackthorn.

She turned the page, the parchment crackling under her touch. More words waited, a history that stretched back centuries, a lineage once honored but long since drowned in ambition.

The Blackthorns had not always been feared. Once, they had been revered as keepers of Sylvancrest's mystical balance. But power is fickle, and in time, duty had given way to hunger. No longer content to protect the forces of magic, they sought to command them, to bend the untamed wilds of the enchanted world.

Magnus had been born into this inheritance. He had been shaped from boyhood into a weapon and sharpened by blood. His mother had whispered to him of destiny, of a throne rightfully his. Power was meant to be taken, not feared, she told him.

His father had not agreed. The war within his own family had forged his resolve and kindled the hunger that would one day consume him whole.

Autumn reached for the loose papers tucked between the pages, unfolding them with careful hands.

Letters. Her eyes traced the flowing script.

"My dearest Magnus…"

She lifted another page.

"Opal, my love…"

She read on, the fragments of a lost story rising from the dust. Magnus had loved a woman named Opal Starlight. The letters spoke of devotion, of longing, of something once whole and then shattered beyond repair.

Madness had taken Magnus. Their final meeting had not been a lovers' reunion but a reckoning. A battle fought with the weight of all that had been lost between them.

And Opal, said to be the first Fireborn, had taken from him the thing he coveted most.

His power.

Autumn turned the page with care, the old ink breathing to life beneath her fingers. She read the words aloud, her voice low, as if afraid to stir whatever lingered in the shadows of the room:

"In the days when the forest yet held its ancient strength, and the moon rode low over the woods of Whispering Pines, there came a night of sorrow to the Emerald Glade.

Magnus Blackthorn stood alone at the water's edge, his dark cloak stirred by the wind. The pond, clear and deep, mirrored the heavens above and the turmoil within his heart.

And from among the trees came Opal Starlight, fairest of the forest's guardians. Her hair shone like the rivers of starlight, and her gown glimmered with the pale hues of the moon. Soft was her tread upon the moss, and sorrowful were her eyes as they met his.

'Have you come with an answer?' Magnus called unto her, his voice broken by longing and despair.

Opal took his hand and spoke: 'The forest is not a crown to be worn, nor a kingdom to be ruled. It is a gift, and no hand may bind it without peril.'

Long did Magnus plead with her, but her heart was steadfast. 'I shall not forsake the freedom of the wood for the hunger of one man's will,' she said. And though tears glistened in her eyes, she turned away, vanishing into the mist."

Autumn shifted her weight, her fingers tracing the delicate lettering. She read on:

"Thus was Magnus left alone, and heavy grew his heart. In bitterness, he withdrew to his dwelling, and there he gave himself over to the old and hidden arts, which wise folk fear to name.

Shadows lengthened in Whispering Pines, and the roses of blood-red hue sprang up where none had planted them. Their thorns gnawed at stone and timber alike, heralding the sorrow that had taken root in Magnus's soul.

Long years passed, and Magnus grew mighty in dark craft, yet hollow within. When at last he returned to the glade, the forest shuddered at his coming.

Opal met him once more beneath the ancient boughs. 'Magnus, what evil has taken hold of you?'

Wrath and yearning strove within him, and he lifted his hand against her. Yet the forest rose with Opal, and the battle between them shook the very hills."

Autumn tightened her grip on the book.

"Magnus beheld strange signs upon Opal: scales that flashed with hidden light, wings like mist unfolding. And when at last the dragon came, roaring into the glade, Magnus trembled.

Long they battled, but Magnus faltered before the might of the ancient magic. Cast down at last, he knelt broken before Opal, and the light of the forest claimed him.

'I never wished this fate for you,' she said, and her tears fell as rain upon dry ground.

Thus was the shadow torn from Magnus, and thus did Whispering Pines endure, though scars of that night lingered long.

And Opal wove a great spell, wrought of sorrow and strength, that severed the bond between Magnus and the powers he had sought to bind.

His might was torn from him and hidden away, beyond the reach of shadow, where no darkness could ever lay claim."

The townspeople had built the statue to honor Opal, the woman who had stood against darkness when no one else could. Carved in stone, she held a beautiful dragon, symbolizing the bond between magic and mercy, strength and restraint, the fire that protects rather than consumes.

After his defeat, Magnus refused to look at it. Rage surged through him, and he struck out, shattering the dragon piece. Before he could destroy the rest, the people of Whispering Pines intervened, forced his retreat, and banished him from the town.

The missing dragon piece, the curse, the ancient war… The book did not speak in fables.

He couldn't bear to look at the statue. No wonder he destroyed the dragon. It wasn't just stone to him, it was the woman who chose to stand against him. She ended him, and he's never forgiven her for it.

Autumn swallowed hard. The boundary between legend and truth had shattered before her eyes.

Another page turned beneath her hand, revealing a portrait of a man whose beauty did little to soften the malice in his gaze. High, noble cheekbones framed his face, his jawline sharp as a blade, but it was his eyes that held her fast. Cold. Calculating.

The air froze in her throat, and for a heartbeat, she forgot how to breathe.

The portrait of Magnus Blackthorn bore the face of Maxwell Wolfsbane.

No.

Autumn's grip tightened. A distant uncle, perhaps. A grandfather. Just an old drawing, a trick of artistry. Coincidence.

But those eyes... She knew those eyes.

No. Impossible.

How could Magnus be alive after all these years? It had to be hundreds. And there had to be some sort of magic behind it. Maxwell Wolfsbane lived and breathed—no myth, no legend.

All these secrets have been buried for so long. Dragons, power, and curses, no longer myths, but truths carved in blood and stone.

Not figments of fevered imaginations nor the ramblings of drunken storytellers, but real, as true as the earth beneath her feet and the book that sat heavy in her lap. Whispering Pines had stood witness to their power. And then, in time, it had chosen to forget.

She closed the book, the ancient leather meeting weathered pages, a whisper of secrets reluctant to be sealed away. Dust danced in the light, creeping in through the small window, spinning like tiny spirits disturbed from their long slumber.

A fragment of paper slipped free, floating to the floor almost with intention.

Autumn's fingers reached out, almost against her will. The paper was thin and brittle, the color of old bones. Her skin prickled as her hand closed around it.

The locket at her throat pulsed.

Not a tremor. Not a gentle warmth. A pulse. Like a heartbeat. Like a warning.

Her eyes scanned the faded lines, words rising from the page like something half-buried clawing free:

> "When crimson tears the earth shall weep,
> and shadows stir from ancient sleep,
> a child of realms both near and far
> shall rise beneath the evening star.
> Born of fire, by gold adorned,
> the voice shall wake what once was warned.
> Through forest deep and tangled wide,
> the sleeping flame shall be their guide.
> What once was lost shall be reclaimed.
> What once was stolen, now renamed.
> A harbinger in darkest night
> shall blaze the path to morning light.
> And when the final hour is shown…"

Autumn stared at the gap. The bottom of the page was torn, and the sentence ended mid-thought, as if the words themselves had been swallowed. It was just ink and parchment, brittle with age. And yet…she felt it, that absence. An accident, or something buried on purpose?

The ticking of the antique clock echoed through the room, steady, deliberate, too loud in the quiet. She traced the ragged edge with her fingertip, half expecting the missing words to whisper themselves into her ear.

Her hand drifted to the locket.

Then, a noise. A thud. There, amid a fallen heap of books and trinkets, sat Papyrus, tail flicking, mischief in his golden eyes.

Papyrus approached her with a satisfied purr, unbothered by the chaos he had orchestrated and blissfully unaware of the weight of secrets hidden in the room.

Autumn let out a breath, half relief, half frustration.

Fool of a feline.

But then, if Papyrus had made his way down, the door must have been left open. A cold dread coiled in her gut.

I should have been more careful. If Evelyn came, if anyone came… If they saw me here, with this book, with these stolen pieces of the past, what then?

She fled the room and shut the door, sealing in the ruined pages and the truths no one meant to find. Papyrus pranced at her heels, pleased with himself, while she swallowed down the knot of fear tightening in her throat.

CHAPTER 10:
THE ENCHANTED BLOOM

Blood rushed to Autumn's ears as she climbed the narrow wooden stairs. Her steps were quick, her breath tight. Heat crept up her neck, pooling beneath her collar, a prickling discomfort spreading across her skin. Her clothes clung to her, suddenly too tight, the fabric pressing against her ribs with each sharp inhale. A bead of sweat traced a slow path down her temple, clinging at the curve of her jaw before falling away.

The bookstore still hummed with life with those preparing for the celebration, though none were aware of the terrible knowledge now burning in her mind. Her heart hammered against her ribs like a war drum, and she tasted copper on her tongue. The forgotten words within had stirred something dark and ancient.

Okay, Autumn, just stay calm. She needed a moment, just one moment, to think. But that moment was nowhere to be found. The book had set something in motion, and she could no longer turn away.

"Foolish girl," she whispered.

The truth of it all lay bare on those yellowed pages, written in ink that breathed with strange life beneath her trembling fingers.

Papyrus wound between her ankles. He chirped softly and batted at the hem of her dress. She cast Papyrus a weary glance, offering a soft pat atop his head. "Not now, little fella. I cannot stay in this place. Not with what I now know."

If there was anyone who could unravel these arcane secrets, it was Flora Hawthorne. Her knowledge of plants, herbs, and crystals was the closest thing to magic Whispering Pines had ever truly accepted.

The walk to The Enchanted Bloom stretched long before her. She had never been brave, not truly. But courage often came when fear left no other path forward.

The door's chime rang through the air, a quiet announcement of her arrival into a realm far removed from the ordinary. She allowed the shop's atmosphere to ease the heat prickling at the back of her neck. Here, in this haven of nature's secrets, she could almost forget the weight of the knowledge she carried.

The air inside was earthy, floral, and subtly spiced, each breath a tale of root and leaf, of secrets buried deep in the earth. The walls were lined with shelves, crowded with jars and bottles. Flora had gathered them, tended them, as though the very soul of the woods had been distilled and stored in glass.

There stood Flora Hawthorne, her presence as steady and grounding as the roots of an ancient tree.

Her skin bore the rich, warm tones of the earth itself, reminiscent of the fertile soil along the Starlit Run. Its vitality was akin to the ancient oaks of the forest. Her dark waves cascaded over her shoulders like a river at twilight, while her eyes—a striking fusion of amber and honey—gleamed with the wisdom of centuries past. Her lips, tinted with a deep red hue, were as soft and striking as the petals of the rarest flower in her garden.

Flora's wisdom stretched beyond her years, an inheritance passed down through generations. As an herbalist, an apothecary, and the guiding hand behind The Enchanted Bloom, she was the only bridge between the mystical and the mundane, a living reminder of the pact between man and nature, as old as the first seed that had taken root in the soil.

She was a woman of warmth, her presence as comforting as the crackle of a hearth-fire on a bitter winter's night. Men and women came to her for salves, tinctures, and counsel—for the ailments of the body were often the least of their troubles. Her voice was a balm for wounds unseen.

Flora looked up from her work. "Autumn, good morning. What brings you here today?"

Autumn hesitated, the words tangling like brambles in her throat. She fidgeted with the sleeve of her dress.

"I was just...curious," she began, her voice a tentative whisper, "about...you know, the herbs and flowers here. Do they, um, have special properties? Beyond the medicinal, I mean."

She berated herself internally. *I sound so silly right now. I must look like a nervous wreck.*

Flora's smile was gentle, and her answer acknowledged the unspoken depth behind Autumn's question. Her dress, a rich crimson that deepened toward the hem, swayed as she moved. She looked as if she had been painted into existence by an artist with an eye for the divine.

"Many things in nature hold secrets beyond what we see. Some say there's magic in the very essence of these plants. It all depends on what you're open to discovering."

The heat that had flushed Autumn's cheeks began to fade in Flora's presence. The tightness in her chest eased. In its place, something else stirred: a flicker, faint but undeniable, like the first spark struck from flint in the depths of a dark cave.

"So, in all your time with these plants, have you… So, is there really truth to the tales? About magic and such?"

Say it. Just say it. Tell her about the book. About Magnus. About Magnus Blackthorn.

Flora set down the jar of dried lavender she had been labeling, the glass clinking softly against the worn wooden table.

"Well, that depends on what you mean by magic. There are more wonders in this world than we often acknowledge. The way a seed sprouts into life, the healing properties of a simple herb. Some might call these things magical."

"But I mean, *real* magic," Autumn pressed, her voice growing slightly stronger, emboldened by Flora's open demeanor. "The kind in stories: enchantments, spells, things beyond the ordinary."

Feeling the blush creeping up her neck, she immediately regretted asking the question. *She must see me as a child chasing fairy tales. Please don't laugh at me.*

But Flora was understanding. "In Whispering Pines, stories weave through the very air we breathe. We may dismiss them as mere folklore, but every legend has a kernel of truth. In its purest form, magic is about connection, with nature, ourselves, and the unseen threads that bind the world."

Autumn listened. Flora's words echoed the sentiments of the mysterious book, blurring the lines of reality.

"And have you…ever experienced such things? This…connection?"

"Perhaps," Flora replied softly, her gaze drifting to the window. "Perhaps there's a touch of that ancient magic in every potion I brew and in every plant I nurture. It's not about flashy spells or conjuring illusions. It's subtler, deeper, a harmony with the earth's rhythms."

"So, it's real, in a way?" Autumn asked, almost to herself. Her skepticism battled with the burgeoning sense of wonder that Flora's perspective invoked.

"In a way," Flora affirmed. "The world's magic is as real as we allow it to be in our hearts. And sometimes, in places like Whispering Pines, it reveals itself in the most unexpected ways."

Flora's insights offered no definitive answers, but they opened doors to possibilities Autumn had never allowed herself to consider.

Stop stalling and just ask her.

"Oh, one more thing," Autumn inquired. "Does the term 'dragon whisperer' mean anything to you?"

Flora appeared surprised and slightly amused by the question. "My Aunt Althea used to tell me an old tale about those who could summon a dragon during great times of need. They were known by various names: Fireweavers, Fireborn, Dragonkin. But I'm afraid that one was just a story, one of those typical myths that most likely came from Legends Night."

Autumn stepped closer to the chaos of papers strewn across Flora's desk. The surface was a patchwork of notes and sketches, each one a fragment of the herbalist's world. Delicate drawings of plants spilled across the pages, rendered with such care that they seemed almost alive, petals unfurling, leaves curling, roots digging deep into the parchment. Beside them, Flora's handwriting sprawled in tight, precise lines, cryptic annotations that spoke of properties and potions, of remedies and rituals.

"What are these?" Autumn's fingers hovered above the papers, not daring to touch but aching to trace the lines of ink.

"Ah, just a little project of mine. I've been trying to create a special potion, but it requires a plant that proves to be quite elusive."

Autumn's curiosity was piqued. "What plant is that?"

"It's called the Luminosa Blossom," Flora explained. "It's a rare plant, known for its petals that glow faintly in the moonlight, casting a gentle hue of deep magenta. Legend says it thrives in places where the veil around our world is thinnest.

It's sometimes known as Lady's Embrace because of the way the petals wrap around the stem, almost as if the flower is holding itself in a protective hug. This unique characteristic, combined with its ethereal glow, gives it an aura of mystique and grace, symbolizing the nurturing and protective qualities often associated with feminine energy."

Flora's brows furrowed then. "I've searched throughout Whispering Pines, even venturing into the forest, but to no avail." Her fingers curled into fists at her sides. "It's as if the plant doesn't want to be found, or perhaps it no longer exists in our realm."

Autumn thanked Flora and turned to leave, but Flora stopped her, pressing a bundle of tea leaves into her hands. "The river does not choose where it flows, yet it finds its way just the same," she said.

Autumn nodded, offering a polite smile before stepping out the door. Her first attempt at courage ended in failure and she left The Enchanted Bloom feeling defeated. She could not bring herself to tell Flora about the book, about the truths it had unearthed, about Magnus Blackthorn. The weight of them was too heavy to speak. To say it aloud was to lay herself bare. But the fear of being dismissed, of seeing doubt flicker in Flora's eyes, held her tongue.

CHAPTER 11:
RARE BOOKS AND RARE MEN

Autumn's fingers trembled against the worn leather binding of the book as bodies flowed like a stream around a stone. The lavender scent freshened the old shop, Flora's doing, of course. Paper ribbons and dried garlands lay scattered across the counter.

Evelyn organized books at the display table with mathematical care. Iris hummed softly, a lullaby at first, though it turned strange against the dry snap of stems as she pressed them into their vase. Flora moved between the hearth and the counter, teacups clinking in her hands.

The brass bell jangled, harsh and discordant with each opening door, marking the steady flow of patrons, blind to the weight she carried.

But the activity was distant to her troubled mind. Her thoughts tangled in a web of questions she dared not voice, of suspicions that prickled beneath her skin like the very thorns creeping through the town.

Maxwell. His name scorched her tongue. She yearned to speak of him, but her stomach knotted at the thought of three pairs of eyes turning to her at once, three voices dismissing her fears as nothing more than her usual anxiety.

What would she even say? That trees danced in a painted frame? That a book hissed secrets into her bones? That Magnus Blackthorn might lurk among them, masked in a stranger's name?

Magic? Foolish girl. That's what they'd say.

"The calendar swears it is early summer, but the air tells a different tale, am I right, ladies?" Iris perched on the edge of the table, head tilted so that her golden hair caught what little light filtered through the windows.

Flora stood by the hearth, her words like a knife wrapped in silk. "A creeping chill now coils through the streets," she said, her voice musical as always. "Threading its way through stone and timber, in places where warmth ought to have claimed."

Evelyn brushed her hands on her apron, leaving faint smudges of dust. "The sun has grown timid," she said matter-of-factly. "There's no joy in this day's light." She shrugged. "It must be one of those unusual seasons that come around every now and then. Something to do with weather patterns." Her face brightened momentarily. "I do hope the weather cooperates for Legends Night."

Autumn tightened her grip on the book, her knuckles white like polished ivory. She wanted to believe Evelyn, to accept the comfort of a rational explanation.

Strange weather. Nothing more. But the chill in the air felt wrong. Unnatural. Like a breath from a grave.

Flora's eyes traced the shifting canvas of the heavens as if the clouds spoke to her of something insidious, something that refused to loosen its grip.

The kettle shrieked, sudden and sharp, and Autumn's shoulders jumped.

Flora tended it with care then, engaging in the age-old ritual of tea-making. Autumn watched as she measured water with precision, selected herbs, and steeped them with respect. Each movement spoke of knowledge passed from one generation to the next, of earth's magic woven into the simplest of acts.

The wind stirred outside and set the wind chimes singing. Their melody, once light and whimsical, now keened like mourners at a funeral. The sound raised gooseflesh on Autumn's arms. She studied vines again, following them as if they were a map leading to places unknown. The roses were beautiful, yes, but their thorns looked too sharp, their shadows stretched too long, as if they might pull free from their roots and slither toward the door.

Flora's lips pressed into a thin line as she passed out cups of tea. "A storm is brewing," she murmured. "One not of this world nor of the skies." She shivered, though the fire in the hearth burned bright. "I can feel it in the marrow of my bones."

Autumn's chest tightened like a fist. Words clawed at her throat—about the book, about Maxwell, about the wrongness that had seeped into Whispering Pines like poison.

"I checked on Uncle Henry," Flora said.

Evelyn paused, one hand still holding her steaming cup. Her brow creased. "How is he?" she asked, as if the words might bruise if spoken too loudly. "I miss him here at the shop."

Flora's shoulders sagged, the weariness like a shroud. "He's...not himself," she said. "I went to him yesterday. The garden is overgrown, vines creeping up the walls like they're trying to swallow the place whole. Inside, it's cold. Quiet. He was sitting at the old oak table, just staring at nothing. As if the life has been drained out of him."

Autumn's heart twisted. Henry had always been a beacon of warmth and wisdom, his laughter filling the shop on cold winter days, his stories captivating even the most restless children. To think of him hollowed out by grief made her stomach clench and her throat burn.

"I made him tea, sat with him," Flora continued. "He said that he'd made a grievous mistake. Something that touches the very soul of Whispering Pines."

Autumn's breath snagged like a bird caught in a hunter's trap.

Ask what he meant, her mind urged, but her tongue lay useless in her mouth.

Iris tilted her head, indigo eyes narrowing. "The animals are acting strange too. The birds, the cats, even the dogs. They're restless, like they sense something we can't." She twirled a lock of pale hair around her finger.

Evelyn sighed and took a sip of the steaming brew. "Animals are sensitive to changes in the weather," she said, practical as always. "It's probably just the unusual season."

No, Autumn thought, though she still remained silent.

No. It's more than that. Wasn't it?

The roses with their too-sharp thorns, the vines that seemed to move with purpose, the chill that seeped into her bones. The book, revealing prophecies dark as night. And Maxwell, with eyes like bottomless wells and a voice smooth as silk...

Flora's voice soothed her if only for a moment. "Whatever is coming, we'll face it together, ladies."

Autumn nodded and drank from her cup. The steam rose like ghosts and the old clock ticked, each second bringing them closer to whatever awaited.

And then the bell above the door chimed, a note that set Autumn's teeth on edge. Cool air rushed in, carrying the scent of earth and decay and something else, something that made her heart stutter.

It was no usual patron. Maxwell stood in the doorway, tall and dark against the gray day. Autumn's muscles tensed and her breath stuck somewhere between her ribs. Papyrus sprang down from the faded burgundy armchair, his tread lowered and wary. His tail twitched once, then again, ears pinned flat. A hiss tore from his throat, directed squarely at Maxwell.

"Apologies," Maxwell said. He didn't flinch. He never did. "It seems I've offended the house guardian."

His coat was a deep plum that caught the light like brushed velvet. He looked like something from another time—the kind of man old fairy tales warned against too late.

"Ladies," he said. His gaze brushed over them like the sweep of a blade. It found Autumn last.

"Mr. Wolfsbane," Evelyn said. "We don't often have the pleasure."

"A pity. I thought it time I paid my due. I've been looking for something...specific." He wandered, fingers brushing spines like he was reading secrets in the bindings. But he wasn't really looking. Not at books anyway.

"And what might that be?"

"Something in the realm of folklore," he said. And now he was close. Closer than he needed to be. His shadow brushed Autumn's boots. "Local legends. Prophecies, perhaps. I find myself...curious."

He was standing closer now. Too close. His eyes dropped to the necklace at her throat, as though the trinket held more weight than it ought to. He reached out, not touching, but near enough to feel.

"You wore it again," he said softly. "It suits you."

She didn't step back. Didn't smile. "I wear it every day. It was my mother's. Or so I was told. I'd like to believe that part, at least."

"Autumn, you know... I asked Mrs. Meadows where the shop kept the rare books. She pointed at you."

She laughed—unintended, unwilling. Small, but real. It escaped before she could catch it.

Her face shuttered before the sound had faded.

No. No, no, no. You do not laugh at his jokes.

One look at the others told her it was already too late. Evelyn looked quietly amused. Iris raised one sculpted brow, lips curled. Flora's expression said too much with too little.

The idea made her nauseous.

Not a chance, Mister.

She took a step back as Maxwell returned the book to the shelf, a collection of children's fairy tales. "Nothing useful," he said. "But charming, nonetheless. I've always admired bookshops. So many stories stacked together, quietly waiting to be claimed. Like deeds, really."

He nodded to the group. "They say knowledge is power. Good thing I have excellent taste in real estate."

His coat brushed the doorframe as he left. The door swung closed behind him, its echo lingering long after his footsteps had faded.

Papyrus returned, and brushed Autumn's leg as if in penance.

"Well," Evelyn said, smoothing her skirt and apron. "He's...intense."

"Intense is one word," Iris said. "Wouldn't mind him reading me a bedtime story, though."

Autumn groaned.

Flora didn't smile. "He bought herbs from me last evening," she said. "Calming blends. Nightshade. Bit of valerian. Nothing unusual on its own."

Iris blinked. "Didn't know he suffered from nerves."

"This morning, there was a note at my door, thanking me...and a rose. Red. Perfect. Still blooming."

Autumn's fingers found her pendant as if to steady herself, then looked to the empty doorway where Maxwell had stood. Something was happening. She could feel it—coiling at the edges, curling around their lives like smoke beneath the floorboards. Yet they all played the mummer's farce, named him merely a man. Strange. Bold. Harmless.

CHAPTER 12:

THE EMPTY SHELF

Another day arrived in Whispering Pines and a crowd had gathered in the square, drawn not by spectacle or scandal, but by something far simpler. A man.

A man who, by all accounts, had suddenly done more for Whispering Pines than most of its citizens would in a lifetime.

Autumn arrived at the edge of the square, unseen but listening.

"...repaired the fountain himself, paid for the stone and the labor," murmured Birdie to the baker's wife. "And the library— he's having new books sent from Sylvancrest City at his own expense. Can you imagine?"

"Not just the library," came another voice, a shopkeeper Autumn recognized but did not know well. "The roads near the market—he's funding the cobblestone repairs. Said we shouldn't have to twist an ankle just to buy a loaf of bread."

A hum of agreement rippled through the gathered townsfolk. Autumn gripped the strap of her satchel tighter.

"And he asks for nothing in return! A true gentleman, that one."

Maxwell Wolfsbane stood in the heart of it all, as composed as a king surveying his court, like a wolf in another wolf's clothing. He did not fidget, did not shift his weight. He simply stood, waiting, allowing their praise to settle like dust on a long-forgotten book.

Autumn knew the look of a man accustomed to admiration. Maxwell was not flattered. He was assured.

He stepped onto the raised platform near the fountain then. Its waters ran clear once more, its cracks mended by his coin. A small thing, but symbolic. He was always trying to repair what others had deemed broken.

The murmurs faded. The crowd turned.

"Friends," he began, his voice a silk thread weaving through the stillness. "I do not stand before you as a stranger with coin to spare. I stand as a man who sees the beauty of this town, the strength of its people, and simply wishes to preserve what is worth preserving."

A few approving nods.

Maxwell clasped his hands behind his back, his expression shifting—earnest, composed, so perfectly measured that it could only be intentional.

"But preservation is not stagnation," he continued. "Whispering Pines is steeped in history, in traditions passed down like heirlooms. And yet, we must ask ourselves, do we honor history best by remaining in its shadow, or by walking forward, carrying its lessons with us?"

Autumn stiffened. The words were too carefully chosen, too practiced.

And yet, a part of her stirred at them. She had long wondered the same: if honoring the past meant defending it blindly, or forging something new from its ashes.

A breeze stirred the square, sending a few stray leaves skittering across the cobblestones. No one spoke.

Maxwell let the silence linger, let the weight of his words settle. Then, with the ease of a man who already knew he had won them, he smiled.

"A new shipment of books will arrive next week, filling your library with knowledge from across the kingdom. The roads will be repaired before winter sets in. And as for the upcoming celebration…" He spread his hands as if offering something unseen. "Perhaps it is time we celebrate not just where we have been, but where we are going."

The townsfolk did not cheer, but they did not protest.

Autumn saw it in their eyes—the slow, creeping acceptance. This was how it began. Not with fire. Not with war. But with a man standing in a sunlit square, speaking of progress.

And for one treacherous moment, she understood the appeal. He made it sound so simple. So reasonable. He offered not threats but vision. Not power for its own sake, but power in service of something better.

Her heart beat faster. He was speaking to the part of her that wondered what her life could be if she stopped apologizing for her strangeness, for her strength.

A voice, older than her doubts, whispered: "He sees you. He knows what you are. And he would not ask you to hide it."

She shook her head and pulled her cloak tighter, as if that might still the pull of it. But the seed had been planted.

***

The bookstore welcomed Autumn, though the tightness across her chest remained, stubborn as a mule. At least the air was no longer poisoned with praise for a man who deserved none.

Evelyn sat behind the counter, flipping through a leather-bound ledger. "You look like you've been running."

Autumn pressed both hands against the oaken counter, drawing strength from its solidity beneath her fingers. "Not running," she managed, voice ragged. "Just—" She exhaled sharply. "You were wise to stay away. It was unbearable."

Evelyn hummed low in her throat, eyes still fixed on her numbers. "The speech?"

Sweat gathered along Autumn's spine, her blouse clinging to her back like wet parchment. The shop held the pleasant coolness of stone walls in summer, yet heat radiated from her skin as though she burned with fever.

"The performance," she corrected, the word sharp as castle-forged steel. "He stood there speaking like a man who had already claimed the throne, and no one even questioned him."

Evelyn finally raised her gaze. Her shrewd eyes moved deliberately over Autumn's damp brow, the restless shifting of her weight, as if her clothes had suddenly been tailored for another's form. "You don't trust him."

"Not even a little."

Evelyn leaned forward, elbows resting lightly on the counter. "And why is that?"

Autumn caught sight of the red rose in the vase on the counter, and the words pressed up inside her, too many and too tangled to escape.

Great. Not you too.

"Because he's lying," she said instead, the simplest truth among many.

Evelyn arched a skeptical brow.

Autumn hesitated. She had no proof that would satisfy the small council, let alone Evelyn, with her ledgers and logic. Yet the unease growing within her had sunk roots deep into her bones, tendrils of certainty that would not be silenced.

Say it. Just say it. She lowered her voice to a whisper that would not carry beyond the shelves. "I think he's Magnus Blackthorn."

There. I said it.

Evelyn blinked once, twice, like an owl awakened in daylight. She sighed with the weariness of one who has heard too many tall tales, removed her glasses, and began cleaning them with the edge of her sleeve.

"Who?"

Heat flushed Autumn's cheeks. "Magnus Blackthorn. The book I found. The old history of Whispering Pines, the one everyone seems to have forgotten. He looks exactly like the portrait."

Evelyn pinched the bridge of her nose, her voice gentler now but no less skeptical. "Autumn."

"I found a book, Evelyn. A history of Whispering Pines, one that seems to have vanished from memory. It speaks of Magnus Blackthorn and—"

Her pulse quickened, blood rushing in her ears louder than drums before battle. "He looks exactly like the portrait in the book. Exactly."

Evelyn sat in silence, with the patient look of someone waiting for reason to take hold. As if, at any moment, Autumn might hear her own words, realize how absurd they sounded, and let the matter drop.

"I know how it sounds," she said again, sharper this time. Her skin flushed hot as fire, sweat beading at her temples. "I'm not claiming he's a ghost risen from the crypts. Or—I don't know. Perhaps he is. Or maybe it's his bloodline, some descendant carrying forward the same ambitions, or perhaps—"

Evelyn sighed the sigh of the long-suffering, slipping her glasses back onto her nose. "Autumn, listen to yourself. You're reaching like a child grasping for the moon."

"I'm not reaching. I'm piecing together fragments of truth, and they fit like a well-made sword in its scabbard."

Evelyn studied her with a silence that stretched longer than a northern winter. "And what if you're wrong?"

The thought had never truly taken root in the soil of her mind.

What if I am wrong?

Evelyn leaned back in her chair, exhaling with the patience of one who has seen many summers. "I've heard tales of the Blackthorn legacy from years past, but only that they once stood tall among the noble houses of Sylvancrest City."

Autumn clenched her jaw tight enough to make her teeth ache. Her fingers moved of their own accord to her locket, the metal cool against her feverish skin.

"I just need you to believe me."

Evelyn's gaze softened, but she shook her head with gentle finality. "I believe that you believe it." She stepped closer, tucking a stray strand of hair behind Autumn's ear with the tenderness of a mother.

"Autumn, I've known you for years. Your mind shines brighter than any sun, and your heart holds more courage than many men who claim the title of knight. If the cosmos had ever blessed me with a daughter, I'd hope she'd have your spirit. But I also know that your head soars with the ravens while your feet rarely touch the ground."

Autumn turned away before Evelyn could witness the tears welling up in her eyes. Heat engulfed her, suffocating, as if she had only now realized she could not draw breath.

"He's going to take this town apart," she murmured, speaking more to the watching shadows than to Evelyn. "Piece by piece, and no one will notice until there's nothing left but dust and memory."

The book!

The thought struck her like a blade, sharp and sudden. She should fetch the book. She should show Evelyn. That would make her believe. That would make her see.

Autumn's chest tightened as the idea took root. The sweat on her skin turned cold, clinging to her like a second shadow. Why hadn't she thought of it sooner?

If Evelyn saw it, the portrait of Magnus, the missing pages, the prophecy scrawled in that ancient, spidery hand, she would have to listen. She would have no choice.

Without a word, Autumn made haste toward the back of the shop, her boots striking the floorboards with a steady, determined rhythm. The wooden steps groaned beneath her weight as she descended into the basement, the air growing cooler, heavier.

Her pulse quickened with every step. This would change everything. It had to. She reached the far shelf, her eyes darting to the spot where she had left it, but her fingers grasped at nothing.

The space was empty.

Autumn froze, her hand hovering in midair as if the book might materialize if she waited long enough. She reached again, her fingers brushing against the rough wood of the shelf, searching for something that wasn't there.

No. No, this can't be.

Her heart pounded against her ribs as she dropped to her knees, pulling books aside, checking behind them, beneath them. Dust clouded the air, swirling in the dim light as she shoved volumes aside, knocking over a small stack in her haste. Pages fluttered to the ground like fallen leaves, their whispers mocking her.

Gone. She knelt there, unmoving, her hands pressed against her thighs, her breath coming in short, shallow gasps. The book was gone. Someone had taken it.

Or… Her stomach twisted. Had she imagined it?

No. No, she had held it. She had read it. The portrait of Magnus, the prophecy, the history of Whispering Pines, it had been real. She had traced the words with her own fingers, felt the weight of its secrets in her hands.

But now, it was missing.

She swallowed hard, forcing herself to stand. Her legs trembled, unsteady beneath her. She turned in a slow circle, her eyes scanning the basement for any sign that someone had been here, for some clue, some misplaced book, some sign that she hadn't just dreamed it all.

Her fingers moved with desperate precision as she tore through stacks of forgotten tales. She combed through the dim recesses beneath tables, pried behind crates coated in years of neglect, and even forced herself to peer into the basement's darkest corners, where the light dared not reach. Yet the book slipped further from her grasp with each passing second, an apparition dissolving into the ether.

Nothing. A cold, crawling feeling crept up her spine. Someone else knew. Someone else had seen the book. And they had taken it. She backed away from the empty shelf, her pulse thrumming in her ears. She needed to think. She needed to breathe. She needed to get out of the basement.

CHAPTER 13:

BORN OF FIRE, KISSED BY GOLD

The book had slipped from Autumn's grasp like a greased eel, leaving only the ghost of its weight in her trembling hands. Evelyn had offered no counsel worth keeping. Flora had tried, but her words broke apart like brittle twigs in a winter wind.

Breathe, she commanded herself, but the air tasted thick and stale.

At the edge of the garden, a single rose bloomed. Red as spilled wine. A furious little flame, daring the dusk to smother it.

Her hand moved of its own accord. Pale fingers brushed the petals; soft as silk, treacherous with thorns hidden beneath.

Then something spoke. It did not sound so much as arrive, slithering into the world like breath through fog. Neither near nor far. Neither loud nor soft.

A strangled gasp escaped her lips, and chill crawled down her spine like the touch of a grave-cold hand.

"Ouch!" A crimson bead welled on her fingertip, a mirror to the rose's defiant bloom. "Who's there?" No answer came. Only the rustle of leaves.

Her shoulders sagged and a sigh escaped her then, dragged up from the depths of her soul, weary, defeated. She closed her eyes, seeking a moment's respite, but the exhaustion suffocated her.

She moved to the hearth of her cottage. Her fingers, pale and clumsy, closed around the kettle. Steam hissed, curling like a dying man's last breath. The familiar motions brought no pleasure tonight.

But the first sip tasted wrong, bitter and burnt, like ash from an old fire. Her stomach churned. Bile surged behind her teeth. The cup slipped from her grip, cracked against the saucer, tea spilling like ink across parchment.

Even my tea betrays me tonight.

The room shifted and the walls tilted like ships in a storm. Candlelight bled into shadow. A weight gathered behind her eyes, dragging her lids down as though sewn with stones.

The rose still lay where she'd cast it days ago, its petals bright, its dew unfallen, unmarred by time. No wilt. No rot. Just that same impossible red.

Her knees buckled. The bed rushed up to meet her, and darkness swallowed the room whole.

***

Autumn's eyes fluttered open. First came the weight of her body, then the hard surface beneath her.

"Born of fire, by gold adorned…" It was not quite a sound, not quite a thought, but something between, like the tolling of a distant bell heard through thick fog.

Her consciousness wavered, tethered to her by the thinnest of threads. Her body felt strange: too large, too small, shifting like smoke caught between forms. The boundaries of self blurred, ran like paint left too long in the rain.

A deep hunger gnawed at her, a ravenous beast that sank its talons into her gut and twisted. It clawed relentlessly, a hollow ache that drowned all else. Never had hunger burned so fierce, so raw. It roared through her, insatiable, a fire that devoured reason, as if her very bones were starved.

She tried to speak, but the words came out wrong. Not words at all, but a low, rolling sound that shook through her like the sky before a storm. Thunder, or wind, or fire itself—she couldn't tell, only that it wasn't human. And it belonged to her.

The sound reverberated through her bones, a primal thing that clawed its way up from some deep crypt. Deeper than memory. It was a sound that spoke of ancient things, of roots burrowing through forgotten earth, of winds that carried whispers older than blood.

Her gaze swept the world before her. Towering trees, ancient as the roots of the earth, pierced the rocky expanse, their gnarled branches swayed in a cool wind that kissed her scales—*scales?* Sparse and weathered, they dotted the jagged terrain, and every rustle below snared her attention.

Her skin tightened, no longer hers. A pressure swelled within, vast and unyielding, as if her flesh sought to burst its seams. She lifted her hand to see it, to know it, but no hand greeted her. Claws came instead, massive and cruel, their serpentine skin rippled like a river of molten bronze.

Her breath halted, a snarl in her throat, and realization sank its teeth deep: she gazed through a dragon's eyes.

A hawk sliced the sky. A hare darted in the underbrush, its heartbeat a drum in her ears. The scents flooded her senses: pine, bitter and green, with the cold musk of stone, rich and heavy in her nostrils.

Her massive form prowled the rugged slopes, each step rumbled the earth beneath her taloned feet. The mountain stretched wild and untamed, its untouched corners abound with prey: elk that roamed the shadowed vales, goats that clung to jagged crags, their bleats a siren's call to her rending jaws.

She could taste their fear on the wind, and her maw watered with need. The wilds beckoned, and she hunted, a shadow of scales and flame upon the broken stone.

In the distance, they emerged: deer. A small group grazed quietly among the trees along the mountain's edge, heads lowered, oblivious to the predator watching from the shadows.

The deer bore a mark that spoke of otherworldly things: a white crescent of fur on their foreheads. Some had spectral antlers rising from their skulls—not bone, but something spun from shadow and moonlight.

The herd scattered in a blur of motion then, hooves drumming against the earth, all but one. This solitary creature remained, its dark eyes piercing the veil between what was and what could be.

It showed no fear, no desperate urge to flee. Motionless. Calm. Only the faint flicker of its ears betrayed any movement, as though it understood that some moments are written in blood and destiny.

This singular, impossible thing remained.

Autumn's heart thundered. Her massive frame trembled, every sinew coiled with anticipation. Energy crackled around her like lightning waiting to strike. She remembered venison, tender, seasoned by human hands. But this? This would be different.

What remained of her humanity recoiled at the thought of raw meat, of taking life with her own claws. Yet the hunger rose, a primal thing, both foreign and achingly familiar.

She lowered herself even closer to the ground. Her jaws unhinged. A cavern of ancient hunger. Breath scorched the air. Saliva threaded with something darker than blood. Primal need clawed up from her core—past humanity, past memory. Pure hunger. Pure violence.

The deer did not run then—it waited.

Autumn erupted from sleep, not a gentle rising, but a violent explosion of limbs and ragged breath. Sweat pearled across her skin, cold as grave-dirt. The room spun, shadows twisting like serpents at the edge of vision.

Smoke, thick and heavy, filled her lungs, though no flame danced, no embers glowed. Just the acrid promise of something burned, something destroyed.

Her hands betrayed her. Trembling. A violent, full-bodied tremor that threatened to shake her apart. Fingers splayed like broken branches, skin pale as dead winter light. Each quiver spoke of something fundamental breaking—bones, or will, or the very fabric of what she believed was real.

Then, hands, warm and sure, found her shoulders. "Easy now," came a voice, like velvet pulled through ash.

She froze.

Maxwell.

He was beside her. Sitting on the edge of the bed as if he belonged there. His presence softened the air, stilled the smoke that had no source.

"You were dreaming," he said, brushing damp hair from her brow. His touch was gentle, practiced, like he'd done it a hundred times before.

She wanted to flinch. Wanted to pull away. But her body betrayed her, sinking toward him, lured by the promise of steadiness in the wake of chaos.

"I saw fire," she murmured. "I was…burning. No, not burning—I was the fire."

Maxwell smiled. "Dreams have a way of showing us truths we hide from ourselves."

His eyes held hers. They gleamed like deep water, calm on the surface, concealing fathoms beneath.

She blinked. The shadows shifted.

Something was off; the way the light failed to touch his skin, the way his reflection failed to dance in the mirror across the room.

"Maxwell?" she whispered.

He tilted his head, but said nothing.

The floor creaked behind her.

She turned, just a flicker of movement.

And then—

She woke again. For real this time. Alone. Sheets damp. Heart rattling in its cage. No voice. No comfort. Just the echo of his fingers where none had touched her.

And the distant scent of roses.

CHAPTER 14:

THE BORROWED CHILD

The day of the celebration arrived in Whispering Pines, and by noon, the town had come alive. Music spilled from every corner, a symphony of fiddles and flutes weaving through the crowd like threads of gold. The square pulsed with movement, vendors calling out their wares, children darting between stalls, their laughter high and sweet as birdsong.

The weather had turned out lovely, bright and sunlit, the kind of warmth that settled gently on the skin. The air held the rich scent of popcorn and the buttery warmth of fresh pastries. Cinnamon and honey coaxed even the most resolute passersby to pause, to indulge. It was a siren's call, drawing them in, pulling them toward the heart of the square.

Autumn stood among them, a cup of cold tea cradled in her hands. The chill was welcome against her skin beneath the weight of the sun. She lifted it to her lips, breathing in the notes of dried leaves and faint spice.

Look at them, she thought, *so connected and carefree.*

She couldn't shake last night's dream. His voice still echoed in her thoughts. She kept her gaze moving. Watching. Waiting.

Somewhere among the sea of faces, Maxwell Wolfsbane lingered. She had not seen him yet, but she knew he was there. He always was.

There was Iris, the free spirit. She stood in the midst of a group, her hands dancing through the air as she spoke, her gestures as expressive as the strokes of her brush. Behind her, her latest works were displayed, their colors bold and alive, each canvas a window into her wild imagination.

Then came Sylas Finch. He moved through the crowd like an absentminded ghost. Interpreting her eye contact as an invitation, Sylas initiated a conversation and spoke in his usual riddles.

"Miss Ashwood." He inclined his head. "Have you ever considered the intricate dance between books and destiny?"

Autumn tightened her grip around her cup. *Of course, he would say something like that.*

"Oh, uh…no, not really."

Sylas leaned in slightly as if sharing a well-guarded secret. "Ah, the written word has a power of its own. It can shape destinies, uncover hidden truths, and even bind the fates of those who dare to read between the lines. But be cautious, for not every story unfolds as expected."

"Our destinies?" she asked.

Sylas only smiled. "This celebration is a splendid affair, wouldn't you say?"

He had sidestepped the question with a skill sharpened by years of avoiding direct answers.

Autumn hesitated, then nodded. "It is indeed, Mr. Finch."

Sylas smiled. "Magic. A force that often hides in plain sight, much like the treasures within these books. Perhaps the ink is not always visible."

Autumn lifted her cup in a silent toast, more to end the conversation than to agree with whatever game Sylas was playing.

Papyrus darted into the sun-dappled grass, his sleek form a shadow against the sunlight. His eyes were fixed on the fluttering creature before him: a butterfly. He leaped and twisted, his nimble paws batting playfully at the air as though he and the butterfly were partners in a whimsical dance, a fleeting game of predator and prey.

There was something enchanting about the scene, something that made the weight of the secrets she carried feel a little lighter, if only for a moment. The butterfly's glow pulsed in time with Papyrus's movements, its light casting delicate patterns on the grass, a living kaleidoscope of gold and green.

Another butterfly spiraled around Autumn, its wings flickered like ember-lit silk. A strange feeling stirred in her chest as the butterfly whispered: "What once was lost shall be reclaimed, what once was stolen, now renamed…"

The words threaded themselves into the quiet spaces between her thoughts. Autumn blinked, willing them away, but they clung to her like the last embers of a dying fire, stubborn and slow to fade.

Autumn noticed a child then, alone on the cobblestone street. She looked like a wounded fawn lost in the festival's bustle. Tears streaked the girl's cheeks, catching the light, and her small shoulders slumped as if burdened by a hidden weight.

She knelt, bringing herself eye-level with the girl's tear-streaked face. "Hi there. What's your name?"

The little one sniffled, rubbing at her eyes with a tiny fist. "Aster," she replied.

"Are you lost, Aster?" Autumn felt a sharp pang between her ribs.

The child shook her head, dark curls bouncing against pale cheeks. "No, not lost. Another kid took my chocolate, and now I don't want to play anymore," Aster confessed.

The theft of a sweet seemed a small thing to grown folk, but to a child, it could feel like the end of all joy. She remembered her own childhood hurts, wounds that had seemed so vast at the time.

"It's going to be alright, Aster. Let's go get you another piece of chocolate." The offer came unbidden, surprising even Autumn herself.

Aster's small fingers curled around Autumn's hand with a trust that felt both precious and terrifying. Such faith, so easily given. Autumn knew the weight of such trust, knew how easily it could be broken. Yet she found herself leading the child toward the candy shop, her steps more certain than they had been all day.

Speech had always been Autumn's enemy, so silence now seemed a comfortable companion. She offered what comfort she could, a gentle squeeze of the hand, a soft smile, small gestures that required no speech yet spoke volumes in their quiet way.

The door to the candy shop swung open with a soft chime. Sweetness spilled into the air: dark chocolate, rich as gold coin; sugar spun fine as silk; spices warm and strange, whispering of far-off coasts and markets under foreign suns. The shop was a treasure hoard, no less, the kind even a dragon might pause to admire.

The girl's eyes widened like twin moons, her earlier tears forgotten as she gazed upon glass jars filled with treats of every color.

The shopkeeper looked up as they approached, a woman whose kind eyes had seen many children come and go through her doors. Autumn's fingers gripped the edge of the wooden counter, seeking strength from its solid reality.

"Um," she began, and her voice cracked worse than green wood in a fire. She cleared her throat, painfully aware of the woman's patient gaze. Aster's hopeful eyes lent her a strength she did not possess alone.

"May I get something special for Aster?" she finally managed, the words tumbling out in a rush. Her cheeks burned hot as forge-fire, and she fixed her gaze on the worn counter, tracing the patterns in the wood grain as if reading some ancient text written there.

The shopkeeper smiled and selected a chocolate bar wrapped in paper that gleamed like beaten silver in the shop's warm light.

"This is a special treat, just for you," the woman told Aster.

Autumn watched the girl's face transform again, sorrow replaced by joy as swift and complete as summer replacing winter. Small fingers carefully unwrapped the treasure with a reverence usually reserved for holy relics.

She felt a strange peace settle over her, like finding a hidden pool of stillness in a raging river. There was room for small victories, for kindnesses that cost little yet meant much.

The door chimed again, and Evelyn entered. She wore her usual smile, though Autumn could see the strain behind it, the way a practiced eye might spot a hairline crack in fine porcelain.

"Hello, ladies," Evelyn called out, her voice cheerful despite the weariness that hung about her. "Looks like we're out of marshmallows. The display's empty—thought I'd pop in and grab some more."

Her eyes fell upon Aster, and her brows lifted in question. "And who's this little one?"

"This is Aster," Autumn said, her hand gentle on the child's shoulder. "She was having a rough time, but I think it's all better now."

"Well, it's good to meet you, Aster. Nothing like a little sweetness to brighten the day, huh?"

Autumn moved closer to the librarian, leaning in to speak words meant for her alone. "Um, Evelyn, could you…um, help Aster find her parents? She says she isn't lost, but, you know, just to make sure she stays safe and…gets back to them?"

Evelyn nodded, understanding without need for lengthy explanation. She took Aster's hand with the gentle confidence that came so naturally to her.

"Can you tell me who your parents are, sweetheart?"

Autumn watched them leave, an odd mixture of emotions swirling within her breast: relief that Aster would be safely returned, a strange emptiness at the child's departure, and beneath it all, a quiet satisfaction. In a world full of large and daunting challenges, she had faced a small one and not been found wanting.

***

She felt it as soon as she left the candy shop: the warmth of the day now tempered by a sluggish wind that whispered of rain. The kind that didn't cool, just clung. Clouds gathered at the edges of the sky, not yet dark but waiting.

The festival still hummed with life—fiddles played, laughter rang, and the scent of roasted nuts tangled with woodsmoke. But it all felt distant, like a memory playing too far off to grasp. She kept to the fringe of the crowd, unsure what she was looking for.

Birdie found her first, a bundle of napkins tucked beneath one arm and a pastry half-eaten in her hand. "Are you alright?"

she asked, peering at Autumn with narrowed eyes. "You've got that look. Like you've seen a ghost, or worse—one of those after-season pies Callum insists on baking with leftover fruit."

She still couldn't shake the dream, the way Maxwell had spoken to her in it, voice low and kind, hands gentle in a way that didn't belong to him. It had felt real. Too real. And now, awake beneath the sun, she couldn't decide what unsettled her more: the dream itself...or how much she'd wanted to believe it.

Birdie clucked her tongue and leaned in a little closer, lowering her voice more out of habit than caution. "Actually...you just reminded me of something strange. Meant to tell you days ago, just forgot." She took another bite of her pastry, then wiped her hands on her apron, already deep in her own story before Autumn could answer. "You know me, I keep things to myself about as well as a cracked jug holds water."

Birdie's face was paler than usual now, her brow tight with something held too long.

"I was out in the garden the other day," she continued, "gathering the last of the thyme before the weather spoiled it. That's when I heard them. Voices...from Maxwell's room. And not just idle talk. It was...tense. Like two hounds circling before a fight."

Autumn felt the pull in her chest; a tightening, as though the strings of her ribs had been drawn taut.

"Maxwell's voice was sharp as a blade," Birdie whispered. "But the other man—he wavered. One moment bold, the next near pleading."

Autumn's fingers clutched her pendant. "Who was it?"

Birdie shook her head. "I went to check to see if everything was alright. Just to be sure. But when I reached the top of the stairs...silence." She hesitated, swallowed, then continued.

"Then the door opened. Slowly. Like whatever was behind it wasn't done hiding."

She shook her head as if the memory chilled her even now.

"Sylas stepped out."

Autumn blinked. "Sylas?"

"But not the Sylas we know. Not the one who speaks in riddles and wanders like his feet forget where they're going. His face was wrong. Shut tight. Like he'd swallowed something bitter and didn't dare spit it out. He didn't even see me. Just kept walking, fast, quick as a man fleeing a grave."

Autumn's mouth had gone dry.

"Then the door slammed shut behind him," Birdie finished. "I didn't knock. I didn't dare."

Sylas, who wove words like spider's silk, was reduced to silence. Her stomach turned.

A breeze coiled through the square, thick with the scent of roses—not fresh, not clean. Sweet, but sickly. Something blooming too late, too long. Like rot beneath perfume.

Birdie placed a hand on her arm. "You won't tell him I spoke of it, will you?"

Autumn shook her head, but the unease had already taken root.

What bargain had broken behind that door?

Birdie gave a quick glance toward the sky, where the clouds had darkened at the edges. "Hope the rain holds out," she murmured. "Would be a shame if it ruined Legends Night."

CHAPTER 15:

A NIGHT OF LEGENDS

Autumn watched the first stars pierce the veil of twilight. The hour had come for her to don her costume, to hide behind the mask of revelry while her mind churned with darker secrets. She slipped away from the noise and found refuge in the empty washroom.

Her fingers trembled slightly as she withdrew her dress from its bag, the fabric cool and smooth beneath her touch. A small swell of pride bloomed in her chest—this, at least, was hers. Not borrowed, not gifted by some well-meaning hand, but crafted by her own design, paid for with coin she had earned. In a life where so much remained beyond her grasp, this simple ownership felt like victory.

The mirror offered no comfort. Her reflection stared back, a stranger with familiar eyes. Autumn studied the face that sometimes felt like someone else's: the curve of her jaw, the slope of her nose, the arch of her brows. All pieces of a puzzle with no picture to guide its assembly.

Do I have her eyes? The thought often came when she confronted her own image. She wondered for the thousandth time if her eyes mirrored her mother's, if somewhere in her features lay the ghost of the woman whose blood ran in her veins but whose voice she had never heard. What words might that woman have spoken, had she lived? What wisdom or warnings might she have passed down?

A deep breath filled her lungs. A final glance at the strange girl in the glass before she stepped back toward the celebration that awaited.

Autumn's midnight-blue dress caught the flickering lantern light, its gold and silver detailing dancing like scattered stars in a winter sky. The fabric embraced her form as though woven from the night itself, an embodiment of the ancient myths that Legends Night sought to honor with its frivolous masquerade.

Upon her head sat a delicate crown of stars, tiny points of light twined into a circlet of silver wire that she had bent and shaped with her own hands through long evening hours. She had crafted it with the care of a smith forging a lord's sword, a tribute to the celestial wonders that had always called to her spirit when earthly matters proved too burdensome.

If they only knew what I was carrying. The thought was a cold stone in her belly. *I wish I could share what I know, but who would understand?*

The book's secrets felt heavier than any physical burden, knowledge that changed everything yet could be shared with no one. Not here, not among the laughing revelers with their painted faces and shallow concerns.

The noise of the celebration swelled around her like a rising tide, threatening to pull her under. Fatigue pressed in, a familiar weariness that came with these gatherings, where words must be measured and expressions guarded.

She longed for a quiet corner, a moment to collect her scattered thoughts and draw breath without eyes upon her. Just one moment of peace.

But she straightened her spine and lifted her chin, her star crown catching the light. Autumn watched as townsfolk she had known all her life became strangers before her eyes; delicate winged fairies who normally sold bread at the market, bears with hungry eyes who taught children their letters by day, wizards whose hands more commonly held ledgers than wands. For one night, the burden of time had been lifted from the town's shoulders as if years were merely cloaks to be shed at will.

Flora moved through the press of bodies like a wood witch. Men and women alike parted before her. The forest itself seemed to have claimed her, weaving its bounty into her garments as a lord might adorn a favored daughter with jewels.

Evelyn and Roger stood together near the bonfire like twin stars in the night sky. They had come as the Moon and Sun; she in silvers and blues, he in warm golden hues. Their costumes spoke of the dance between light and shadow that governed all things. Autumn noted how their hands remained linked, fingers entwined like roots beneath the earth, steadfast and sure.

Iris bloomed in deep violet, her gown catching the firelight like the sky at dusk, when day surrenders to night but stars have yet to reveal themselves. Her attire was not a costume shaped by fancy, yet the paint and glitter adorning her face transformed her into something fey and wild.

Henry Hawthorne was absent. Perhaps the weight of his years had finally bent his back too far—or perhaps he knew something the others did not. Old men often had a sense for ill winds before they blew, as if their proximity to death granted them sight beyond the veil of the living.

Autumn took a seat by the bonfire, the flames casting long shadows. The first storyteller stepped forward, a man whose face was lined like a map of ancient kingdoms. He spoke of the Guardian of the Forest, a great bear that once stood between Whispering Pines and the darkness that sought to claim it.

"Gather 'round as I recount the tale of the Guardian of the Forest," the elder began, his voice enveloping the crowd like a warm blanket. "Long ago, a mighty bear stood as protector over Whispering Pines, shielding it from darkness. In those days, magic coursed through the town, as tangible as the air we breathe today. This bear, more than a creature of fur and fang, was a beacon of that magic, a true guardian that walked between the realms of man and the ancient forces of the forest."

He raised his hands, mimicking the bear's powerful stance, and the children gasped. The fire crackled, the flames dancing to the rhythm of his words. Applause followed, murmurs of appreciation rippling through the gathered crowd.

Another storyteller took the elder's place, a familiar young man taking his turn. Known to Autumn for his enthusiasm for magic, wizards, and dragons, he began recounting a tale of a brave hero's victory over a mighty dragon.

He spun a tale of dragon slayers and heroes, their triumphs sung in ballads. The words twisted in Autumn's chest. Not so long ago, she might have smiled along with the rest, but now the story left a bitter taste. The glorification of dragon slaying cast a shadow over her enjoyment of the tale, given her recent discoveries and the newfound understanding of their significance to Whispering Pines.

Autumn pressed damp palms against her skirt and cleared her throat. "May I—may I share one?" she asked.

Old Miller Hawkes, pipe dangling from his lips, chuckled. "This ought to be a good one." Light laughter followed. She stared at the flames, drawing courage from their restless sway. Her fingers now curled around a fallen pinecone, turning it over and over while the hush settled again.

The firelight caught the edge of her boot as she tapped it once, quick, uncertain. The murmurs of the crowd dimmed, and eyes turned toward her. Her voice trembled:

"Many years past," she began, her eyes fixed toward the fire, "a tale of love, betrayal, and a quest for power unfolded. It is a tale few dare to recall, its truths buried beneath the weight of fear and time, yet its echoes linger still, drifting through the years like wind over forgotten hills."

A swallow caught in her throat. She turned the pinecone again, grounding herself as the old rhythm of storytelling took hold.

"There was a man then, tall and proud, with hair as black as a raven's wing and eyes like a starless night. He was a figure of undeniable charm and ruthless ambition; a man who could smile as he stole the ground from beneath your feet."

She paused, as her thoughts drifted to Maxwell and her dream.

"His heart, or what passed for one, was captured by a woman whose beauty was said to rival the stars' soft light upon still waters."

She glanced at the circle of listeners, then quickly back to the fire. A few faces had softened. Encouraged, she lifted her chin slightly.

"He loved her, or so he claimed, though his love was a greedy thing. He harbored a dream that stretched beyond the mere confines of love: a vision to reign over the magical forest that cradled Whispering Pines and, hence, all of Sylvancrest. Once woven from threads of passion and shared dreams, their bond began to fray. She was no fool, though his charm might have deceived lesser hearts."

Her throat tightened. She swallowed again. Her voice no longer faltered.

"She saw the darkness creeping into him, the ambition that poisoned his soul. For she was not merely a woman of beauty; she was something far older, her blood tied to the forest. Her heart recoiled at the darkness that sought to consume the purity of their beginning.

The day came when he laid bare his ambition before her, a plea for her to stand by his side as he bent the forest's magic to his will. Her refusal was as sharp and final as a blade, a chasm that could never be bridged again."

Her fingers clenched around the pinecone, its rough scales pressing into her palm.

"What followed was not love turned to hatred but something colder, more dangerous, a war of wills that would shape the fate of Sylvancrest. Fueled by the bitter taste of betrayal and the sting of rejection, he spiraled into madness, consumed by an insatiable thirst for power."

A breeze stirred the fire's edge, and with it, her hair brushed across her cheek.

"Their final confrontation came in the heart of the forest. She stood alone against him, the first of the Dragonkin, called upon the ancient rites and secrets known only to those whose fates were entwined with the dragons of old."

Now her voice had settled into something sure.

"She wove a powerful spell, severing his connection to the forces he sought to enslave. His powers were torn from him in a torrent of fire and shadow. Broken and defeated, he was banished from the kingdom, cast out to wander as a hollow shadow of the man he once was."

She shifted her weight.

"The woman took what remained of his power, hiding it where no darkness could ever claim it. Her name faded into legend, her deeds remembered only by the line of dragon whisperers who followed her: a sacred lineage sworn to protect Sylvancrest."

Her voice softened now, almost reverent.

"Thus, the prologue to the saga of Whispering Pines was written not in ink but in the echoes of a battle fought beneath ancient boughs, where myth and reality often walk hand in hand; the story of a woman and the man she once loved serves as a reminder that the heart of Sylvancrest is, and always will be, protected by those who command the ancient magic of the dragons."

When the final word passed her lips, Autumn exhaled. She dropped the pinecone, fingers trembling.

Her voice faded. Sparks drifted upward, mirroring the quiet that fell across the gathering. For a moment, no one moved. Then a single clap sounded, another followed, and the applause continued—softly.

Out of the circle stepped a young girl garbed in orange and black, silk wings stitched to her sleeves. She curtsied, eyes shining. She began the tale of a prince whose bravery and kindness outshone any crown, and the night's stories rolled on.

The prince, she said, had set out to save his town and the forest from an endless winter, armed with nothing but his wits and a heart unafraid to feel. Through trials and shadows, he had won the trust of the forest's creatures, learning that strength lay not in swords but in understanding and compassion.

The prince's loyalty, his love for his people and the land, stirred something deep within Autumn; a memory, sharp and sweet, of Philip. Her chest tightened, a bittersweet ache blooming as she thought of his laughter.

But Autumn couldn't listen any longer; the polite clatter of applause rang hollow, as though her tale had fallen on deaf ears. She rose from her place in the circle and walked through the square, letting the swirl of masked revelers and bright costumes tug her mind elsewhere.

Maxwell. He did not emerge from the dark so much as arrive. It was as if the night had made space for him, and he'd only now chosen to fill it. The golden wolf mask concealed all expression, but his eyes, dark and unreadable, found hers at once.

He wore a long coat of midnight blue, nearly the exact shade as her own dress. Too close to be a coincidence, though she doubted he'd admit to anything so deliberate. It felt like a trick, a spell laid without her knowing.

His gloves were black, his boots polished to a mirror sheen. Over his face, he wore a wolf's mask: gold, smooth, and expressionless. Not snarling. Not baring teeth.

Just watching. Always watching.

The music changed. Slower now. "Miss Ashwood," he said. "May I have this dance?"

She should have said no. She meant to. The word hovered on her tongue, trembling, ready to leap.

But she didn't speak it.

He extended his hand. His fingers were steady, unhurried, as though he knew the answer already.

"I don't think it's a good idea," she murmured.

"But you do think about it," he said. "That counts for something."

Her hand met his before she realized she had moved. His grip was firm, cool through the leather. He guided her gently to the center of the square.

Maxwell's hand found the small of her back, guiding her into the slow rhythm of the music as though it were second nature. They began to move. And the world folded in.

This is a mistake.

He danced like a man born to it—not rigid, not overconfident, but precise. Her body knew the rhythm, but he led it. As if he knew her rhythm already.

The lantern light from the square flickered across his face, gilding the hollows of his cheekbones, the sharp line of his jaw. The world narrowed to the space between them.

"You look stunning tonight," he murmured, his voice a low current beneath the music. "Stunningly beautiful."

I don't want to enjoy this. I don't want to feel safe here.

Autumn said nothing. She focused on the steady pressure of his hand, the feel of his coat against her fingers, the way his gaze did not drift. It stayed fixed on her, unwavering.

"I heard the story you told by the fire," he added. "Quite the tale."

Still, he did not name it. He let it hang between them.

Then, softer: "You look like the night sky made flesh. Bearing the weight of distant stars. And like those celestial bodies, you shine, despite all that darkness pressing in around you."

The music slowed. Around them, the revel continued, laughter, the clink of mugs, the occasional snap of firewood, but it all felt muted, distant.

"You don't belong among them," he said. "They see your kindness. They don't see your strength."

She said nothing.

"You walk through their little world pretending to fit," he continued. "But we both know better. You feel it. Don't you?"

He was too close. And yet not close enough.

"Feel what?" she asked.

"The weight of it. The eyes. The blood in your veins that remembers things you haven't yet learned."

He leaned in near enough that the mask brushed her temple.

"You could be so much more," he whispered. "You already are."

The music swelled, rich and aching. Autumn's fingers curled tighter against his shoulder, her knuckles pale beneath the lantern light. She hated that she wanted to know what he meant—hated more that some secret part of her, buried beneath caution and pride, agreed with him.

The words slid beneath her skin like a blade eased into velvet. How did he know the shape of the ache in her so well? How did he speak to the hollow places she dared not name? And why did part of her wish he didn't wear that mask?

Guilt struck sharp, sudden, like betrayal rising in her own chest. Not of the town. Of herself.

She drew in a breath that trembled on the way out. "I know who you are," she said.

His reply came softly, almost amused. "Do you now?" Then his voice darkened, subtle as storm clouds gathering beyond the horizon. "But do you know who you are? Because I do."

She looked up.

And the wolf looked back.

The music faded. The dance ended. Autumn stepped away before the silence could stretch too far, before her legs betrayed her and the truth broke free. She didn't curtsy. Didn't thank him. Her fingers unclasped from his as if from a wound.

She turned and walked toward the edge of the crowd, the press of bodies and firelight suddenly distant, unreal. Her pulse thrashed in her throat, wild and uneven, as though it no longer answered to her.

Keep walking. Just breathe. Just get away from him before he says more. Before I want to hear it.

Behind her, Maxwell did not move. He stood where she'd left him, a carved figure in midnight cloth and silver edges, smiling.

Watching.

CHAPTER 16:
THE MAN WITH THE KEYS

The night carried a bite that did not belong to this time of year, a sharp coolness that pressed against her skin, creeping beneath the folds of her dress. But the air was changing; growing humid, heavy. Clouds now smothered the stars, and the warmth of the firelight behind her felt distant, as if the world had drawn a curtain between what was and what would come.

Autumn passed Flora, radiant in her joy, lost in conversation with her beau. They sat on a bench outside the bakery, sharing bread and ale. She continued toward the food displays, where spiced cider steamed in wooden cups and the scent of roasted nuts wafted through the air.

A pastry called to her, a simple thing, golden and dusted with sugar. She bit into it, savoring the cinnamon and apple filling. Then she saw him.

Sylas Finch.

He stood across the square, unmoving, silent. Light from a nearby lantern brushed against one side of his face, leaving the rest of him swallowed in shadow. He wore no costume, no mask, no mark of the celebration.

And he was watching her.

Not with the idle curiosity of a nobleman inspecting his estate, nor with the sharp amusement he so often carried, as if the world itself were some grand jest. No, this was something else.

Something about the way he looked at her set her pulse skittering. Not fear, not quite. But something close.

Then, without a word, he was gone.

He didn't turn. Didn't step aside. One moment he was there, the next he had vanished, leaving only the space where he had stood.

Autumn swallowed, the last bite of pastry suddenly dry on her tongue. He wanted her to follow.

She hesitated. A moment. Two.

Then—a flicker of movement at the edge of her vision. She turned, catching only a shadow vanishing between the stalls.

A fox, perhaps.

"Autumn, I'm glad I caught you." Evelyn's voice pulled her back, snapping the thread of her focus. Her presence was as sudden as a hand on the shoulder in the dark. "It turns out that Aster doesn't have any parents. She is a resident of the Ashwood Group Home for Girls."

"Ashwood?" Autumn echoed softly.

Evelyn nodded. She lightly touched Autumn's hand before continuing on her way.

Laughter and music twisted through the open square, a fiddle's high, bright notes rising above the murmur of voices. It would be easy to stay. To turn back to the warmth, to the faces she knew.

But some paths, once glimpsed, refused to be ignored.

The lantern glow faded as she slipped between the buildings, where the festival's noise became softened and distant. Shadows pooled in the narrow spaces between shuttered shops, their shapes shifting as she moved. She glanced behind her once, twice, searching for the familiar sweep of a coat, the glint of an eye watching from the dark.

Nothing.

She pressed forward, boots light on the worn cobblestones. Sylas had led her here, but to what end?

Where are you, Sylas?

Somewhere ahead, the faintest sound: a rustle, a step, perhaps a boot scuffing against stone. A gasp cut short. Then— silence fell heavy as a castle gate. She turned her head slightly, straining to hear beyond the quickened beating of her own heart. No voices. No footsteps. Just the town at her back, the empty street ahead.

What am I doing? Chasing shadows, they'd say. I should go back.

Then she caught a scent—roses, earth, leather, faint but unmistakable. Her fingers grasped her locket, a habit she did not want to break.

The wind stirred again, shifting the darkness before her. She was not alone.

"Maxwell, is that you? Sylas…?" Her voice sounded like a child's plea in the dark.

What is happening to me?

A shape lay upon the ground ahead, half-hidden beneath the glow of a distant lantern. Something small, abandoned or discarded in haste.

She knelt, fingers trembling, and lifted the single torn page. The parchment felt warm against her skin, as if recently held, recently read. The ink was familiar. The words burned beneath her gaze then, branding themselves into her memory:

"When crimson tears the earth shall weep,
and shadows stir from ancient sleep,
a child of realms both near and far

shall rise beneath the evening star.
Born of fire, by gold adorned,
the voice shall wake what once was warned.
Through forest deep and tangled wide,
the sleeping flame shall be their guide.
What once was lost shall be reclaimed.
What once was stolen, now renamed.
A harbinger in darkest night
shall blaze the path to morning light.
And when the final hour is shown…"

Sylas had this page. He'd tried to show her something.
Does he have the book?

Heat crawled up Autumn's neck, settling in her cheeks like coals beneath the skin. She gritted her teeth, tried to still it, as if she'd been caught trespassing in some truth meant for no one else.

The prophecy echoed in her mind.
Born of fire, by gold adorned…

Sylas was gone. Swallowed by the shadows. But he had left her this—this scrap of truth, this curse in paper form.

A single raindrop fell, cool and quiet, settling on the page like the first toll of a bell, as if the sky itself had begun to turn.

***

The sky withheld its deluge, though the air flicked cold droplets against her cheeks, sparse and sharp like coins tossed by an idle hand. There she sat, knees drawn tight to her chest, the cobblestones becoming slick beneath her, their dampness seeping through her gown. In her fist, the parchment crumpled, its edges sodden and soft.

How long she'd crouched there, lost in the grey twilight, she couldn't say. Time slipped through her grasp, fluid and false.

Why? Why did it summon her, this unseen current, this whispering dread that coiled in her gut when all others were deaf to its call?

Why me? Why now?

A flicker caught her eye: a golden butterfly, its wings aglow with a fire that should not be. It danced above her, flitting silently against the sodden nightfall. She'd seen its kin before, hours past, when Papyrus had chased it under the sun. Its beauty pricked at her. A marvel, or a terrifying omen?

Voices swelled from the square beyond, a murmur at first, low and restless like the sea before it turns cruel, then sharpening into a clamor of delighted tongues. She moved toward it, drawn as if by a thread stitched into her bones.

Henry Hawthorne stood before the gathering residents, shifting his weight from foot to foot like a boy caught pilfering fruit. His usual jovial mask had slipped, leaving behind a man worn thin, his gaze skittering away from the faces turned towards him. Shame sat heavy on his slumped shoulders, or perhaps it was exhaustion. Or fear.

He knows something is coming.

Henry cleared his throat. "Friends, neighbors… Thank you for gathering. There's…there will be a special announcement. Shortly. We're just…waiting." He stalled, his words clumsy, buying time he didn't seem to want.

Then the crowd rippled, heads turning, a path opening like a wound. Maxwell Wolfsbane strode through, his steps sure as a wolf's despite the breath he chased. His dark hair lay tousled by the wind, his fine jacket askew, but he paused, smoothed his lapels, raked fingers through his locks, and smiled.

As if summoned by the expression, thunder rumbled low and long, a growl from the belly of the bruised sky.

"Thank you all for your patience," Maxwell declared, his voice slicing through the murmurs, smooth as honed steel. He stepped beside Henry and clapped a hand on his shoulder. This made the smaller man flinch so slightly that she nearly missed it.

"It's been a long road, fraught with…complexities. But I am thrilled, truly thrilled, to finally make it official." He paused, letting the anticipation build, his eyes sweeping the crowd, lingering perhaps a fraction too long on Autumn.

"I've claimed Whispering Pines Bookstore and Library," he announced, his tone rang with feigned warmth. He gestured grandly at Henry, "with many thanks to Mr. Hawthorne, of course."

Lightning cracked overhead, a jagged white sear across the darkening sky.

"It's been my quiet dream," Maxwell pressed on, his voice dropping slightly, pulling them close, "to help preserve the unique history of our Whispering Pines. To keep its tales breathing." He waved toward the shop. "To honor what was…and forge what will be." His smile widened, pulled them into his web. "Stories matter here. I'll ensure they endure."

The air turned to grave soil, crushing Autumn's chest. Her refuge, the scent of brittle parchment, the dust swirling in slanted light, the magic lived in its corners—was hers no longer.

Why hadn't he told me when we danced?

He owned it now, this man who walked like a storm given flesh. Clapping broke around her, polite at first, then eager, a tide of relief she could not fathom.

Blind fools, she thought, her lungs burning. They see nothing. They feel nothing. She was drowning in a sea of smiling faces, utterly alone in her terror.

The truth struck her then, a blow that buckled her knees. This was no whim, no savior's gift. Maxwell Wolfsbane was no stranger, no distant kin come to claim a prize. She knew it now.

Magnus Blackthorn stood before her, grinning through that borrowed face, his charm a mask over rot.

Legends Night was over. Maxwell clasped hands and drank their praise.

Rain now lashed the forsaken town, a cold, spitting shroud. Townsfolk scattered like rats from a sinking ship.

"No," the word escaped her lips, a choked whisper. "No, no..." She backed away, stumbling, heedless of the people pushing past her. The rain plastered her hair to her face, cold trails snaked down her neck.

Shouts and curses rose as cloaks were yanked tight, boots slipping in the muck. Autumn stood rooted, the downpour soaking her hair, her dress, her bones. She saw Henry Hawthorne ahead, hobbling fast as his cane allowed, the wood tapping sharp against stone. Flora gripped his arm, her face pinched beneath a hood, guiding him through the flood.

"Mr. Hawthorne! Henry!" Her voice broke free, thin against the storm, and she lunged forward, skirts dragging wet and heavy. They turned, faces slick with rain, eyes meeting hers through the blur.

"I know what the bookstore means to you, and to this town," Henry said, his voice rough, leaning hard on his cane. "But I did what I thought right. I'm not young anymore. It's beyond me now."

"But—" The word slipped out, a plea half-formed.

Henry stiffened, jaw tight. "Mr. Wolfsbane has good intent. That's enough."

"Please, Mr. Hawth—" She reached, desperate.

His eyes flashed, cutting her sharp as a blade. "I've decided. No more."

"Please—"

"I said no!" His shout cracked through the rain, a whip of sound that struck her mute.

She'd never seen him like this, a stranger in the old man's skin. Shame burned in her chest, hot and bitter, tangling with the old dread of raised voices, of words that bruised. She shrank back, breath catching, tears welling despite her will.

Flora's soothing voice brought no comfort. "I'm sorry, Autumn. I need to get him home, out of this wet." She tugged Henry's arm, and they turned away, swallowed by the storm's grey veil.

Autumn stood gasping, sobs tearing free as rain plastered her face. Words had failed her again, left her raw and exposed, a child lost in a squall. She spun away, boots splashing, unable to choke down the grief. Tears bled into the rain, salt on her lips.

A stranger's hands now laid on her soul's last anchor. Betrayal gnawed at her, deep as a wound, splitting the town's heart in two. She stumbled through the deluge, alone with the ache, the rain drowning all but her silent scream.

A sharp tug at her hem broke her spiral; Papyrus, pawing at the soaked folds of her dress. His claws snagged the fabric, insistent, his golden eyes looking up through the rain. Autumn knelt, mud sucking at her boots, and scooped him into her arms. His fur pressed wet against her chest, warm despite the damp, a faint rumble stirring in his throat. She clutched him close, fingers sinking into his sodden coat.

Her feet skidded on the slick stones as she ran, crashing hard into the statue at the square's heart. She recoiled, and a lightning flash split the sky.

The weathered stone face twisted, screamed in silent torment, its eyes gaped wide, its hand clawed outward in anguish, a desperate, silent plea. The golden butterfly darted near, brushing Autumn's cheek, but she swatted it away, a snarl tearing from her lips.

"Not now!"

"Autumn! Wait!" Evelyn's voice barely cut through the noise, but it drowned in the downpour, lost to the thunder hammering her skull.

***

Autumn burst into her homely cottage, drenched and trembling, and the door banged shut behind her. Her sanctuary was tainted.

Run away. Just run away. Foolish girl.

Her numb fingers fumbled with her bag's latches, yanked clothes free, crammed them in without care.

A soft glow halted her. The golden butterfly hovered beside her; its light kissed her icy skin.

"You followed me home?"

It dipped lower, toward the pocket of her gown. Autumn reached in and felt the damp press of parchment. She drew it out slowly, water beading on the surface, though the strange, archaic ink had not run. Her hands trembled as she unfolded it. The butterfly landed gently in the center of the page and spoke.

"It is you, foretold from near and far,
The child who will rise under an evening star.
With the power to awaken what lies within.
Autumn. Fireborn. Dragonkin."

The truth sank deep, a blade slipping between ribs. The whispers, the pull. They were not signs of madness. They were this. She smoothed the page; her eyes traced the words etched into her marrow:

Born of fire, by gold adorned…

Reacting would not serve. Running would not save her. Magnus Blackthorn stood here, in flesh and lies, and the prophecy, sodden in her grasp, demanded she rise.

But as who? And at what cost?

If my path is written, if I was born for this, were my choices, my solitude, my wish to just be me—ever really mine?

CHAPTER 17:

CLOSED FOR REMODEL

From the perspective of Evelyn

Evelyn crossed the square with her cloak drawn tight. Three days gone, and still no sign of Autumn. The worry had settled low in her belly, a hard stone that no warmth could soften.

The wooden sign of the bookshop swung above the door, its iron fastenings groaning with each shift of breeze. Whispering Pines Bookstore, the paint long faded, the edges split with age. It had watched the town grow fat and thin again, had seen children turned to widows and bright lads to broken men. It had been hers, in all but name.

A second sign had joined the first now; newer, crude by comparison, nailed to the door with fresh iron tacks. "Closed for Remodel," it read.

Henry owed her nothing, she knew. Still, years spent beneath that roof, cataloguing spines, tending shop while storms howled through the pines, ought to have counted for more.

She paused at the door and smoothed the front of her dress. The navy wool had faded at the hem, but the pockets were deep, stitched for use, not show. Her fingers brushed the brass key tucked within, worn smooth from years of turning. Henry had given it to her the day she turned eighteen, saying little, only nodding once as he passed it into her palm.

She had opened the shop alone every morning since. And for the last five years, Autumn had been there too, setting the kettle on and readying the shelves before the first customer crossed the threshold.

The key still fit. Of course, it did. Maxwell was no fool. Locks were changed by men afraid of being robbed, and Maxwell feared no thief.

She twisted her hair, rich as ground coffee beans and just as stubborn, into a knot and pinned it with two wooden quills, carved by her husband last winter. Evelyn's hands remained at her nape a moment longer than needed. Then she pushed the door.

The hinges complained as they always had, but the scent was wrong. Beneath the leather and dust and ink, something else clung to the air—roses, heavy and perfumed, and beneath that, something faintly sour.

He stood at the far end of the shop, one foot on a stool, reaching for the top shelf. Morning poured through the high windows, casting him in silhouette. Tall, deliberate, dressed in black from throat to heel, save for the deep crimson lining of his doublet. His cloak lay draped over the back of a nearby chair. Not a wrinkle, not a speck of dust.

"You've arrived," he said without turning, as if he had eyes in the back of his head. Perhaps he did. Stranger things had happened in this world of theirs, though Evelyn preferred explanations rooted in reason rather than mystery.

"I work here," she replied, dropping her satchel behind the counter with a thud that was perhaps louder than necessary. "Six days a week, from dawn bell to evening bell. As I have for twenty-three years almost."

He turned then. His eyes found her like a hawk finds a hare: quietly, without effort, and all at once.

"Indeed." His mouth curved, though it did not warm his face. On another man, it might have passed for a smile. On him, it looked like a blade being drawn. "Your devotion to this little establishment is...well recorded."

Maxwell's face was carved from handsome bones and careful calculation. He was a thing made to be looked at, though there was no kindness in him, only sharp edges.

Evelyn opened the ledger, the spine creaking beneath her hands. She gave him no answer, only turned a page. "The collection from Mr. Harwick's estate arrived two days past. Still unsorted. There are also four special orders pending collection." She ran her finger down the column of inked names and numbers, her own script, neat and sure.

"How fortunate I am," Maxwell said, "to have inherited not only the books but such a meticulous keeper of them." His words, polished and precise, carried the faintest edge. "Though I had expected two such keepers. Where is the girl?"

"I don't know where she's gone. It isn't like her to miss a day." Evelyn said.

"Perhaps she's found livelier employment."

Beneath the counter, Evelyn's hands curled into fists. "And what of Papyrus?" she asked, deliberately changing the subject. "That cat has been the bane of mice in this shop for as long as I can remember."

Maxwell's expression soured, if only for a moment. "The beast took an immediate dislike to me, remember? I assumed it followed your friend when she left."

"I should check on her," she murmured, less to him than to herself. "If she's taken ill—"

"Your concern is touching," he said, the words hollow as a mock blessing. "But I'll require your attention here today. I'm converting the old office into a study."

That room had been Henry's. His coat was still hung by the door, and his papers were still scattered across the desk. He had not used it often the last couple of years, but he had never let it go. Now, Maxwell meant to claim it.

Evelyn bit her tongue. She had no true claim here, not in any way that mattered. Her knowledge of the shelves, her years behind the counter, her care for the books and the stories they held—it all weighed less than a signed deed and a name written in blood.

She turned toward the eastern chamber, chin high. But before she reached the threshold, Maxwell's voice followed her like a knife at her back.

"You said your friend's absence was unusual," he called. "How unusual, exactly?"

She stopped. The fine hairs on her neck rose as she looked over her shoulder. "Autumn has never missed a day without sending word," she said. "Not once in five years."

He nodded slowly as if tasting the weight of her words. "And the animal. This Papyrus. It was close to her?"

"Papyrus is…selective," Evelyn said. "But yes. He adores her. Would curl up in her lap while she worked, some days."

Maxwell's face revealed nothing. The light caught in his eyes, but they did not reflect it. "How curious," he murmured. "And she lives alone? No kinfolk nearby? No…protectors?"

Evelyn's spine stiffened. "She tends for herself, as many women must."

"Indeed." Maxwell turned away, seemingly losing interest.

Evelyn rolled up her sleeves and set to work clearing Henry's old office, sorting volumes that had gathered more memory than use.

They worked in near silence, the scrape of furniture and the soft thud of books the only sounds to fill the room. Dust hung in the air like smoke, disturbed from years of stillness. The space had once belonged to a man of quiet habits. She folded Henry's woolen coat, threadbare at the cuffs, with care and set it aside. Maxwell said nothing. He took the shelves with the cold precision of a man arranging a tomb.

Between tasks, Evelyn paused to tend to the business at hand. She unpacked the crates from Mr. Harwick's estate, each book carefully wrapped in cloth and string, many bound in cracked leather or marked with strange, curling script. Some she recognized; others bore titles she would need to transcribe and research.

She stacked the four special orders beside the counter, wrapped them in brown paper, and marked each with the customer's name in her fine, practiced hand.

By midday, her arms ached, and her brow shone with sweat. Dust clung to her skin, and her knuckles had gone red from lifting and sorting.

At last, Maxwell excused her. He stepped into the office— no longer Henry's, not in truth—and closed the door behind him. The latch clicked, and he was gone.

Evelyn stood alone in the main chamber. Her thoughts wandered back to Autumn.

Perhaps I'm overreacting, she told herself. The girl could have taken ill. Or traveled, though Evelyn knew she had no family; still, she would have sent word. She always did.

There could be a dozen innocent reasons. And a dozen more that are not so innocent. She felt it like a change in the weather—subtle at first, then impossible to ignore.

A knock, sharp against the glass, made Evelyn jump. She turned, brow furrowing, and spotted a familiar shape in the window. Iris stood outside, waving with both hands as though she meant to summon a storm.

Evelyn crossed the room and unlatched the door.

"Thank the stars you're here," Iris said, sweeping in like wind through a chimney. "I was halfway through glazing a set of tiles when I thought, Evelyn's probably starving, and that was that."

She held up a cloth-wrapped bundle like it was a sacred offering. The smell of warm bread and herbs chased out the dust and old glue.

Evelyn managed a tired smile. "You always seem to know."

"I listen to my bones. They creak when friends forget to eat."

She was a striking figure, even now in the golden twilight of her years. Her hair, mostly gold with threads of silver, had been twisted into a loose braid that hung over one shoulder.

Her eyes, somewhere between violet and dusk, scanned the shop. "Place looks different," she murmured, looking toward the rear chamber. "New hands leave different fingerprints, I suppose."

"He's turned Henry's office into a study," Evelyn answered, voice low. "Wants to be left alone."

Iris pulled two apples from her shawl and set them beside the wrapped bread. "Come. Sit with me and eat something before you turn into a ghost."

Evelyn poured two cups of tea and they settled near the window. While storm clouds gathered, the warmth of Iris's presence filled the shop more surely than any fire.

She broke the bread with practiced hands and handed Evelyn the larger piece, as always.

"You look bone-weary," she said, her voice softening. "Have you been working like this all morning?"

Evelyn nodded. "Harwick's estate arrived late, and the orders are still waiting to be collected."

Iris bit off a piece of apple and gave a quiet hum. "Books may not bleed, but they still ask for your life."

They ate in companionable silence for a moment, the sounds of chewing and the creak of old wood the only conversation. "Autumn still hasn't come round?" she asked.

Evelyn set down her bread. "No word. No message. Nothing."

"That's not like her," Iris said at once, brows knitting. "She's steadier than sunrise."

"I know," Evelyn replied. "I've been telling myself it's nothing. Illness, a trip, something simple. But it doesn't sit right."

Iris leaned forward, elbows on the table. "Evelyn, I'd wager she's just sulking at home... Still brooding over Maxwell buying the shop. Has anyone gone by? Knocked on the door, peered through the windows?"

"I haven't had the time," Evelyn admitted.

Iris reached across the table and took her hand. Her grip was warm, firm. "She'll come back when she's ready."

Evelyn looked toward the rear of the shop, to the door that now stood closed: Maxwell's study, though she still thought of it as Henry's room. She remembered the way Autumn had looked at him that first day he arrived. There had been something in her eyes, something Evelyn hadn't wanted to name.

What if she was right about him?

No. Maxwell was cold, prideful, and arrogant, but nothing more. Autumn had always seen shadows where there were none. Books, after all, made it easy to believe in monsters.

CHAPTER 18:

A PAINTED MEMORY

From the perspective of Iris

Iris pressed the latch of her satchel until it clicked, then slung it across one shoulder. "If I stay another minute, Evelyn, you'll have to fetch a wheelbarrow to cart me home," she said with a wry smile, brushing the crumbs from her skirts.

Evelyn's smile was more a crease at the corners of her lips than a true grin. She remained seated, fingers resting near the rim of her emptied teacup. "You always feed me too well," she murmured. "Keep doing it."

Iris leaned down, pressing a kiss to the crown of the woman's head. Then she turned from the table and from warmth and words, out into the grey world beyond.

The rain had come and gone, though it had left its mark. The cobbles glistened beneath the pale sky, slick as polished slate. Roses, those infernal, persistent things, had pushed their way through the fractures in the stones again, blooming where they had no business to. Their scent chased her down the lane like perfume spilled in mourning.

She unlocked the door to The Spellbound Canvas; the chime from the bell sounded like the sigh of an old friend. The air inside greeted her with its usual perfume: turpentine clinging to the rafters, the dry musk of old dust, and, faintest of all, the lavender sachets she kept tucked into the corners of drawers and shelves.

Iris exhaled. The space held her like a well-worn coat.

The windows drank in the overcast light, casting silver onto the floorboards and the stacks of brushes and paints that filled every shelf like old bones arranged for divination.

Paintings leaned against the far wall; landscapes, portraits, one commission she hadn't yet touched, all rendered in her steady, practiced hand. There was peace in this place, built brushstroke by brushstroke over years of solitude.

She unfastened her cloak with a sigh, hung it on its peg, placed her satchel below, and turned to the canvas she'd left unfinished on the easel.

It should have been a coastal study, waves on rock, or some memory of the eastern cliffs—but the thing she had painted was a forest. Deep and strange. No true light touched the boughs. At the center, figures picnicked beneath trees that bent too low, with baskets and bunting, laughter half-lost in the stillness of the glade.

I didn't paint this.

Had she?

She couldn't recall starting it, no sketch, no underpainting, no memory of mixing those particular hues. The canvas had simply…been there. Waiting. As though it had summoned her, rather than the other way around.

She had always known her paintings captured more than the surface of things. A line of light in a still life might reveal a lie unspoken. A portrait's eyes might shift if the soul it depicted was troubled. But this…this canvas felt like a door she had not meant to open.

Or perhaps it was not a door at all, but a window, and something was looking back.

She lifted her brush, but it stilled in her hand. The colors blurred at the edges. Then the memory came.

It was Flora's tenth nameday, a bright, windy afternoon, held in Althea and Henry's garden behind the old Hawthorne house.

All-white linen tables strewn with ribbons and sweet cakes and garlands strung between trees. Laughing children danced like sprites among strings of paper lanterns.

Althea, stately even in grief, had hired her for face painting. Iris had refused payment, but the woman insisted. Tradition, she had said, though her eyes had held the weariness of those who know how little tradition keeps.

That was when she first saw the child with a stillness in her that did not belong to children.

Autumn, a strange little thing, nine years old, with wild ginger hair and curious eyes. Most children asked for butterflies, unicorns, or stars. Autumn had asked for a dragon.

"It has to be gold," she'd said, climbing onto the stool. "Because gold dragons are the rarest, and they guard secret names."

Iris remembered the weight of those words even now.

"Do they now?" she had asked, brush held midair.

"They know the true names of things," Autumn said, "even the sky."

Iris had paused, measuring the girl. "That's a kind of magic, isn't it?"

"What is?"

"Believing there's more than what you see."

The girl had blinked. "Like a painting?"

"Exactly."

She had painted the dragon along the curve of the girl's cheek, its body coiled, its head resting behind the ear as if it were whispering to her.

The memory might have ended there. But another face came to her now. That same day, after the music faded and the children's laughter gave way to dusk, a man walked her home.

She had packed her brushes and tucked away her paints. The man had stood by the gate, boots clean, coat too fine for a common traveler. Polite. Curious.

"Maxwell Wolfsbane." He had introduced himself with the ease of a man who had worn many names.

"Just visiting," he said. "Curious about the past."

She answered him. Cautiously. Thought he might be a chronicler, a scholar, some lord's scribe chasing legends. But his smile had lingered. Not kind, not cruel. Just there, like mist clinging to the skin after rain. He'd thanked her for the conversation. Tipped his hat. She hadn't seen him again, not until years later, when he returned to town for good.

Now, sitting before the forest she had painted and did not remember beginning, her brush trembled in her hand. Autumn. Maxwell. A girl who believed in dragons. A man who hunted old names.

Evelyn had told her what Autumn suspected. That Maxwell wore another name beneath his skin, that he might be a Blackthorn. Might be Magnus himself, walking the world once more in borrowed flesh.

Iris had scoffed then. Laughed the way a widow laughs at the idea of ghosts.

Her eyes fixed on the canvas. The longer she stared, the deeper the trees seemed. She did not move, yet the path drew nearer. The paint no longer lay flat, almost breathing. The light in the room bent, faint and wrong.

The sound hit Iris like a slap—a wet, guttural cry. The brush slipped from her fingers, clattering against the floorboards. Three strides took her to the door. When she threw it open, the world beyond had changed.

The sky had dimmed unnaturally. Clouds sagged heavy and low, their bellies torn with a strange gray light. Rain had stopped, but the air hung thick and sour. Every rose in sight had turned toward the alley, their red blooms split wide like mouths mid-scream.

Another shout rang out. She gathered her skirts and ran, boots slapping through puddles, skirts dragging through muck and scattered petals. She turned the corner and found chaos waiting.

Tobin, the butcher's boy, hung suspended in the narrow alley, vines wound tight around his chest and arms, hoisting him off the ground like some grotesque marionette. Thorns punctured his sleeves, threading blood into his tunic in slow, dark blooms. His face was pale beneath a layer of sweat.

He didn't scream now. Just kicked.

Thomas grunted from below, hacking at a vine with a cleaver already slick with green sap. Birdie had her apron wrapped around her hands, yanking a coil from Tobin's leg with all the strength her frame allowed.

"Tobin! Don't move!" Iris shouted, pushing forward.

One vine uncoiled from the bricks and slithered toward her like a serpent. She met it with steel. The canvas knife came free from her belt, and she slashed in a wide arc. The vine hissed and recoiled with a shudder.

The roses twisted on their stems, petals splitting at the edges. A single blossom, full and black-veined, turned to follow the motion of her blade.

She gritted her teeth and lunged for Tobin. The vines around his torso resisted. She cut again, and again—green sap spattered across her wrists, and with a snap, the final vine split. Tobin dropped like a sack of grain into Thomas's waiting arms.

"I've got him!" Thomas grunted, staggering back. "Is he—?"

"He's breathing," Birdie said quickly. "But his arm, look at his arm."

"No time," Iris said. "Get him to The Healing Hall. Now."

"What is this?" he asked.

"I don't know," Iris answered, though her voice said otherwise. "But it's awake."

Birdie helped haul Tobin upright, their footsteps dragging over slick stone. Iris stayed behind, heart hammering.

The alley groaned. Vines slithered across the walls now, crawling toward second-story windows. One latched onto a shutter and pulled it closed with a snap. Another wrapped itself around the handle of a rain barrel and crushed it like tin.

Slow and deep, like something vast and slumbering had just turned over in its sleep.

Iris looked toward the old stone well. The roses had spread there, too, curling along the rim. Their petals unfurled with impossible speed. Dozens of them, blooming in unison. All open. All turned toward her.

Iris wiped the sap from her hands and sheathed the knife.

She started toward the square. Then stopped. The brush she'd dropped earlier was back in her pocket.

She hadn't put it there.

CHAPTER 19:

THE WORDS THAT NAMED HER

The world continued on, unbroken. Shopkeepers thrust open their doors, hinges groaning in the damp air. Children raced through the square, muddied ribbons streaming behind them. Autumn heard them from her cottage, echoes through the warped glass. Yet the town felt skewed, its bones shifted, as if a hand had tilted it and left it leaning. She felt it in the air, sharp and wet deep in her marrow.

She brewed some tea, the steam curling sharp with herbs, and watched dew bead on the window, tracing paths left by last night's rain. No downpour now but dampness clung, to the walls, to her skin. The candle before her sputtered as if it too were hesitant to burn.

Papyrus prowled the windowsill, his tail twitching each time a bird's shadow flitted too near. He'd not settled since dawn.

The torn page lay on the table. She hadn't touched it since Legends Night, yet it bore a weight beyond its frail edges, pressing against her chest like a stone lodged beneath her ribs.

What frightened her was the idea that she'd already been living toward the prophecy without knowing. That all her not-quite-belonging…had always been a path she didn't choose. Was this what she'd fled from, all those years of solitude, of being the odd duckling? Talking to creatures that said hello? Or had she been running toward it, blind as a child chasing shadows?

She struck a match, lit a fresh candle, and reached for the parchment. Her fingers uncurled it slowly, carefully, as if it might tear beneath the burden it bore. She smoothed it flat and spoke the lines aloud, soft at first, then again, tasting them in her voice:

> "When crimson tears the earth shall weep,
> and shadows stir from ancient sleep,
> a child of realms both near and far
> shall rise beneath the evening star.
> Born of fire, by gold adorned,
> the voice shall wake what once was warned.
> Through forest deep and tangled wide,
> the sleeping flame shall be their guide.
> What once was lost shall be reclaimed.
> What once was stolen, now renamed.
> A harbinger in darkest night
> shall blaze the path to morning light.
> And when the final hour is shown…"

The words sank into her, coals beneath flesh; quiet, glowing, perilous. Papyrus leapt to the floor, brushing her leg with a low rumble. The candle flickered, casting jagged light across the page.

A child of realms both near and far…

That was her, wasn't it? Whispering Pines—near. Known, its dirt under her nails, its wind in her lungs.

But something else stirred beneath the surface, cold and distant: frozen rivers glimpsed in sleep, gates crumbled under frost, an endless sea of snow where voices wailed beneath the ice.

Born of fire, by gold adorned, the voice shall wake what once was warned...

But gold adorned... That felt gentler. Like a crown. Like a light held close.

She put her hand to her locket.

Like...a locket.

What once was lost shall be reclaimed. Not given—taken back. A name. A truth. What once was stolen, now renamed. Her voice, perhaps, silenced too long? Or the bookstore, snatched by Maxwell's grin?

A harbinger in darkest night shall blaze the path to morning light. A herald, not a savior. One who walks before, who bears the storm.

The words ended there, torn at the edge. Autumn traced the jagged line with a finger, then leaned on the table, elbows braced, forehead pressed to her hands.

What if I've never been free? What if magic had chosen me, not the other way around?

What if the prophecy only opened the door, and she was still the one who had to walk through it?

She'd always heard the trees bend in still air, the sigh of roots beneath dirt. The page had called to her, and she'd answered, blind. But now she wondered: Was it a warning scratched in ink? A command carved by dead hands? A map she must tread—or burn? Her heart pounded, not at who she was, but at who she might become if she let it claim her whole.

The page didn't answer. But the candle guttered.

She didn't know if she'd gotten any of it right. Most of her was certain she hadn't; she didn't trust a word of what she'd pieced together.

Papyrus brushed against her ankles again, his fur a mere whisper against her skin. He pawed at the hem of her nightgown, then sprang into her lap, curling easily into her welcoming arms.

"You're the only one who understands me."

The cat purred in reply.

***

Autumn loved her cottage, truly she did, but its walls had begun to press in, as if the house itself wished to swallow her whole. Three days she had lingered there, a prisoner not of lock or chain, but of worry. The rain had not ceased. It came and went as it pleased, soft enough to blur the windows, steady enough to sink into her bones. She moved through the hours like a ghost, brewing tea, feeding Papyrus, whispering the same line of prophecy beneath her breath again and again.

When crimson tears, the earth shall weep...

It echoed now in her chest, in her ribs, as if the prophecy itself had carved a place within her body. It had named her, somehow. She knew that. But it left no map behind.

She walked barefoot across cold wood, the floor creaking beneath each step. The locket tapped softly at her collarbone. Papyrus watched her from the arm of her chair.

The torn page still lay on the table beneath a heavy book, its corners curled from damp. She had read it a hundred times. Traced the words. Spoke them aloud, as if voice alone might give them meaning.

Her thoughts circled again to Sylas. He had left the page. She was sure of it. But why? He knew something. He always had.

Not just about the prophecy, but about her. The way he watched her. He collected things. Books, forgotten truths, strange relics, names that once meant something. If anyone could read the prophecy's meaning, it was Sylas.

But Sylas had vanished. No letter. No word. As if the fog had risen to claim him, as it did so many forgotten men.

Perhaps he was angry. The sale of the bookstore had broken something in her; perhaps it had done the same to him. He loved that place. The bones of it. The ink and the dust and the centuries living between pages.

I need to find Sylas.

She had never visited his home, but Evelyn once gestured beyond the mill, where fences yielded to ivy and no hand kept the wild at bay.

Autumn looked out the window. No rain, but the sky hung heavy and pale.

Papyrus jumped down, circling her ankles.

"I'm done hiding," she whispered.

She pulled on her boots and reached for her cloak, still faintly scented of cedar and old leaves. Beneath it, she wore a simple dress, deep green like pine needles after rain, the hem brushed from old wear. She slipped the torn prophecy page into her satchel.

Then she knelt beside Papyrus and ran her hand along his back. "Stay here. Watch the house." The cat blinked once, then padded silently to the hearth.

She stepped outside, and the door closed behind her with a sound that felt like the end of something. She passed beneath the trees, gnarled limbs arching overhead. The mill sagged in its rot, forgotten by time and men. Beyond the mill, the road narrowed. Trees leaned closer. Their wet limbs arched above her like ribs. Dusk crept in behind her, soft-footed and watchful. No lanterns lit the way.

She almost missed the gate. It leaned half-swallowed in ivy, wood splintered, hinges rusted. No name. No mark. Just a thin trail winding into the brush.

She pushed. The gate groaned, slow and reluctant, like something long asleep.

The house stood as stone ought to stand, weathered, clinging to its secrets. Vines gripped its bones like veins through a corpse. A crow watched from the chimney. One window hung ajar, its curtain unmoving.

This is the place.

She moved slowly, her hand brushing her locket. The door bore symbols. Old ones. Like the ones Evelyn had once shown her in books too brittle to lend. Wards. Of warning. Or protection. Or both.

She knocked. Once. Twice.

"Sylas?"

The wind answered in branches, bones rattling overhead.

The door sighed open.

Inside, dust clung to every surface. Books crowded every wall, stacked in uneven towers on the floor. A kettle sat cold on the hearth, half full. The scent was thick, dried herbs, wax…and something metallic beneath it.

She stepped lightly through the room, careful not to disturb the clutter. On the desk were quills, scraps of parchment, and stones covered with sigils. And on the wall above it, pinned carefully: a freshly-written copy of the prophecy. Lines were marked. Symbols circled.

Her name had been written in the margin.

A lantern sat by the door. She lit it with shaking hands.

The further she walked, the more wrong it felt. Not abandoned…interrupted. A cup beside the chair, half full, long cold. A cloak folded by the door, untouched by dust.

She moved into the hall behind the main room. The air grew colder. Shelves lined with brittle flowers sagged under age. A writing desk had been ransacked. Drawers yanked open. Pages scattered across the floor as if someone had searched for something, or torn through the place in anger.

"Sylas?"

Then she smelled it.

Roses. Faint. Not of garden or perfume. Old leather, fresh-turned earth, and roses. A scent like mourning. A scent like Maxwell.

Her stomach turned to stone.

Birdie had spoken of a quarrel between Maxwell and Sylas, voices sharp and low behind locked doors. Had it happened here too? Perhaps worse.

Her throat tightened. Maxwell. He had done something.

She closed her eyes, her jaw tightening. The answer was becoming clear. The house he wanted restored. The one he used to live in—as Magnus.

She didn't want to go there. But Sylas was missing. And the bookstore, her home, was no longer safe ground.

Maybe Maxwell would be there. Maybe not. Either way, she had to find Sylas. Autumn turned back toward the door. The rain had stopped, but the wind had returned.

CHAPTER 20:

SILVER TONGUE AND GOLDEN FIRE

The place felt familiar in the way ghosts sometimes do, haunting not the hall, but the marrow. Autumn had not set foot here in years, since when the other orphans whispered tales of curses and vanished girls.

But someone had tamed the ruin. Weeds had been stripped away. New planks patched the steps. The air held the tang of polish and old wood.

A shiver coiled at the base of her spine. That, she thought, was exactly what Magnus wished to do with the world.

The dust had not been cleared; it had been arranged and brushed into corners, out of sight but not forgotten. Order imposed upon decay.

A fire crackled somewhere deeper in the house, yet its warmth hadn't touched her skin. She followed the sound past walls mottled with damp and bearing the claw marks of time, or something older than time. Her boots creaked over floorboards that bowed beneath her weight. The scent of scorched iron lingered in the wood; ash and old blood, buried deep in the grain. It clashed with the polish laid over it, like perfume on a corpse.

"Sylas?" she whispered.

But when she reached the hearth, he was already waiting.

Maxwell. No. That name had burned away like paper in flame.

Magnus.

He stood with one hand upon the mantle, his dark coat pristine, his hair too neat for someone born of ruin. He looked at her as though she were late to her own undoing, eyes like tempered steel catching the firelight and holding it fast.

There it was. The old book lay on the mantle. She felt the heat rise in her chest, but she gave it no room. She did not speak. Did not move. To react would be to cede the ground first.

"You came," he said.

"I...I'm not here for...pleasantries."

A chuckle, smooth and unbothered. "You never are."

Her eyes took in the room—the bones of the house laid bare. Heavy beams overhead. Stone crumbling in one corner. The faded outline of something long dragged across the floor. Blood or soot, she could not say.

"That color," he said, his eyes trailing the line of her sleeve. "It suits you." A smile touched his lips as if the dress said more than she'd intended.

"Um... You've been fixing up the place," she said, her fingers curled into her palms.

"I built it once," he replied, still turned half toward the flames. "Before the town called it cursed. Before your council marked it abandoned. But it was never abandoned, Autumn. Just misplaced. Like so many things of power."

He turned slowly, and the fire painted shadows along his jaw. "Like prophecy. Like truth. Like you."

Her throat tightened.

He tilted his head. "And now here you stand. Curious, isn't it?"

The fire hissed, and something old stirred behind the walls. Autumn could smell the heat now—burnt things. Charred parchment. Bone dust.

"I'm not afraid of you."

He stepped forward, slow, like a serpent offering fruit. "Your trembling lip says otherwise." He reached out and brushed her lower lip with his thumb.

She didn't flinch. Didn't step back. Still, some part of her whispered: This was a mistake.

"You and I," he said, his voice low and velvet-slick, "are not so different. You hear it too, don't you? The fire in the deep places. The song beneath the bark and stone. You've always known they were more than bedtime tales."

Then his hands rose, slowly, reverently—as if she were something sacred or cursed. His fingers traced the line of her jaw, thumbs resting just beneath her cheekbones.

He leaned closer, and she caught the scent of him: pleasant now, disarmingly so. Fresh roses. Earth still damp from rain. A whisper of aged leather worn smooth by time. It unsettled her more than any of his cruelty might have.

She could feel the tremor he did not show, the restraint in him pulled tight as a bowstring. His breath mingled with hers, warm and unhurried.

Their foreheads nearly touched. His lips were so close she could taste the word he hadn't spoken.

She almost leaned in but she pulled away.

"I don't want what you want."

"How can you know that?" he asked, almost gently. "You don't even know what you are."

She hated how his words echoed things she'd thought in the dark.

"Tell me, Autumn, when did you first feel it? That hum in your blood, that itch behind your ribs? You walk the edge of the world, and you never once asked why?"

"I know enough," she said.

"I know your blood," Magnus said. "The first time I saw you, I felt it. Fireborn. Dragonkin. The bloodline that once held kingdoms in balance and bent storms to its will."

Then his mouth parted, just slightly. There was something else he meant to say. She saw it flash across his face, unguarded, for the space of a single breath.

"Though how…escapes my knowledge. I thought I—"

He caught himself. Too late.

Her eyes narrowed.

"You look at me like I'm the villain in a fireside tale," he murmured. "But I'm doing what no one else dares to do. This world is splintered. Bound by rotting oaths and old superstitions. Tell me, girl, what have your lords and kings preserved, besides their own decay?"

She didn't answer. She couldn't.

He stepped past the hearth. "The forest. The flames. Prophecies penned by madmen. You saw it, didn't you? On the map."

She blinked. "Frost…?"

His smile curved like a blade unsheathed. "So you have seen it."

"The open border?"

"Let me show you the rest," he said. "Let me show you what power does when it chooses you back."

That was his gift. Words spun like silk, soft and strong, until they closed around your throat. He didn't burn his enemies. He rewrote them.

"People don't need chains," he said. "They need the right story. Told well. Told often."

"You mean *your* story."

He inclined his head. "If I shape the tale, I shape the future. I won't burn the world, Autumn. I'll cleanse it."

"And those who disagree?"

"I won't erase them," he said, like a lie wrapped in silk. "I'll give them purpose. A place. A better ending."

He stepped closer once more, and the space between them drew taut. "You're standing on the edge of something ancient," he said. "Wouldn't you rather be the hand that shapes it...than a forgotten name in someone else's song?"

What if fate isn't a path? she thought. *What if it's a noose?*

The fire in the hearth now burned too hot. Or perhaps it wasn't the fire at all. Perhaps it was fear, or nerves, or something else entirely. She couldn't tell the difference anymore.

A bead of sweat traced a slow path down Autumn's chest, and Magnus watched its descent as it slid past her collarbone and came to rest against the locket. She had feared this moment, not because he was wrong, but because he almost made it sound right.

To burn was one thing. To become the match in someone else's hand? That was something else entirely.

"No." The word was soft but final.

"No?" he said, as if tasting the word.

"I may not know what I am. But I know I will never become you."

He looked at her, eyes narrowed as if he'd just found a lock he couldn't pick. "You could be the flame or the kindling," he said. "Don't walk away and become ash."

"I'd rather burn on my own terms than live by yours," she said. Her eyes did not waver. "Just like Opal."

The name landed between them like a blade. She saw it then, the glint in his eyes, the tightening of his jaw, too brief for most to catch but not lost on her. The words had struck true. And she regretted them the moment they left her mouth.

The fire snapped sharply. A gust of wind howled through the chimney and set the coals hissing like serpents.

"Do not ever speak that name in my presence," he said. His voice was no longer velvet. Iron now.

That was it. She'd done what needed doing: She had stood before him, spoken the truth, denied the crown he tried to place upon her head. But the cost of defiance now coiled tight around her throat.

He knew. He knew she was Dragonkin. What reason would he have to let her live?

The door slammed behind her, and she ran, head down into the dusk, her breath sharp in her chest. She didn't know where her feet carried her. Only that she had to move. To stop was to be caught. To be caught was to be unmade, in one way or another.

Her lungs burned. Her shawl slipped from her shoulders. Still, she ran.

Then—hoofbeats. Distant, but gaining.

Magnus. He was coming. He knew she would falter. Knew she had nowhere to go.

He's coming for me, she thought, heart hammering wildly as a trapped bird. She turned and ran again, legs aching, dress catching on brambles as she pushed beyond her limit toward the treeline.

But it wasn't the Emerald Glade she reached. It was a different entrance. She'd seen it in Iris's painting.

The woman in the woods.

The forest before her was wild and untouched. Vines curled over one another, a snarled green menace. No obvious path. No gentle welcome. The tendrils shifted as though mocking her, daring her.

Autumn hesitated, caught between the known and the unknowable. Between the man who pursued her and the wild that offered no guarantee of mercy.

Her fingers found the pendant at her throat. It reminded her she was not prey. She was not alone.

"Please," she whispered. She didn't know to whom. And then, light. A flicker. A butterfly, its wings a shimmer of molten sun, appeared before her, rising from the air itself. It circled her once. Twice. Then drifted forward, toward the twisted wall of vines.

And the vines slowly parted. The path revealed itself. The hooves were louder now. Closer. No more time to hesitate. Autumn stepped forward and the forest accepted her.

She looked back once as the hooves broke through the last bend in the path, just long enough to see the shape of him, high in the saddle, watching as the last of the green knit shut between them.

"Think about my offer," he called to her, his voice chasing after her like a shadow that refused to let go.

Autumn's knees gave way. She fell back, the earth cool against her spine, her arms splayed at her sides. Above her, the first stars peered through the violet sky. Her breath came ragged, her ribs rising and falling like a wounded thing.

The butterfly danced in frantic circles, but she hadn't the strength to watch. Not now.

Her body ached. Her pulse slowed, then quickened again. For a moment, stillness settled in her chest until the leaves rustled behind her. Too deliberate for wind. Too measured to dismiss.

No shadow emerged. No voice called out. But Magnus had never needed to be seen to be known.

He's coming for me.

Her body moved again before thought could follow. She stood upright, legs shaking, and walked deeper into the woods, where the trees grew ancient. She didn't know this path. Had never dared it as a girl. And yet…there was something familiar about it all the same. The trees ahead were older, stranger. Vines twisted thick as rope. Each branch seemed to lean closer, and each leaf turned toward her like a silent jury waiting to judge.

CHAPTER 21:
THE FOREST'S GIFT

The forest air prickled against Autumn's skin, though not unkindly. The earth beneath her feet felt alive, not dead soil and cold stone, but something that breathed.

A whippoorwill called in the dark. A nightingale answered, their voices weaving through the trees like sacred songs. From beyond the tangled branches, a barred owl's deep cry rolled through the night. Even the brook found its voice: water tumbling over worn stone in a language no man remembered.

In the shadowed undergrowth, wood orchids lifted pale faces toward what little moonlight pierced the canopy. Wild bluebells clustered in hollows, their slender heads nodding in the faint breeze. Buttercups scattered like stars fallen to earth, while trillium, maroon and white, pushed up between gnarled roots. Lady's slippers, rare as dragon's eggs, nestled beneath thorned brambles, shy and hidden.

The golden butterfly returned, dancing before her eyes. Moonlight caught its wings, but the light was wrong. Not the silver-blue of night, but the fierce, caged gold of warmer days. It hovered, waiting.

"Thank you for helping me," Autumn whispered, extending her hand.

But what landed on her palm was no butterfly. It stood upright on legs, each toe tapering to a needle's point. Its skin beamed like gold leaf. The scent of honeysuckle rose from it, thick, sweet, and cloying, as if the warmth of summer lived inside its tiny body.

Wings arched from its back, thin as knife-blades, veined like ancient glass. They caught the light and fractured it: blue as deep water, green as new leaves, purple as dusk on the horizon. Hair spilled over her tiny shoulders, pale as cream against gold. Its lashes were a cat's delicate sweep, but the eyes—the eyes burned like twin stars fallen from the heavens.

"Are you…a fairy?"

The creature tilted its head, studying her as a raven might study a dying man. "Something like that." The voice reminded her of leaves rustling in her garden, of wind sighing through the summer grass. "We are keepers of forgotten tales. Whispers in the breeze. The unseen guardians of Whispering Pines."

Two more of the golden creatures emerged from the shadows, their arrival sounded like distant harp strings plucked in the dark. The trio circled Autumn as if she were the center of some strange ritual. Their bodies shed threads of golden light that vanished in the air behind them.

"Um, where should I go from here?" Autumn's voice sounded childish in her own ears, a girl's question in this ancient place.

The fairies halted mid-dance, frozen as though bound by an unseen hand. One by one, their eyes were drawn to the pendant resting against her skin.

"The forest holds the power to reveal what lies hidden in plain sight," said the first.

The second fairy flitted closer. "Only those who have the courage to seek the truth may unlock its secrets."

The third, smaller than its companions, chimed in: "You have embarked on a journey that few have tread before. To unveil the secrets hidden within, you must follow the path of whispers and shadows. Seek the heart of the enchanted forest, where truths and revelations await."

It paused, eyes old as the forest and just as full of secrets. "But remember, not all that gleams with magic is true, and not all that hides in shadows is false. Trust in your heart, for it alone shall guide you through the maze of illusion."

"Illusions?"

Autumn could not help but think of tales spoken at Legends Night, of creatures of the forest, and wondered if these beings were their kin, or something older still, from the dawn of days when magic walked among men.

A sound. She froze—a whisper of leaves where no wind blew. Her eyes searched between the trees behind her. Nothing stirred but shadows and the sway of ancient branches. A raccoon, she told herself. Or perhaps some other forest creature going about its nightly hunt.

The fairies continued their procession, oblivious or unconcerned. Their wings caught moonlight and scattered it across the forest floor like broken glass. If they heard what had startled her, they showed no sign of it.

Autumn finally took one more step forward. Another. And another. The path before her was dark, the way home growing distant behind. But the golden light of her strange guides pulled her onward.

Darkness was already pooling beneath the trees, and even if she turned back now, she would never find her way home before nightfall claimed the forest completely.

I can't go back just yet. Magnus could be waiting for me.

The fairies beckoned her forward. The smallest fairy circled back, hovering so near she could feel the warmth radiating from its tiny form. The shadows no longer seemed so deep, the night no longer so absolute.

She would trust them, for now—these fairies with star-bright eyes and voices that echoed ancient things.

What choice did she have? The path ahead was unknown, but the way behind was no safer now. The forest had its own rules, its own dangers.

Autumn had never been fond of dark corners. The bookstore basement had been dark, too, and there had been no moonlight to guide her steps.

The stairs had creaked beneath her weight, each step a complaint voiced in ancient wood. Cobwebs had clung to her hair and brushed against her cheeks like ghostly fingers. The darkness had pressed against her eyes, thick as wool, heavy as a winter blanket.

Her heart had pounded then, just as it did now. Her hands had trembled as she moved between towering shelves packed with forgotten volumes. The scent of old paper and leather and secrets had filled her lungs.

And then she had found it—the old book. It called to her, just as the forest had called to her.

She had faced shadows before and found treasure within them. Perhaps these fairy lights would lead her to something just as precious, just as ancient. At least with these guides, she might survive until dawn's light found her again. Her pendant grew warm against her skin at the thought, as if in agreement.

But as quickly as they appeared, the fairies vanished, like candle flames snuffed by an unseen draft. They had flitted ahead or disappeared entirely; whichever it was, Autumn stood alone now, abandoned to the mercy of the night. The thought settled like a cold hand at her back, the touch of a long-dead king.

"Hello?" Her voice wavered. "Fairies?"

Only silence answered. She blinked hard, willing the sting behind her eyes to vanish.

"Oh no...no. I trusted them," she whispered, her voice small against the vastness of the ancient wood.

Her breath quickened, shallow and sharp. Fingers clenched at her sides, then opened again, restless. She turned in place, heart thudding louder with each step—no sound, no light, nothing but trees pressing in.

Then, just as her pulse threatened to drown her thoughts, the forest shifted. A path unfolded before her, pale and unnatural, its twists and turns shaped by something more than mere roots and stone, as if some forgotten craftsman had laid this trail in the days when magic still flowed freely through the realm.

The whispers came next. Soft, slithering things that wound through the trees like threads of smoke, rising from the very marrow of the forest as if old wizards were stirring beneath the soil. They beckoned, murmured, not words exactly, but something close. Not entirely inviting. Not entirely cruel. But there, curling through the night like a breath on the nape of her neck, cold as the grave.

A shape, low to the ground, conjured itself from the air, born of stardust and shadow. It moved like liquid night, sleek and silent as it slipped across the forest floor. A fox, or something that wore the shape of one.

Its coat shifted hues of green, pink, and violet as if the cosmos itself had spilled upon its fur. Its edges blurred as though it had never quite chosen whether to belong to this world or the next.

The earth seemed to twist now, reshaping into something new, and an illusion summoned itself into being.

The path ahead dissolved, and in its place stood Ashwood, the orphanage where Autumn had grown up. The air was clean, filled with the scent of sun-warmed grass and the distant laughter of children, untainted by the sour bite of poverty that clung to such places. In the vision, she was a girl again. Her hands bore no calluses; her eyes had not yet learned the weight of sorrow.

The other orphans played around her. It was a scene of companionship, of innocence—the very thing time had stolen from her.

And there, moving amongst them, was the celestial fox. It wound between the children, its form casting long, flickering silhouettes that twisted and stretched, mimicking their movements. Its gaze held no pupils, only white light, unnerving, unreadable, as though it saw everything and nothing at once.

It was a trickster's gaze. A keeper of secrets. A reminder that the warmth of this vision was only that: a vision. A beautiful deception, spun from memory and magic, meant to draw her in. To make her forget, if only for a moment, the truth that waited beyond the veil, patient as the executioner's blade.

Autumn laughed. For a moment, just a moment, she let herself believe that the past was not lost. That the warmth of camaraderie wasn't some fleeting thing, bartered away like grain in winter. She was home. She belonged.

The celestial fox slithered through the scene, its phantom form a mischievous specter at the edges of her vision. Its shadows stretched and twisted, drawing paths where none had been, erecting obstacles that hadn't existed moments before. It played its game well, this creature born of neither flesh nor truth.

But beneath the joy, beneath the glow of memory reborn, something stirred in her breast, cold as a raven's call. The fox's movements were just a breath out of rhythm with the light that birthed them. It was guiding her, yes, leading her through the tangled corridors of her own past, but whether to reveal or to deceive, she could not yet tell. In the courts of kings, such uncertainty often came just before the fall of empires.

"Autumn, come play with us!"

The voices rang out, a melody spun from the golden threads of childhood longing or as sweet as the songs of maidens that lured knights to their doom in the old tales. The children reached for her with small, pink hands extended in friendship. Their laughter meshed into the world around them, and the illusion billowed with color.

The celestial fox prowled at her side, its gaze unreadable as ancient runes; its tail, had it ever had one, was a flicker of darkness against the glowing air. The children beckoned. The forest whispered. Reality and dreams intertwined together.

Was this not what she had always wanted? To belong. To be wanted. To be loved. The orphaned child's eternal hunger was sharper than any blade forged in the fires of the master smiths.

Her heart wavered, drawn toward the promise of warmth, of acceptance. And then, as if exhaled by the forest itself, the children's smiles unraveled, dissolving like mist in the first breath of morning, like armies scattered by a battle they had no hope of winning. Laughter faded, sinking into hollow echoes.

The playground was gone. The past was gone, banished once more to the realm of memory where all dead things dwelled. Only the celestial fox remained, watching her with sly eyes that had witnessed the rise and fall of kingdoms.

Maxwell Wolfsbane stepped forth from the crumbling illusion, his form cast in golden light, warm and steady against the shifting dark. The echoes of trickery dissolved like frost under the first kiss of dawn. From a distance, the celestial fox watched, its sleek shape curling at the edges of the dream as it unraveled.

"I only want what's best for the town," Maxwell said. His eyes glinted like polished steel catching firelight. The mirage around him melted away, revealing not deceit, but a vision of trust and partnership.

He extended a hand, palm up, open, and the illusion beckoned. "Let's take care of the bookstore together."

The words curled around her like warmed wine on a cold night. The vision wove its web with practiced care, offering a glimpse of shared burdens and soft alliances—a world as rare and fragile as peace between ancient foes.

Maxwell gestured toward a path. An invitation or a challenge? The weight of choice settled on her shoulders, heavy as a knight's armor before battle.

She stepped forward with the same resolve that had carried her through every lonely year since Ashwood. The path unfurled beneath her feet, moonlit and waiting. Maxwell walked at her side, the scent of roses, rich earth, and aged leather clinging to him in the most pleasant way.

Whispering Pines Bookstore emerged from the mist ahead, its doors flung wide, glowing with hearthlight. A sanctuary offered freely. A dream made real.

But the whispers stirred. Low at first, then louder and urgent. One urged her forward. The other warned of knives in the dark. The earth beneath her boots shifted, uneasy. Like the hush before battle, when armies wait for the horn that will carry them toward glory…or ruin.

And then—

The fox.

It slipped past like a ripple in the air. A breach in the illusion's veil. Maxwell vanished. The bookstore dissolved. Stone, timber, memory…gone, like castles dreamed by sleeping children.

Autumn stood alone once more in the ancient wood, with only the night and the stars to bear witness to what had nearly come to pass.

The shadows twisted, flesh forming where only darkness had been moments before. A woman stood where nothing had been—tall and proud as any queen of old. Her golden-strawberry hair caught what little light filtered through the ancient trees, with a warmth that reminded Autumn of her own reflection.

Brown eyes soft as a doe's. Delicate lips that could have sung the old songs of hearth and harvest. Her gown was a gentle shade of peach, like the sky just before dawn breaks.

The heart-shaped locket rested at the woman's throat, the very same that had been Autumn's only inheritance from a life she'd never known.

Autumn's feet were rooted to the forest floor like the ancient oaks surrounding her. Her breath caught. "Who are you?" The words scraped her throat raw.

"Autumn." The woman's voice sounded like honeyed tea on a cold morning. "Look inside your heart."

Her hands trembled. Her knees weakened. She found herself moving forward without command, drawn by something primal and hungry.

"Mother?" The word escaped her lips before she could trap it.

The woman's smile widened. "I've always been here with you." She extended her arms, the fabric of her gown rippling like water. Autumn's nostrils filled with scents of sugar and honey.

A sob built in her throat.

"The orphanage…" Autumn's voice cracked. "Why did you leave me there?"

Instead of answering, the woman's lips parted in verse:

"When the fire calls and the shadows cry,
You'll stand where roots and ruin lie.
One hand will beckon, one will burn.
Choose the one that does not yearn.
Stone remembers. Flesh forgets.
The true path waits where silence rests."

"I...I don't understand." Autumn stretched forward, her fingers reaching for the mother she'd dreamed of a thousand nights. Her hand met something warm—not flesh, but not emptiness either; like touching sunlight, if sunlight could be held.

A flash of cut through the vision. The fox darted between the trees, weaving a path around the woman's feet. Where its tail brushed, shadows curled like smoke from a burning village. Its eyes were white and cold as winter stars.

More illusions bloomed around them, springing from the earth like soldiers from an ambush. The children from Ashwood appeared again, their laughter echoing against the trees. Maxwell was there too, hand outstretched. They surrounded her, pressing close as if to welcome her into their fold.

But beyond them, the other path waited—dark and unwelcoming, offering no promises, no visions of belonging.

The pain in Autumn's chest twisted like a dagger. Every muscle strained toward the illusions offering everything she'd ever wanted. Love. Family. Purpose. The visions closed in, a noose tightening.

She squeezed her eyes shut. Hard. A tear broke free, cutting a path down her cheek like a river carving through stone.

You're not real, she thought. But the illusion pressed in, the whispers, the shadows, the voice that wore her fears like a second skin.

Then she felt it. The locket. Cool against her skin, where it always rested. Steady. Real.

Her fingers found it by instinct, curling around its familiar shape, the chain warm from her body. She had held it a hundred times before, through sleepless nights, storms that shook the windows, days when she didn't know who she was or what she was meant to become.

It had always brought her back. Now, it anchored her again.

"You're not real," she said, her voice finding steel. "None of this is real."

When she opened her eyes, her mother's face contorted. The warmth drained from her like blood from a mortal wound. The woman tore the locket from her throat. Her arm extended, fingers unfolding to reveal the golden heart, then released.

The necklace shattered against invisible stone. Gold and amethyst fragments flew like sparks from a smith's hammer, then vanished between one heartbeat and the next.

Wind ripped through the glade, a howl of rage or mourning—Autumn couldn't tell which. The children scattered like leaves. Maxwell dissolved to mist. Her mother remained longest, eyes burning with accusation before she too was torn away by the gale.

Silence crashed back into the clearing. Autumn stood alone, as she always had. The path that had hidden in shadow now lay bare before her, illuminated by morning sun. The forest no longer whispered false promises; it simply existed, as real as the dirt beneath her boots.

It's morning already? It can't be.

Then she saw them. At the base of an oak grew a cluster of delicate flowers, their petals emitting a faint, magenta-like glow.

They were the very flowers she had seen in Flora's sketches: the Luminosa Blossoms. She carefully picked several, handling them with the care they deserved. She placed them gently into her satchel, ensuring they were secure for the journey home. She could already imagine the joy and surprise on Flora's face and the happiness such a rare find would bring the magical woman.

CHAPTER 22:

THE SERPENT'S TONGUE

One by one, the fair folk returned, lantern-limbed and light as breath. Autumn had not expected to see them again. She had thought them lost to that place of shifting lies and vanishing paths, too fragile or fey-bound to pass through. But here they were, hovering above fern and root, their laughter like wind chimes. They had not abandoned her, and their delight upon seeing her again was proof enough.

The forest murmured. A rustle, faint but purposeful, disturbed the undergrowth behind her. Not the idle stirring of wind, nor the aimless scurry of prey; no, this sound had intention. She stiffened, the hair at her nape rising like bristles on a hound sensing danger.

She had heard it before. Several times since running into the forest, always behind her, never near enough to see. A watcher, perhaps. Or a warning.

"Who's there?"

The fairies stilled mid-flight. Even the trees seemed to lean back, their branches withholding judgment. Somewhere high above, a bird took wing in silence. The forest itself listened.

The fairies darted toward the thicket where the sound had come again. Autumn watched, her body as tense as prey deciding whether to bolt. The bushes stirred louder now, as if something within had tired of subtlety.

A shape broke through the foliage, black as pitch, swift as nightfall.

Papyrus.

The cat leapt forth with the elegance only a creature of his kind could claim, sleek and sure, a whisper stitched into flesh. Sunlight slipped across his back, catching on the curve of his spine.

Relief came suddenly. Papyrus trotted to her, tail high and curved like a scythe, his purr already rising—a low, rumbling spell.

She crouched, hands slipping into the warmth of his fur. It was like grasping memory: soft, real, anchoring. He pressed his head against her knee, a gesture so ordinary, so familiar, it almost broke her.

"And here I thought I'd been left to face this cursed wood alone," she said to him. "Have you come to join me, then? My silent knight, my shadow-footed guide?"

He did not answer, save with a nudge of his head and a flick of his tail, as if the question was foolish for needing to be asked.

The fairies, pleased by the reunion, circled him in playful arcs. Their glow danced upon his coat like firelight on polished stone. Papyrus ignored them with the dignity of a prince long accustomed to adoration.

The path ahead was no true path at all now, only the ghost of one. Roots gnarled like old hands clawed across the earth. The ground sloped and twisted, led more by instinct than design. Autumn rose, brushing her skirts clean, and followed where the cat led.

He moved ahead, pausing now and then to glance back, ears twitching, as though measuring her pace. "Follow me," his eyes seemed to say. "I've walked this way before."

She believed him.

Something had changed since the maze. The forest felt denser, older, as if the trees themselves bore witness. And Papyrus, who had once been content to sleep in bookshop windows and chase the shadows of moths, now strode as one who knew secrets and had chosen, at last, to share them.

Autumn followed, heart lightened but wary still. The forest did not welcome easily, and what was welcomed once could betray just as quickly. But with Papyrus before her, and the fair folk flitting near, she no longer felt entirely alone.

And yet, the feeling lingered that she was being watched not just by trees or beasts, but by something deeper. Something buried in root and shadow, waiting.

Waiting for her to come closer.

She walked until the green swallowed all signs of what lay behind. The fairies kept close, their light dimmed to a soft, steady glow, as though they, too, sensed the shift in her.

Papyrus padded ahead, unhurried now, his tail low, movements fluid as water. He led her to a clearing ringed with old stones sunk half into the moss—altars or markers, perhaps, placed by hands long returned to soil. Here, even the air felt older.

At the center of the glade, beneath the tangled arms of ancient pines, rested a stone coffin raised upon a weathered granite. Dragons coiled along the sides, their bodies wrought with a craftsman's care, each scale carved with patient precision. Their eyes gazed east and west, guardians locked in silent vigil.

Stars and crescent moons arched above their heads— celestial shapes picked out in faint, half-worn relief. The lid itself bore an inscription, words eroded by centuries of wind and rain.

Autumn stepped beside the tomb. Papyrus circled it, ears flicking as if attuned to voices she could not hear. Here lay no hero sung by minstrels, no tyrant crowned in iron. The presence was quieter, but it weighed upon the heart.

She traced the dragons with careful fingers, feeling the cold bite of ancient stone. Between them, a single star had been cut deeper than the rest. Beneath it, the barest suggestion of a name, lost to time.

A gust shivered the branches overhead. Autumn looked up, uncertain if she was trespassing on holy ground or simply walking in the memory of someone who had once mattered more than kings.

"Opal, is that you?" she whispered.

It could be no other. The dragons, the star cut deep at the heart, the air thick with secrets. All of it pointed to her.

A snake coiled down from a gnarled branch. Its descent was slow, deliberate, its gleaming eyes fixed upon her, though there was no threat in its movement.

Its scales were a hypnotic vision of emerald, rich as the heart of the forest itself. Streaks of gold ran along its spine like ancient runes, each motion catching the light, glinting like the first rays of dawn cresting the horizon.

But it was the eyes that held her still.

Molten orange and yellow, twin embers lit from the same fire that first awakened the world. In their depths she saw movement: branches swaying in long-dead seasons, stars shifting across skies untouched by maps, faces she did not know yet somehow recognized.

The snake watched her, but Autumn did not flinch. Her breath slowed. Her hands hung loose at her sides.

It drew closer still, its body winding around a stone near her feet. Then it stopped, tongue flicking once. Waiting.

She knelt.

She had read of omens like this, ancient creatures bearing messages from the deep world, from roots and rivers and time itself. But no tale had prepared her for the one the snake offered.

Their gazes met again, and something passed between them—wordless, vast, and final.

Autumn bowed her head. Whatever force had summoned this creature, it did not see her as lost. It saw her as chosen.

It hissed and then it spoke. "They called you foolish. Mad. Lost in fancies and phantoms. But when you spoke, the wind listened. When you feared, the trees reached for you."

She closed her eyes.

"What do you see when you are no longer trying to be seen?"

Her fingers curled into the moss. All the names they had given her came back, not one had ever fit. But they had shaped her all the same.

"Turn your eyes to mine once more. Look not outward. Look...beneath," the snake said to her.

She looked deep into the snake's eyes and saw herself as she was. Not as the town called her, not as the orphan girl who spoke to trees and dreamt of things too wild to speak aloud. She saw the way her steps had always matched the rhythm of the wind, the way her thoughts reached places others would not tread. She saw every time she'd quieted her voice and folded herself smaller for the sake of being left alone.

And still, *still*, the fire had endured.

She was not broken. She was forged. "I see a girl who was never lost," she whispered.

Papyrus returned to her side, rubbing along her legs before settling on his haunches.

"They were never meant to understand me," she whispered. "And he—he thought I'd never find the pieces. But I've had them all along."

The snake asked again, "What do you see when you are no longer trying to be seen?"

"I see...I see that I do not need to be fixed, for I am not broken," she said.

The snake remained coiled at the foot of the stone, its golden-streaked body resting like a crown around old moss. The weight of its gaze had not lessened. If anything, it pressed heavier now—as though it waited to see what she would do with the truths it had given.

Autumn rose, brushing the moss from her palms. She set her gaze beyond the ancient grave, beyond the circle of stones, to where the forest shadows deepened.

"I know what must be done," she said. "I do not yet know whether I have the strength, but I'll see it through, one way or another. If ever a dragon listens, let it be now."

Papyrus watched her, tail curled close, as if he too understood the weight of it.

She turned to the fairies, who hovered in a lazy ring of light, their wings humming like distant bells. "Do you know the way to the Emerald Glade?" she asked.

They giggled, three voices in three different tones.

One flew a slow circle around her head and whispered, "Follow the root that drinks no rain."

Another chimed, "Chase the shadow that blooms at dawn."

The last somersaulted midair and added, "Where silence sings, the path begins."

Autumn blinked. "That doesn't mean anything." They only laughed again, swirling upward like falling stars in reverse.

She sighed. "Of course not," she said, and then asked the snake, "Do you know the way to the Emerald Glade?"

The serpent's tongue flicked once, tasting her question in the air. "The way is not walked. The way is remembered."

She let herself fall into those ember eyes, and this time, the vision did not stop at what she had been. It reached forward— through the shrouded path, the gnarled roots, the fire-lit night still to come. She saw the glade not as it was, but as it remembered itself to be. A place of beginnings. A place of endings.

Autumn looked to Papyrus. He sat waiting, tail curled neatly. He had walked with her through root and bramble, illusion and hush. But she saw his motive now for what it was.

Curiosity.

The kind that pulled cats into cupboards and kings into ruin, because he wanted to know what might be found.

"Well then," she murmured, crouching beside him. "You did well. But we'll lead from here."

Papyrus gave no sign of protest. His tail twitched once, as if in agreement—or amusement.

The snake had begun to move again. The forest deepened around them, the sun bleeding low through the trees, turning bark to bronze and shadows to ink. Each step felt slower than the last. Branches reached overhead like the ribs of some ancient creature, and the air cooled with the coming of night.

The fairies trailed behind now, weaving in and out of sight, their lights dimming to a glow barely brighter than fireflies.

Autumn raised her chin. "Do you want to play a game of riddles?"

The fairies stilled, then burst into delighted motion, circling her head like storm-blown leaves.

"A game!" one cried.

"A riddle!" shrieked another.

"Only if we win," said the third, grinning far too wide.

Even the serpent shifted, lifting its head from the ground, tongue flicking as if amused.

Autumn smirked. "Then let's begin." And she recited:

"I am the season that comes to pass,
when shades of green turn gold and brass.
I precede the coming of the snow,
after summer's final glow.
What am I, with harvest moon so bright,
when days are shorter than the night?
I herald the end, yet also a beginning,
in the cycle of seasons, my foliage thinning.
Who am I, who neither sows nor reaps, awaiting the
blanket that winter keeps?"

The fairies spun again, circling one another, whispering nonsense in old tongues. Then, one darted forward. "It's a festival! The night of lanterns!"

"No," said the second, somersaulting midair. "A scarecrow!"

The third struck a triumphant pose. "Clearly...it's a bonfire."

Autumn arched a brow. "Is that your final guess?"

They tumbled into each other, laughing like wind through empty branches.

Then the snake lifted its head. "You are Autumn."

The fairies stopped their laughter, blinking wide-eyed as though only now realizing the shape of the game.

Papyrus blinked once, slow and feline, as if he'd known all along.

Autumn smiled, not shyly, not as one exposed, but as one finally seen.

She bowed her head to the snake. "Well played."

The snake's eyes glowed brighter, as if in approval, and it lowered its head in return.

It studied Autumn, its tongue flicking once, then twice, as if tasting not the air, but the space between her thoughts.

"Now mine," hissed the snake. He continued:

> "No flame I wield, no wings I wear,
> yet through the air, my words do bear.
> A silent pact, a secret bond,
> across the veil of which I'm fond.
> What am I, who, with no roar,
> commands the sky and so much more?
> A secret keeper, a silent guide,
> in whom the ancient beasts confide?"

Autumn thought for a moment before speaking. "A shadow," she said at last. "Or...the wind?"

Without acknowledging her response, the snake went on:

> "No scales upon my skin you'll find,
> nor wings to soar through skies unkind.
> Yet dragons heed my silent call.
> With me, they rise, and with me, they fall.
> What am I? Who walks not with might,
> but in the shadowed land takes flight.
> Binding beast with a gentle word,
> a kinship unseen but felt and heard?"

The answer was not hidden. It had always been her. She raised her eyes to meet the snake's. "Dragon Whisperer."

The snake lowered its head. The fairies gasped, all at once.

One placed a tiny hand over her heart. Another knelt midair. The third dimmed entirely.

Autumn stood straighter, though her hands still trembled. The word felt vast in her mouth, old and heavy. Not a title. A truth.

The snake wound itself once more, slower this time, almost tender. "Now you remember."

Papyrus flicked his tail. Autumn turned to say something to the snake...but he was gone, vanished into the green as though it had never been.

But the fire it left in her remained. The trees ahead thinned without parting. The forest gave no farewell. It simply let her pass, as if it had shown her all it meant to show.

CHAPTER 23:

ASHES AND THORNS

It was dusk once more and Autumn watched from at the edge of the crowd, half-shadowed beneath the overhang of the old bakery.

They hadn't noticed her yet—not Evelyn, not Iris, pale and tight-lipped near the front. That suited her just fine. She wasn't ready to speak. Not yet. Her hand curled around the locket hidden beneath her cloak.

"Mr. Wolfsbane! Tell us what is going on!" Heads turned. Callum stepped forward. He looked older than she remembered. His voice, though worn by cigars and ale, rang out clear and sharp. He pointed a shaking finger at the man in the center of the square. "These changes only started when you arrived in town."

Maxwell stepped forward, his posture calm, but she saw the tension in his shoulders. The flicker in his eyes.

Relief hit her first—swift, unwelcome. Her breath caught at the sight of him, tall and composed, the firelight brushing gold across the planes of his face. He was still handsome, infuriatingly so. Still steady in a world that felt as if it had tilted sideways.

Don't be glad to see him.

The thought struck hard.

Don't be foolish.

She clenched her jaw, forcing down the flutter in her chest. *He is the danger. Not the refuge.*

He spread his arms like a priest before the pyre, inviting both worship and surrender.

"I understand your fear," he said. "But I assure you, I am here to help."

Autumn nearly laughed. A dry, brittle sound she swallowed back.

Samuel's voice cut in, booming and raw. "Since you've come, the town has been overrun by these cursed vines and this...this darkness."

Faces twisted with fear, voices sharp with anger. The chorus rose fast, too fast, and for a moment Autumn hoped the truth might crack through on its own.

But Maxwell held. He didn't shout. He didn't fight. He spoke. Measured. Steady.

The lie slipped from his tongue. "The roses," he said, "are part of the enchantment that binds this place. They were summoned to protect us. There is a beast...a great beast...older than you can imagine. It threatens everything we hold dear."

Autumn clenched her fists.

He spun them a tale of ancient danger, of thorns woven for their protection, of sacrifice and unseen war. The crowd began to waver, just as he knew they would. People who had once trusted their own senses now doubted what they saw with their own eyes.

She could feel it, the way their anger gave way to fear. How that fear turned inward, twisting into reluctant trust.

They want to believe him, she thought, *because the truth is worse. Because the truth meant they'd let him in.*

A tap on her shoulder pulled her from her thoughts.

Flora. Eyes wide, breath tight in her chest. "Autumn, where have you been?" she whispered. "Everyone's been—"

Autumn didn't answer. Her gaze flicked once toward the square, then back to Flora. Without a word, she pulled the satchel from her shoulder and placed it into Flora's hands.

"Take this," she said, her voice low, steady. "You'll want to see what's inside."

Flora looked down at the worn leather, confused. "What is it?"

Autumn looked toward the front of the crowd, toward the man she was about to name.

"Autumn, wait…"

She walked forward, no longer unnoticed, boots scuffing the stone, her voice ringing out like a strike of iron.

"Maxwell Wolfsbane is Magnus Blackthorn," she declared, arm outstretched, finger pointed like a blade. "He hides behind a name, behind charm and coin, but he is the same tyrant who sought to break this town once before. And now he's come to finish what he started."

No tremor touched her voice. No fear showed in her stance. She stood with her shoulders squared, eyes alight with fury and fire. The wind caught her skirts, sweeping them around her legs in sharp, snapping folds. Her hair lashed about her face like a banner in a rising storm.

Above her, the fairies circled in allegiance, their golden light weaving through her hair, forming a flickering crown of wings and wonder.

"He failed before," she said, her voice carrying over the crowd, "and he will fail again."

A few townsfolk turned away, muttering under their breath, shaking their heads as they slipped down side streets, unwilling to be drawn into whatever drama she had stirred.

Evelyn's voice rose above the growing murmurs, strained with confusion. "Autumn? What are you doing?"

Autumn didn't flinch. Her eyes never left him.

Magnus stood in the center of the square, smugness pulling at the corner of his mouth, but irritation tightening the lines around his eyes. The wind caught the hem of his dark coat, snapping it like a banner.

He stepped forward, slow and graceful, as though this were all some game he'd already won. "Ah, Miss Ashwood," he drawled, "how dramatic. If you wished for an audience, you might've simply scheduled a reading."

She pointed at him again, her voice slicing through the murmurs like a blade. "Don't listen to him. He is Magnus Blackthorn, a thief of lives, a wielder of forbidden power. He's here to finish what he began years ago, to drain this town dry and bind it to his will."

No denial came from him. "Secrets, my dear," he said, voice like velvet over broken glass, "are the lifeblood of this town. The bookstore, the forest, even the air you breathe—they all hold untold tales. Tales that, with the right touch, can unravel the very fabric of what you call reality."

He stepped forward again, his tone turning colder. "You should be careful with accusations. Some things, once spoken, cannot be unspoken."

From the edge of the crowd, Sylas Finch stumbled forward, breath ragged, eyes wide. His coat was torn, one sleeve ripped at the seam, and a frayed rope hung from his wrist like the tail of a broken leash.

"Stop," he rasped, drawing every eye. "She's telling the truth."

Autumn turned sharply. "Sylas—"

He nodded, breath shallow. "He is Magnus Blackthorn."

A fresh wave of whispers surged through the townsfolk. The name passed from mouth to mouth like a curse recalled from childhood, half-remembered but feared all the same. Faces paled. Others stiffened. The name stirred something old and uneasy in their bones.

Magnus turned, his smile gone. His stare locked onto Sylas with such force that the air seemed to still. The temperature dropped. "So, they let madmen walk freely now? Did you wander out of…or perhaps escape from the…what do they call it now, the sanctuary for the fevered mind?"

He moved like a striking viper, crossing the space in a heartbeat. He seized Sylas by the front of his tunic and yanked him forward, their faces inches apart.

Sylas faltered, his usual riddles swallowed by the weight of that gaze. His voice broke. "I followed your orders," he whispered. "But she…she was just a child. I couldn't do it. I couldn't take it that far."

Autumn stepped forward, her heart pounding. "Who was a child?" Her voice cracked. "Sylas… What are you saying?"

His eyes met hers. "Autumn, I…"

CHAPTER 24:

THE PRICE OF SILENCE

From the perspective of Sylas

Sylas could feel the charge in the air. A wrongness crawling through Whispering Pines like mold through old wood.

The townsfolk murmured like bees in a shaken hive. And now they were here. Waiting.

Maxwell stood at the center like a stone in a swollen river, no longer masked by polite smiles and purchased charm. He looked like a predator disturbed mid-meal.

"Sylas," Magnus said, "what is it you need to explain?" He released his grip, then reached forward with mock gentleness to smooth the front of Sylas's rumpled coat. His fingers brushed the fabric with exaggerated care before giving Sylas's chest a patronizing pat, like a master humoring a disobedient hound.

Thunder groaned above.

"I…" Sylas stammered, the riddle-wrapped certainty of his usual speech nowhere to be found. "I followed your orders."

Magnus's grip tightened around Sylas's coat again.

"But she was only a child."

"Who was a child?" Autumn repeated. "Sylas, what are you talking about?"

The crowd fell to silence, waiting for the answer. Sylas looked at her, and the past rushed up to meet him.

He remembered the path. Narrow, hidden beneath overgrowth. Leading to a cottage near the edge of nowhere, swallowed by wildflowers and vines.

He had gone alone. The task was simple. A name. A location. A command: "The line ends here."

Magnus had offered him a prize, the Chalice of Immortality, a thing of legend. A vessel said to restore youth, preserve power. A relic Sylas had sought for years.

He told himself it would be a clean ending. Quick. Silent.

She answered the door with a wary sort of kindness, as worn by those who had learned to live alongside fear but not be ruled by it. Her hair, long and unbound, held the hue of wheat caught in the first light of morning: soft gold threaded with copper. Her eyes, a deep, weathered brown, reminded Sylas of ancient tree bark, steady, scarred, and quietly wise.

She wore a gown the color of ripened fruit just before harvest, a muted blush that caught the evening light like flame behind silk. And at her throat rested a golden heart-shaped locket.

She studied him for a moment, then stepped aside and gestured for him to enter. "Would you like tea?"

He had followed her in, saying little. The cottage smelled of sugar and honey. Books lined the shelves. Herbs hung from the rafters. There was no fire in her gaze—no threat. Just weariness. And wisdom. And something ancient, quiet, and unafraid.

But Magnus hadn't asked for a reckoning. He'd asked for silence. And Sylas had delivered it.

He still remembered the feel of the air as she fell. The word she spoke as the light fled from her eyes.

"Autumn."

He'd turned and seen the child. No more than two. Ginger curls. Bare feet. Sitting on the floor, stacking worn wooden blocks into a crooked tower.

Sylas had not known about the girl. And something inside him, something long buried, broke.

He just scooped her up, wrapped her in the blanket nearest the hearth, and walked out beneath the cover of night.

He left her on the steps of the orphanage, tucked the locket into her pocket, and said nothing of what had come before.

Sylas reported the elimination of the woman but kept the existence of the little girl a secret. And the chalice he had been promised never came.

Magnus, young as ever, untouched by time, never spoke of it again. And Sylas grew older. Year by year, wrinkle by wrinkle. Forgotten. Used.

"Sylas... What did you do?"

He swallowed hard. "I took your mother's life."

A collective gasp broke from the crowd. Evelyn covered her mouth. Iris gripped her arm.

"I was sent by Magnus," Sylas continued, his voice hoarse. "Promised something rare, something I had long sought. I accepted. But then I saw you. You looked up at me...and I couldn't."

His hands trembled at his sides. "I couldn't finish what he truly wanted. So I spared you."

He met her eyes then, eyes so much like her mother's. "I am ashamed of what I've done," he said, the words cutting him more deeply than any blade. "Over the years, I pulled away from him. From everything. My heart, what was left of it, began to soften."

His voice faltered, but he pushed on. "I watched you grow. From a girl to a woman. Ginger hair and a curious gaze. Every time I saw you, it was a reminder of the night I chose betrayal over mercy...and the moment I tried to make it right."

CHAPTER 25:

THE HEART OF WHISPERING PINES

Whispering Pines now stood in the wake of one truth too many. Some looked to Sylas with disbelief, others with fury. But all turned, in time, to Autumn.

She felt their eyes on her like the weight of a hundred stones. But it was nothing compared to the heaviness inside. Her eyes stayed locked on Sylas, the man who had lied with every glance.

Tears didn't come. Not yet. Her eyes remained dry, wide, and unblinking, as if grief had frozen the part of her that once wept. But inside, a storm raged. Betrayal burned like iron in her chest, and disbelief clouded her vision, turning familiar faces to ghosts.

Every memory, every gesture, every faint smile he had ever offered her, refracted now through a lens of unbearable truth.

She clutched her locket. When she finally spoke, her voice was quiet, but sharp enough to cut bone.

"All this time?" Her lips trembled. "How could you? Every time you looked me in the face, you lied." She took a step forward. "My whole life, I've searched for answers, scraps of the past, anything to tell me who I am. And you—" Her voice broke. "You took that from me. You took my mother. You took everything."

The crowd stirred again. Some wept. Thomas and Samuel stepped forward, each taking Sylas gently but firmly by the arms. They led him away, slow and grim, to ensure he wouldn't escape consequence.

Magnus did not move. His expression remained unreadable, no outburst, no denial, not even surprise. But Autumn saw it: the subtle clench of his jaw, the flicker of disdain in his eyes as if watching a pawn break formation on a game board he'd long mastered.

He turned to the crowd, slow and deliberate, his voice calm as ever. "So this is how it ends...for him. Spilling secrets like a butcher gutting a fish, hoping to wash away the blood with confession."

No one answered.

Autumn's eyes turned to the faces that remained, familiar, weathered, beloved, and yet strangers all the same.

"You all looked at me," she said, louder now, "and saw a foolish girl who chased stories."

A murmur rippled through the gathered townsfolk.

"Even the kind ones—" Her eyes found Evelyn, Iris, Birdie, Flora. "You smiled. You listened. But you never heard me. Not really."

She took another step forward. The wind caught her skirts. The moon broke through cloud and haloed her in silver.

"You didn't want to believe. Because if you believed, then you'd have to see it all: the rot under the roots, the truth that we were never safe. That this town has always been sleeping beside a monster."

A silence fell. Thick. Shamed.

"You called me strange. Said I was dramatic. Said I dreamed too much. You made me doubt my own eyes." She was trembling now. "And when I tried to tell you something was wrong, when I begged you to look closer, you didn't even consider I was right."

A sob broke somewhere in the crowd.

Autumn looked out at them all, heart pounding in her ears. "Even if you didn't believe me, I deserved for you to believe in me."

Magnus smiled, thin and sharp. "Do you all feel better now? Safer?" He stepped toward Autumn, unhurried and composed, a smirk curling across his face like smoke.

"Perhaps," he murmured, voice almost honeyed, "something good may come of this after all." He leaned closer, his words a low thread of silk. "The strength we could wield... The things we could accomplish... Think of the power we'd have...together."

He let the pause hang, then added, softer still, "And I would never doubt you or lie to you, Autumn. Not like they have." His voice was warm and inviting. But the promise behind it was a razor.

She struck him across the face. The slap rang out across the square like thunder.

"How dare you," she said, her voice steady, ice in her veins. "You think I'd stand beside the man who murdered my mother?" He didn't flinch, only smiled.

Magnus leaned closer, his breath brushing her cheek. "The strength we could wield... The things we could accomplish..." His voice dropped, a thread of silk wrapping tight. "Think of it,

Autumn. No more being dismissed. No more being silenced. We could reshape the world."

She froze. The words struck something raw, not with fear, but with the sharp jolt of seeing her own hunger mirrored in his.

"And I would never doubt you," he said, softer now, "never lie to you. Not like they have." He touched her pendant then, just the edge. "They fear what you are. I would honor it."

Her hands curled into fists at her sides to still the tremble of temptation.

"You were never meant to kneel before their small, frightened lives."

She looked at him now, really looked. He was beautiful, in the way fire is beautiful before it devours. His voice held comfort, promise, and ruin. He offered understanding. And that made it worse.

"You want to matter," he said. "To shape your own fate. So do I. You carry the storm just beneath your skin. I could teach you to wield it. Not in shame. Not in silence. But in sovereignty."

Autumn's lips parted, but no words came. Because it was true. A part of her wanted what he offered—not the power, but the freedom. The clarity. To stop shrinking. To stop asking permission.

"I know what they called you," Magnus said, his voice suddenly tender. "Mad. Strange. But I see what you are. You and I... We were made from the same fire."

She looked away. "You want to shape the world in your image. Burn the old legends and wear their bones like crowns."

"And you don't?" he asked, quietly. "Not even a little?"

She stared at him, eyes sharp now, voice steady. "I want to shape myself. That's the difference."

A shadow passed through his expression, swift and bitter. "You'll find the world has little mercy for those who go it alone."

"We'll see," she said.

Then he chuckled—low, cold, amused beyond reason. "So," he said, stepping back, "tell me, Autumn. Where is your dragon? Have you not called it yet?"

His eyes flicked toward the black cat at her feet, and he sneered. "That little thing? What a disappointment."

The prophecy echoed in her ears like a chant lost in the dark.

What once was lost shall be reclaimed, what once was stolen, now renamed...

Magnus came closer again, until his presence was suffocating. The scent of him filled her lungs—earth after rain, crushed roses, aged leather covered in dust. Wild and refined. Beautiful. Terrible.

"Well," he whispered, "it looks like your dragon isn't coming to save you."

He grabbed her wrist. The pain was immediate, his grip cruel, bruising. His voice dropped to a hiss. "Or maybe you're no Fireborn at all."

A wave of whispering broke over the crowd. "Fireborn? Dragonkin? Could it be true?"

"Let her go," Iris called, stepping forward. "Now."

Magnus didn't turn. He didn't loosen his grip. His eyes stayed locked on Autumn's, but his voice rang out, sharp and cruel as snapped bone.

"Stay out of this, wench," he snarled. "This doesn't concern painted old fools clinging to past lives." His fingers dug deeper, demanding more than blood—he wanted submission. Answers. "Now," he growled, "tell me. Where is it? Where is what belongs to me?"

Autumn stared into his eyes, her expression blank but burning beneath. Even if she knew, she would never tell him.

And he saw it in her eyes, that stubborn refusal, that defiance she wore like armor. It was louder than any spell.

He snarled. "Where is it?!"

Papyrus moved. Low to the ground, tail lashing, he circled behind Magnus like a shadow grown fangs. A growl rose from his throat—deep, guttural, almost too large for his feline frame.

Magnus now looked to the pendant resting at Autumn's throat. Something in his posture changed. His expression, once mocking, narrowed. No more games. No more words.

The locket pulsed faintly against her skin, as if it too sensed danger drawing near.

His hand shot out. She slapped it away. He grabbed again, faster this time, and seized the chain. Autumn's hand flew up, clutching the other end, and they struggled, locked in a desperate tug-of-war. The chain dug into her fingers as it twisted between them, the locket swinging wildly between their chests.

"Let go," he growled, his voice trembling now with hunger.

"No," she spat, her grip tightening.

The chain strained. She could feel the links bending, feel the moment stretch thinner than thread. His eyes, locked on the locket, burned with more than rage. It was an obsession, something primal and panicked beneath the mask.

With a final, brutal wrench, the chain snapped. The locket flew from their hands, struck the stone path, and broke open. Gold cracked. Amethyst scattered across the ground. A faint pulse of heat rippled outward, then vanished.

Autumn stared at the shattered pieces, her mouth slightly parted, breath caught somewhere between a gasp and a cry. The fragments of gold and amethyst lay at her feet, each one a splinter of something sacred, of a life, a mother, a name she'd never had the chance to speak.

Threads of gold unfurled from the wreckage, rising into the air in shimmering arcs.

Magnus stared, momentarily stunned, as the magic surged toward him. It poured into him like fire through open veins, filling every hollow with strength that burned and bloomed. His eyes widened, catching the light as it coursed through him, feeding the hunger written into his bones.

But as the last of the golden glow vanished into his chest, the radiance shifted, darkening, deepening—until what remained within him pulsed red, like molten ember beneath skin.

Then he laughed. Low, unearthly, and cold, the sound rolled out in waves, sending a shudder through the onlookers. Power had returned to Magnus Blackthorn. And it no longer wore a golden face.

The broken locket's shards glinted like fallen stars on the cobblestones, cold and lifeless as winter bones. Autumn sank to her knees, fingers trembling as they swept across the jagged pieces. She felt each edge cut into her flesh, though no blood flowed. Pain of a different sort coursed through her veins.

Mother's pendant. The thought threatened to drown her. She had carried the weight of it against her breast her whole life, through summer's heat and winter's chill, through feast and famine alike.

Grief came swift and raw, curling through her like smoke through an open window. Tears fell freely now. The pendant was gone. No spell, no metal, no binding left to save. Just fragments. Just memory. The only tangible piece of her past, now shattered beneath her knees.

The wind picked up, carrying the scent of coming rain. Storm clouds gathered like a flock of ravens above the old square, black against the fading sky.

And yet—

"Look inside your heart, Autumn."

The voice echoed not in her ears but in the hollow spaces between thoughts, soft as a whisper across still water; her mother's voice she'd come to know in the illusionary maze.

She closed her eyes, feeling a lone tear trace the curve of her cheek before the wind claimed it. Her head bowed over the broken locket.

The moon hung low, its light thin and silver, a last lantern before the storm. Thunder growled in the distance like some great beast stirring from slumber. The wild roses that climbed the broken walls hissed and shuddered in the strengthening gale.

When Autumn opened her eyes, Papyrus was pawing at the base of the statue—Opal, or what remained of her. The dragon half had been destroyed long ago, the stone fractured where its wings once rose. But the woman's hand was still outstretched, palm open. Waiting.

Her mother's words rose in her like breath returning to the lungs:

> "When the fire calls and the shadows cry,
> You'll stand where roots and ruin lie.
> One hand will beckon, one will burn.
> Choose the one that does not yearn.
> Stone remembers. Flesh forgets.
> The true path waits where silence rests."

Autumn pushed herself to her feet. Her skirt clung to her legs, wet and streaked with mud. Lightning split the sky like a woodsman's axe.

Her lips parted. "What once was lost shall be reclaimed, what once was stolen, now renamed." The words felt right upon her tongue, as if they had been waiting all her life to be spoken.

She stepped forward, breath steady now, and placed her small hand within the statue's weathered stone palm.

Though she had never spoken the words before, they came as naturally as breath, as if written in the very blood that flowed through her veins:

"Through blood and breath, through fire and flame,
By heart's command, I speak thy name.
Bound by oath, we rise or fall.
By bond unbroken, heed my call."

The shape was now whole again. Woman and dragon. Flesh completing stone. The forgotten made living.

Papyrus completed a thankful rub against her legs.

"Enough!" Magnus's voice cut through the twilight like a blade of ice. He stood at the edge of the square, his black robes billowing in the wind. With a twist of his gnarled fingers, he hurled a bolt of crimson light toward the cat.

The spell missed its mark, shattering part of the statue with a sound like mountains breaking. Shards of rock flew in all directions.

Papyrus bolted down the path, his dark form streaked with light, tail held high in defiance.

"Papyrus!" Autumn cried; she ran after him, leaving the sorcerer cursing in her wake.

She pursued the cat beyond the twisted oaks that marked the boundary between the known and unknown. The path narrowed beneath her feet, winding ever downward toward the Emerald Glade.

Behind her, she heard Magnus shouting and the thunder of boots upon stone. He would not be far behind, and with him, the full weight of his sorcery. Time was as scarce as mercy in the game they now played.

Chapter 26:
Nightmare and Smoke

Autumn stumbled into the Emerald Glade, breathless, her boots slick with mud and rain, and her hair plastered to her flushed cheeks. Even beneath the damp shroud of night, the ancient glade held its terrible beauty. Mist clung to the low branches like torn veils of some ghostly bride, and the stars, fierce and cold, mirrored themselves in the black glass of the lake.

So fair, it might have been a reflection of the heavens, or perhaps a portal to some other realm altogether—one where the old magic still walked freely upon the earth.

Papyrus cried out, an unearthly sound that was neither feline nor human. The sound rippled across the still waters of the lake.

It began as a low keening that split the night air like a blade through silk, then rose to a wailing screech that vibrated Autumn's very bones. Before her eyes, his form buckled and writhed, the delicate frame of the feline unraveling as though some unseen force had gripped its spine and was drawing forth a monstrous thing.

She dared not move, dared not flee. Some instinct older than fear rooted her to the spot, as a sinuous shape rose where once small paws had trod. Bone and sinew twisted, reshaping in ways that no natural creature could endure. His spine lengthened, his limbs tore free of their old forms.

A dragon rose from the ruins of the cat, black as the void between the stars, massive and terrible in its beauty.

His wings unfurled, revealing rich, beaten copper, veined with molten fire that pulsed like blood through living flesh. They stretched wide enough to cast the entire glade in shadow, had the sun been high. Only the eyes remained unchanged, those same golden eyes, burning with a light no earthly thing could kindle.

The prophecy had spoken true after all.

The dragon lowered its massive head until his golden eyes were level with her own. Steam rose from its nostrils in twin plumes, hot breath meeting the cool night air. It smelled of cinder and iron and something untamed and ancient.

Autumn's hand rose, trembling with the burden of fate, and came to rest upon the creature's scaled snout. Warmth radiated through her palm, banishing the chill of the rain and years of doubt in a single moment.

Footfalls crashed through the brush, breaking the silence that had settled between woman and dragon. Magnus came first, his fine clothes torn by thorns, the embroidered sigil at his breast half-obscured by mud. His boots sank deep in the damp soil with each furious stride. Behind him, torches bobbed like fireflies in the gloom as the townsfolk followed, their faces painted in fear and wonder by the flickering light.

One by one, they staggered to a halt at the clearing's edge, as though an invisible barrier had sprung up between the Emerald Glade and the world of men. Their eyes, previously narrowed against the night and rain, now stretched wide as copper coins.

Magnus seized the moment. "Well, folks, there is your BEAST!"

A collective gasp rose from them, the sound of a hundred held breaths released at once. Before them stood a legend made flesh, a creature from the oldest stories told by grandmothers on the longest nights of winter.

The dragon's massive form glistened under the cold gaze of the stars, each scale a testament to powers forgotten by most men. Those scales rippled with every breath the beast took, scattering the moonlight as though he bore the sky's own treasures in his skin.

None had seen the transformation—none but Autumn. To the rest, it was a marvel born of the mist and the old stories they had long learned to doubt. Some fell to their knees in the mud, lips moving in silent prayers to gods whose names they scarcely remembered. Others clutched at talismans worn beneath rough-spun shirts, trinkets passed down through generations against a day none truly believed would come.

Magnus showed no fear. His face hardened into something like stone. The rain had plastered his dark hair to his scalp, and rivulets ran down his face like tears, though his eyes remained dry and cold.

"Stand away from the beast, girl," he commanded, his voice carrying the weight of authority that had cowed lords and peasants alike. "This is no pet to be coddled. This is an abomination of the old magics."

The air crackled with power, and a bolt of lightning filled the glade.

Autumn did not move. The rain had soaked through her garments, but she felt only the heat lifting from the dragon's massive form. Her hand still rested upon its scales, warm as sunbaked stone beneath her palm.

"Foolish girl," Magnus spat, taking another step forward. The mud sucked at his boots, reluctant to release him. "That creature has no name we can speak. It is a remnant of days better forgotten. Your mother knew the danger. She died trying to keep it hidden—"

The dragon's growl rumbled through the glade, deep as thunder and twice as threatening. The sound vibrated in Autumn's chest, in the very marrow of her bones. Several of the townsfolk retreated a step, their courage faltering in the face of such primal power.

"He will burn this land to cinders," Magnus warned, his gaze fixed not on the beast but on Autumn herself. There was something in his eyes she had never seen before, something that might have been desperation. "Everything you know, everyone you love. Dragons bring only fire and blood. The histories are clear on this."

"The histories were written by men like you," Autumn replied. She thought of her mother's broken locket, of the words of the prophecy, of a thousand small moments that had led her to this glade on this night. "Men who fear what they cannot control."

Magnus's face contorted with rage. "Step aside, or you will share its fate."

The great beast bowed its crested head yet further, and the scales rested against the damp earth. Autumn hesitated, just a breath, then climbed onto its back, her fingers finding purchase against the rough ridges of scale. The dragon's hide was alive beneath her body, with a heat that chased the chill from her bones.

Philip would never believe this, she thought, a breathless laugh almost rising to her lips. The girl who wouldn't even ride a horse...

The dragon stirred beneath her, a living mountain, and she tightened her grip, feeling its strength rise up to meet her own.

The dragon's wings unfurled to their full span, copper veins glowing like embers against the night sky. He arched his great neck and bared teeth like polished daggers, each one longer than a man's hand.

Autumn caught sight of Evelyn and Iris in the crowd, their faces pale and stricken, and Flora edging toward them with the same dazed disbelief. They had not expected this; none of them had.

But if they had ever tried to understand her, truly understand, perhaps they would not have been so easily undone by the truth laid bare before them.

Magnus struck then. The magic he conjured was no clean thing, no flash of light or gentle force, but a seething mass of crimson, thick as spoiled blood, twisting the very air as it tore through the glade.

The bolt slammed into the dragon's skull; its head snapped back with a crack of force that shook the earth.

From deep within its throat rose a sound, a furious roar, ancient and terrible, like stones grinding beneath the weight of a mountain.

The crowd broke. Their wonder turned to terror in an instant as they scattered, clawing for cover, tripping over roots and one another in their blind panic. They dove behind the battered fruit stands, hid beneath skeletal trees, their screams mingling with the sickening crunch of splintered wood and trampling boots.

Magnus laughed, a sound sharp enough to split bone. With a slow, serpentine motion, he raised his arms.

From the edges of the glade where the shadows clung thickest, ravens erupted into the air, but these were no living creatures. They were things born of malice, stitched together from nightmare and smoke.

Their feathers drank what little light remained, and from their hollow forms bled a pulse of dull, blood-red fire, as though something wicked beat within their chests.

Their eyes gleamed, red and sharp—not mindless but hungry. They circled Magnus so tightly knit they seemed a single living shroud, awaiting his command.

At the flick of his wrist, they broke apart, diving toward the dragon with the speed of knives loosed from a butcher's hand.

The air sizzled around them, the stench of burning air and damp earth rising like a funeral pyre. They came not like birds, but like curses given wings.

Autumn could only hope the fairies understood the peril and had found refuge beneath the leaves of a nearby bush, their delicate lights hidden from the ravenous shadows, lest they be mistaken for fireflies and snatched from the air.

CHAPTER 27:
THE BELLY OF THE BEAST—
PART ONE

Magnus's laughter echoed through the glade, a sound that set every spine to shivering. His body convulsed, muscles twisting beneath his skin, until a grotesque tearing split the night.

From his back erupted a pair of massive wings, black as the void, their edges frayed into tendrils that drifted and re-formed with every beat. Veins of faint, pulsing light threaded through them, his dark magic woven into every fiber.

He lifted into the air, leaving the onlookers frozen in their terror. Each slow sweep of the wings sent a ripple of something ancient and unclean over the earth. Magnus's eyes, once sharp with ambition, had become pits of darkness, reflecting nothing but chaos.

Magnus hovered above, wings slicing through the mist, his laughter curling across the glade. The shadow-born ravens streaked around the dragon, weaving tight, dizzying circles, their blood-red currents leaving trails that seared against the night sky.

The dragon snapped at them with his fangs, his massive head swinging as he tried to track their swift movements.

Autumn clung to the ridge of his neck, pressing low against the armored scales as the ravens blurred her vision and twisted the world into a whirl of wings and malice.

Magnus flung bolt after bolt of dark magic, each one ripping through the sky with a crack of splitting stone.

The strikes carved smoking scars through the glade, setting the ground trembling with their force. Heat shimmered off the earth, warping the air into waves of flickering shadow.

The dragon growled and fought to stay aloft. Each bolt hammered against his scales, driving him sideways, staggering him in midair. He roared, a deep and furious bellow that shook Autumn to the marrow.

She tightened her grip, feeling the vibrations shudder through his powerful frame. He tried to retaliate, snapping at the circling ravens, but they darted and harried him without rest, dragging his focus away from Magnus's strikes.

Autumn cursed under her breath.

She could feel the dragon faltering under the assault, feel the weight of the magic trying to drag him from the sky. If he lost his clarity now, if he faltered even for a breath, they could fall.

"Find yourself," she urged. "Find your fire. If I can do it, so can you."

A raven dove toward the dragon's golden eye, but he slammed a clawed foot down, pinning the creature to the earth with a sickening crunch. The raven shattered into mist, its broken form vanishing on the wind.

Magnus hurled another bolt, black lightning hissing through the night. The dragon tucked his wings and dove, the attack missing him by inches, burning the air where they had been.

Autumn felt the dragon's heart surge beneath her—wild, fierce, unbroken. And still, she held fast, refusing to fall.

The dragon fixed his eyes on the circling ravens. He opened his jaws wide, and with a swift lunge, he swallowed the first raven whole.

The creature flailed for an instant, its wings thrashing in vain, before vanishing down his throat.

The second raven beat its wings frantically, trying to escape, but the dragon snapped his jaws shut. Feathers and shadow dissolved between his teeth.

The third raven, crackling with blood-red electricity, let out a piercing caw. The dragon struck with brutal efficiency, consuming it as he had the others.

As he devoured each one, their malevolent energy shuddered through him, darkness absorbed and broken by the sheer force of his will.

The dragon slowly turned his head, his eyes gleaming with renewed strength. The power that once sought to overwhelm him now burned inside, subdued and conquered.

And Autumn, clinging to his back, felt it too, the shift, the hardening of something vast and unstoppable.

But the victory against the ravens was fleeting. Magnus descended to the rain-soaked earth, his sinister wings dissolving into the shadows as if they were no more than smoke.

His eyes burned a fierce red, and as his arms again rose slowly, Autumn watched smoke and shadows twist and churn at his command. They writhed like tormented spirits, shaping into three enormous, menacing wolves. Their fur was as black as the void from which they emerged, and their eyes glowed with the same fierce red as Magnus's, that sent a shiver down Autumn's spine.

The spectral wolves stood ready, embodying Magnus's resolve to overpower the dragon. Their guttural growls, a sinister symphony of aggression, filled the air, a sound that promised violence and death. She could see the glint of their teeth as they bared them, poised for the attack.

Then the wolves sprang forward, launching themselves at the dragon. Their bodies blurred into streaks of shadow, moving with a speed that belied their size.

Autumn steadied herself, tightening her grip on the dragon's scales. She would not be defeated by Magnus or his shadow spawn. The battle was far from over; she would fight with every ounce of her newfound strength.

The dragon met their charge with a ferocious roar. His scales, the color of midnight, shimmered as he swiped at the wolves with claws that could have been plucked from legends.

The wolves lunged, their jaws snapping. The dragon dodged and weaved, a dance of desperation and agility.

The clash in the glade became a whirlwind of motion, sound, and elemental fury as the wolves dissolved into smoke, only to reappear a moment later, unscathed and relentless.

Their bodies, though formed of shadows, were as lethal as any creature of flesh and blood. Their attacks were a study in coordinated savagery.

Each swipe of a wolf's claws cut through the air, a tangible threat of violence aimed at the dragon. But agile and determined, the dragon dodged the lethal strikes, weaving around the wolves' attacks with a speed that spoke of his indomitable feline spirit.

The wolves' teeth found their mark more than once, but the dragon fought on, his loyalty and determination shining as brightly as any hero's. The struggle was intense, a true test of wills, where the line between victory and defeat was as thin as a razor's edge.

A growing warmth stirred deep within the dragon's chest, a primal force clawing its way to the surface.

Flames licked at the edges of his jaws, a fierce promise of the inferno to come and Autumn felt the heat building beneath her.

She pressed a hand against his scaled neck, leaning close to his ear.

"Don't hold back," she urged, her voice raw and certain. "Let it burn."

The dragon answered with a deep, guttural roar that shook the trees to their roots. He threw his head back and opened his jaws wide.

A torrent of fire burst forth, a searing stream of orange and gold that lit up the glade like a second dawn. The blaze poured into the night, a living river of heat and fury.

Her dress snapped and billowed under its force. Autumn shielded her face with her arm, the blast of heat stealing the breath from her lungs.

The wolves reeled back, their forms flickering and shrinking before the onslaught. The fire drove them into retreat, their shadows melting under the relentless tide of flame.

"Focus," she whispered fiercely against his scales, her hand pressed flat against the ridge of his neck.

"Let it build—but guide it. Make it yours."

Autumn felt it deep within her bones; Papyrus's dragon fire had awakened, and with it, a new balance between them.

Each breath of flame he unleashed pushed the wolves back, keeping them at bay, shaping the battlefield to their will.

She leaned low and urged him with her touch, guiding his focus.

"There—left—strike!" she cried as a wolf circled wide.

The dragon obeyed, sweeping a broad arc of flame that sent the beast howling into the night. He fought now with growing precision. Focused streams of fire carved swaths through their enemies, driving them into retreat, cutting down their numbers one by one.

Each wolf found itself outmatched, the flames scouring their shadowed forms until they faltered and broke apart.

The more the dragon fought, the stronger he grew, his power tempered by Autumn's will. Through the haze, Autumn glimpsed Magnus standing rigid near the trees.

The firelight flickered across his face, casting deep hollows in his features. Sweat glistened on his temple, and she saw his hands clench into fists, the tremor of fear tightening his jaw each time a wolf fell to the flames.

She knew he felt the tide turning against him.

The dragon expelled another blast, hammering the wolves back in a wave of blistering heat. The last wolf staggered, singed and howling, but instead of fleeing, it lunged in a final, desperate attack.

"Now!" Autumn shouted.

The dragon met the charge head-on, unleashing a torrent of fire so fierce it turned the night to blazing gold.

The wolf's death cry echoed once, a long, broken howl, before it dissolved into ash and smoke, carried away on the rising wind.

Silence fell.

The glade, scorched and smoldering, lay beneath them.

The dragon stood triumphant, sides heaving, smoke curling from his nostrils. Autumn pressed her forehead against his neck.

Chapter 28:
The Belly of the Beast—
Part Two

The dragon soared above the glade, Autumn clinging to the ridged scales along his neck, the night air rushing past them. The sensation of flight gripped her, fierce and wild, the earth falling away as the sky opened before them.

Beneath her, scales caught what little light remained, a living blaze of iridescent color against the darkening sky.

Together, they rose, a fusion of light, magic, and the fire of something newly born.

But their triumph shattered with a crack of dark energy. Bolts of magic lanced up from below, searing into the dragon's hide, and he shuddered under the assault. Autumn tightened her hold, her fury rising hotter than fear.

"Down," she urged, voice fierce against the wind. The air screamed past them as they plunged, the glade surging up to meet them. Autumn locked her gaze on Magnus, who stood at the heart of the chaos, black robes billowing, arms raised.

The dragon spread his wings wide, hovering just above the torn earth, and he unleashed a torrent of flame.

The roar of it drowned the world, the fire lashing forward, illuminating the glade in a searing wave of gold and crimson.

Magnus threw up his arms, a dark shield snapping into existence around him, but the flames rolled over him and beyond, striking the old market shelter at the glade's edge. The weathered wood, dry from too many seasons, caught like tinder.

Embers spiraled into the night, painting the sky with sparks.

Cries rang out as Iris, Evelyn, and the others rushed into action.

Autumn saw Iris, her face flushed in the firelight, sprinting toward the fountain with a battered bucket in hand. She plunged it into the water, hoisting it back with trembling arms, and raced to douse the nearest blaze.

Evelyn, calm even amidst the chaos, barked sharp orders, rallying the villagers into a rough bucket brigade. The rhythm of sloshing water and urgent footsteps filled the glade, a pulse of hope against the creeping fear.

Pockets of fire dimmed and died under their efforts, though the smoke still coiled thick around them, choking the air.

Above it all, Magnus remained untouched. The fire recoiled from him, sliding harmlessly off the shield of dark magic that glowed a fierce, poisonous red. He stood at the center of it like a man crowned in ruin.

Autumn gritted her teeth. The dragon reared back and loosed another blast of flame, a wave of raw fury aimed straight at their enemy.

The fire struck the shield with a deafening crack, and dispersed, swallowed, as if it had never touched him at all.

Magnus smiled beneath the dark light, and Autumn felt the first chill of doubt creep into her bones.

Magnus was drawing strength from an unknown source, its impenetrable surface defying even the most savage assaults. Where once his magic had been formidable but familiar, now it bore the taint of something older and fouler, a power not meant for mortal hands.

The dragon attacked again and again, his fiery breath lighting up the night sky like a second dawn. Copper-veined wings beat the air as he circled above, each pass bringing another torrent of flame that crashed against Magnus's shield.

Yet for all its fury, the fire could not pierce the barrier. It merely flowed around it like water over stone, scorching the earth beyond but leaving Magnus untouched within his arcane cocoon.

With each failed attempt, the dragon's determination only grew stronger, the relentless spirit of his kind driving him forward despite the formidable challenge before him. His roars of frustration echoed across the glade, sending birds fleeing from distant trees and causing the very ground to tremble.

"How is he doing this?" Autumn whispered. "The old book spoke of no such magic. How are we to stop him now?"

It was clear now that the very magic they wielded in defense could just as easily harm those they were desperate to save. With each fiery blast that rebounded from Magnus's shield, the risk of collateral damage increased, threatening to engulf the nearby settlement of Whispering Pines in chaos and flame.

The glade, already scarred by fire, teetered on the brink of devastation. Ancient trees that had stood for centuries now smoldered and cracked in the heat. The townsfolk who had followed Magnus now fought valiantly to extinguish the spreading flames, passing buckets of water from the nearby stream and beating at smaller blazes with dampened cloaks.

But their strength was waning, and exhaustion was setting in. Fear had replaced awe in their eyes, and Autumn could see some casting furtive glances toward the path that led back to the safety of their homes.

Henry crouched low behind a toppled barrel, using it as a makeshift shield against the encroaching flames. The old man's weathered hands gripped the worn wood as if it were the only solid thing in a world gone mad.

Fear flickered in his wide eyes, his brow furrowed deeply, while his trembling lips hinted at words he couldn't bring himself to speak. This was a man who had survived many tough years, yet now he quaked like a child after a nightmare.

Autumn caught sight of Flora's face suddenly brightening, as though illuminated by some inner revelation rather than the surrounding flames. She was always quick of thought, if not of tongue, and hurried back toward town, clutching Autumn's forgotten satchel close to her chest as she disappeared among the trees.

"Whatever she's thinking, I hope it bears fruit quickly," Autumn murmured, turning her attention back to Magnus and his impenetrable shield.

The sorcerer stood his ground within the shell of his magic, boots sunk deep into the scorched and crumbling earth. Smoke curled around him, clinging to his cloak, yet he remained still, untouched by the ruin he had wrought.

His voice cut across the glade, low and clear, carried not by wind or will, but by the strength of certainty. "You see it now, don't you?" he said. "The folly of old magics…and older creatures. They were never meant for the hands of fools. They tear the world apart when left to those who know nothing of their weight or how to bear it. Surrender the beast to me, and I will spare what remains of this place."

Autumn felt the weight of every eye upon her, the frightened townsfolk, the exhausted dragon, even Magnus himself seemed to be waiting for her response.

She reached for her throat, fingers seeking the locket. But there was nothing—only bare skin and the sharp, cold sting of its absence. It was the first time she had reached for it and found nothing waiting for her.

Her hand dropped to her side. She drew a breath, slow and shaking, and when she spoke, her voice was iron.

"No," she said. The word fell like a hammer. A single syllable, yet heavier than any chain she had ever borne. "I will not."

Yet despair coiled deep in her chest, a heavy, grinding thing.

Magnus's shield still stood—untouched, unbroken, indifferent to all they had thrown against it.

Magnus called to his roses. Their thorny vines lashed out across the glade, snaring the townsfolk where they stood, dragging them back from the fires they struggled to fight.

Cries rang out as the thorns bit deep, the roses winding tighter with every frantic movement.

"Autumn!" She turned at the sound of Flora's voice, sharp and breathless. Flora knelt in the dirt. From a pouch at her belt, she pulled a small vial, the glass catching the light in a sickly purple gleam and took the Luminosa Blossoms from Autumn's satchel.

She muttered words too low to hear, and the petals shivered at her breath. Steady hands poured the potion over the blooms. The blossoms drank it in greedily, their color deepening, their light sharpening to a fierce, unnatural glow.

Flora raised them to her lips and blew. A rush of petals spun into the air, carried by a current that smelled of copper and rain.

The rose vines stirred, as if roused from a long, uneasy sleep. Then they moved—twisting, writhing, reaching.

The blossoms, now pulsing with the magenta of Flora's alchemy, called the vines forth like hounds on a scent. They let go of the townsfolk and slithered across the wet ground, swift and hungry, straight toward Magnus.

He saw them too late. His eyes widened, the first true flicker of fear breaking across his face. His own vines struck, coiling around his boots, climbing with frantic speed. Their thorns bit deep, tearing through leather, through cloth, into flesh.

Magnus stumbled, gasping, as the thorns rooted themselves in him, dragging him down. The shield still flickered above him, but now the earth itself fought back.

The vines climbed higher, coiling around Magnus's chest, pinning his arms tight against his sides. He strained against them, muscles bulging, teeth clenched, but the more he fought, the tighter the grip became.

The glow of the vines deepened, their magic sinking into him, leeching the strength from his limbs and the darkness from his shield.

Panic flashed in Magnus's eyes, a brief, naked thing, before he crushed it beneath a snarl. He reached for his magic, clawing for a spell that might tear the vines away, but each effort drained him further. The shield he had wrapped around himself flickered, faltered, and was absorbed by the relentless grip of the Lady's Embrace.

The harder he fought, the worse it grew. The thorns dug deeper, biting into flesh, drawing blood. His movements turned frantic, no longer measured, the last shreds of his composure falling away.

The glow of the vines clashed with the seeping blackness of his power, twisting the glade into a battlefield of light and shadow.

And still the vines pulled tighter.

The dragon's eyes locked onto Magnus, now bound and broken. He descended slowly, wings folding against his sides.

Each step toward Magnus was deliberate, the ground trembling under his weight. Heat coiled within him, rising to his throat, ready to be loosed in a torrent of fire.

His body shuddered from the strain, muscles taut, every breath searing. The air quivered around his jaws, the fire gathering at the cusp of release.

But Autumn saw them, the townsfolk, scattered among the ruins of the glade, watching.

Their faces shone in the flickering light, wide-eyed and hollow with fear. She sat atop a creature of legend, forged by magic older than crowns or kings. Yet she was no monster.

The thought of Magnus's body burning wrenched at her chest. She could see it already—the horror burned into their faces, the stain of it on her soul.

She could only imagine how frightened Aster must be at this very moment.

"Wait!" she said.

A soft whimper rumbled from deep within the dragon's chest as he exhaled, the fire bleeding away with a hiss between his teeth. The glow in his throat dimmed. Autumn leaned into him for a heartbeat longer, letting the anger drain from her bones.

The dragon lowered his massive head, and she swung down from his back, boots sinking into the torn earth. The wind caught her hair and her skirts, whipping them about her as she strode toward Magnus.

He sagged in the grip of the vines, blood streaking his torn clothing, his breath ragged.

"Autumn...please..."

She heard the desperation in his voice, but she did not waver. She raised her hand, arm outstretched, and pointed at him.

The magic stirred in her blood, and she spoke old words, answering the call of the earth beneath her feet, of the sky above:

"By root and stone, by blood and bone,
By flame that sings and earth that groans,
By river's course and raven's cry,

By all that lives and all that dies.
Let light unmake what shadow claimed.
Let power fall as ash to rain.
I bind thee, Magnus Blackthorn.
I strip thee of thy might."

The dragon stepped closer, his nostrils flaring as he breathed in the air around Magnus. He inhaled, deep and slow, and from Magnus's battered form, a stream of smoke and crimson energy tore free. It flowed into the dragon's lungs like a river of shadows, drawn down, consumed.

Autumn watched as the dark power bled out of Magnus, leaving him pale, shaking, hollow.

The vines tightened, still glowing from the magic blossoms, binding him hand and foot. Whatever spells he might have summoned were swallowed before they could even take form.

Magnus sagged, his strength spent, the last of his magic ripped away.

The glade grew still. The fires guttered out. The echoes of their battle faded. Magnus crumpled to the earth, a broken man, stripped bare of all he had once been.

The dragon stepped back, claws sinking into the soil. With a low rumble deep in his chest, he leapt skyward, wings unfurling in a great sweep of power. The dragon roared once, a sound that shook the bones of the earth, and vanished into the night.

CHAPTER 29:
THE WEIGHT OF MERCY

The first light of dawn crept over the Emerald Glade, casting the scorched ground and broken vines in a soft, golden haze. The flames had died out in the quiet hours, leaving only the blackened remnants of the night's fury behind.

Autumn stood weary to her bones. The cool air washed over her, carrying away the last traces of smoke.

The land itself breathed again, slow and tentative, as if testing the morning for dangers that had passed.

Townsfolk gathered in small clusters, their faces drawn and pale, their clothes streaked with ash and dirt. They moved among the wreckage, checking on one another, pulling away dead vines, righting toppled carts.

Evelyn brushed soot from her blouse with trembling hands. Her eyes swept the clearing, wary and uncertain. "Is everyone all right?" she called out.

"We're all here," Clara answered, offering a tired smile. "Just shaken, that's all."

Flora knelt by a withered patch of roses, her fingers trailing over the brittle remains. "Look at them," she muttered.

"They fought against us last night. Now they're just…dead." She shook her head, brushing the dust from her palms. "We'd best clear them away before they rot where they stand."

Evelyn made hesitant steps towards Autumn. "Autumn," she began, voice soft, "there's much we ought to—"

"Not now," Autumn said, cutting her off with a slow shake of her head. "Let's clean up what we can."

Evelyn nodded, and said no more. The work was grim and silent. Each severed vine, each patch of ash scraped away from the stones, felt like reclaiming a piece of the town they had almost lost.

Slowly, beneath the ruin, the glade's old beauty began to show itself again. Thomas wiped the sweat from his brow and leaned on his shovel.

"With care," he said, "this place'll heal. Might take time, but it'll come back."

Iris and Flora worked side by side in the cobbled streets, dragging away the last stubborn vines that clung to the stones.

"How did you know what to do?" Iris asked, panting slightly as she yanked at a particularly twisted root.

Flora grinned without looking up. "It's all in the ingredients," she said, teasing a dead tendril free. "And knowing when to use them."

She shot Autumn a sly wink as she spoke, and for the first time that morning, a breath of something like laughter stirred the tired air.

"Put Magnus with Sylas," Autumn said, her voice low but unyielding. She didn't look to see who obeyed, only braced her hands against her thighs for a breath. "Even without his magic…he's dangerous. Don't leave him alone. Someone stays. Always."

"We can't keep him here long," Samuel said bluntly. "Not safe. Not for us, not for him."

"We'll write to Sylvancrest City," Birdie said. "They'll have men who know how to deal with the likes of him."

No one argued.

Evelyn pulled her spectacles from her pocket, smudged with ash. "I'll see to the letter straightaway," she said, already turning toward the bookstore.

As the sun climbed, its light revealed more than broken branches and scorched earth. It revealed *them*, more villagers gathered at the edges of the glade, silent, wide-eyed, ash-smeared. They did not cheer. They did not speak. They only *watched*.

Some held their children back with gentle hands, as if the air still smelled of danger. Others gripped tools like weapons: pitchforks, hammers, kitchen blades—half-forgotten in their trembling hands.

Autumn moved among the wounded, her steps careful, her voice quiet. Offering cloth, water, and steady hands, to remind them she was still one of them. Still Autumn.

Some flinched when her fingers brushed theirs. One child stared openly, whispering, "Is she a witch?" before being hushed.

Another voice, a woman's, spoke louder: "She saved us."

And that shifted something. A murmur rippled through the gathered crowd, soft at first, uncertain. Then someone began to clap. Another joined. Then another. The sound swelled, awkward and uneven, but real. Grimy hands met in tired applause.

Autumn bowed her head, just slightly. It was all she could manage. Her eyes drifted to Magnus.

Floren and Callum had taken up his arms, dragging him from the glade with the care one might show a wounded beast. He did not fight them. His gaze was lowered, his mouth slack, as if the weight of loss had settled deep into his bones.

She hated him. And yet…she imagined a world where he had chosen differently. A world where he had used his power to protect, not consume. Where he stood beside her, not across from her.

But that world did not exist. She turned to Samuel. "Burn that old house to the ground."

Samuel then gave a single, grim nod.

Without another word, Autumn walked away, the applause still echoing behind her. She did not look back.

CHAPTER 30:
ASHES IN THE WIND

Autumn withdrew to her cottage, a place untouched by the ruin. Weeks slipped past unnoticed, the days folding one into another like pages left to yellow and curl.

She did not return to her old routines just yet. How could she, when everything that had once been certain now lay scattered like ashes in the wind? She spent her time on small, simple things. Mornings steeped in tea, the cup warming her fingers and the drink soothing her soul. Afternoons spent sitting on the riverbank of Starlit Run, her feet trailing in the cool water, watching the current carry broken leaves downstream.

The summer heat pressed down from a cloudless sky, heavy and slow, but she welcomed the sweat on her brow and the warmth on her skin. It was real. It reminded her she was still alive.

Where do dragons go once the fighting ends? To the mountains, perhaps, as they did in the old songs. To the places where men's worries could not follow.

Papyrus had flown away after the battle, vanishing into the high skies without a word of farewell. Autumn did not blame him. There was a part of her that wished she could have flown away, too.

But the river sang to her in its soft, endless voice. The trees whispered as they always had. And so she stayed, mending herself in silence, piece by slow piece.

Some days, when the sun grew too hot and the river's song could no longer quiet her mind, Autumn retreated inside.

Her old book, *Enchanted Realms: Tales of Wonder and Whimsy*, waited for her on her dresser, its pages worn soft by her hands, the ink faded but stubborn against the years.

She read by the open window, the breeze lifting the edge of the parchment, stirring the scents of moss and river stone.

The stories inside the book spoke of old magics, of battles fought in secret, of choices made when there was no good road left to walk.

She understood them better now than she ever had before.

At times, she would close the book and sit in silence, the words still heavy in her hands. On those days, she would open the top drawer of her dresser and look at the picture of Philip. He had looked at her through those worn strokes for years, unchanged while she had grown older.

She traced the edges of the picture with her thumb. The sight of him ached like an old wound, one that time had not healed so much as made familiar.

But the day came when Autumn felt strong enough to return to town, to the bookstore she loved and the quiet order she had left behind.

She had missed it more than she would admit. But she had needed the time. No one could mend shattered things by rushing them back into place.

One morning, she woke before the sun, slipping from the tangled warmth of her blankets into the stillness of her cottage.

The floorboards, worn smooth by time and habit, creaked beneath her bare feet as she crossed to the washbasin.

She bathed in silence, letting the warm water banish the weight of sleep, scrubbing away the half-remembered ghosts of dreams. Outside, the world stirred in quiet symphony, the distant trill of a morning bird, the gentle murmur of the Starlit Run. She soaked it in, letting the sounds settle around her like a second skin, grounding her in the waking world.

The morning light slanted through her window, painting gold across the wooden walls, catching in the strands of her long ginger hair as she combed through them with careful fingers. There was a rhythm to it, a quiet order to be kept—each strand untangled, each motion deliberate. She had always found comfort in small things, in tasks that could be done with steady hands and an unburdened mind.

Her hand reached out of habit to the little dish by the mirror. To the place where the locket should have been.

But there was nothing. And there never would be again.

She froze for a moment, hand suspended above the empty space, feeling the ache rise up in her chest. The locket was gone, lost or perhaps freed. It had carried Magnus's darkness without her knowing, but its absence left her lighter...and lonelier.

Autumn let her hands fall back into her lap.

Her mother had known the risk. She had died for it, died to keep her daughter safe. Magnus had said as much.

And Sylas held the rest of the story locked behind his eyes. She could have visited him. She'd had time, opportunity, a thousand chances to demand the truth. Who was her mother? What was her name? Who had been her father?

But she hadn't gone.

She'd waited her whole life for answers, yet now that they lay within reach, she hesitated. Perhaps out of fear. She couldn't explain it—only that some part of her wasn't ready to look Sylas in the eye and see the ghost of the man who had murdered her mother, behind whatever regret he wore.

***

Autumn looked around Henry's old office. The chamber, once claimed by Magnus. Dust drifted in the slanting light from the high window, catching on the tattered remnants of a better age.

Evelyn's hair, half-unraveled, hung loose against the nape of her neck; wisps of hair framed a face at once sharp and tired.

By her side clung the child, Aster, small fingers knotting in the folds of Evelyn's simple gown.

The girl's wide eyes flickered from wall to wall, drinking in the strangeness of a place she had never known.

Evelyn offered a small, fleeting smile and set to her work. She gathered the leavings Magnus had abandoned: scraps of parchment scrawled with sigils and half-born designs.

Piece by piece she fed them to the waste basket, every discarded scrap a small rebellion, a chisel chipping away at the usurper's hold.

She placed a bouquet on the desk: purple violets, soft pink peonies, and blue asters, flowers that spoke of roots, resilience, and memory.

The room, once hollowed by sorrow, seemed to breathe again.

Evelyn took Aster's small hand and gave it a gentle squeeze. "We're going to make this place wonderful again," she said.

Autumn scrubbed the heavy oak desk, her cloth cutting through the greasy smear left by Magnus's touch.

The wood, old and familiar, seemed almost to shudder under her care, like a hound welcoming the return of a master long thought lost.

She thought of all the words he had spoken in this room, each one soaked in charm and poison. The lies he'd spun like silk. The bargains he'd struck. How close she had come to believing him.

The wood beneath her fingers had once seemed part of her world, familiar and safe. Now it was a place that had harbored a predator. She paused, fingers tightening. A part of her still wanted to understand him, and that frightened her more than any shadow he'd cast.

Was it weakness to feel that? To imagine, even now, what he might have been, if not for his hunger? She pressed harder, her rag catching on a gouge in the surface. The scar would remain, no matter how hard she scrubbed.

So would his.

Shelves and furnishings followed. The dust gave way beneath her hands, and the room began to breathe again.

A pang gripped Autumn's chest.

She could see it still, Henry, seated at that very desk, the sun spilling across the floor, catching in the silver threads of his ebony hair.

"I can almost hear Henry's voice again," Evelyn said, "weaving tales of daring and distant shores, the low rumble of it echoing through the rafters like smoke from a hearth-fire. The way his eyes would sparkle when a good story caught hold of him, the way he would lean back and listen, smiling."

This had been a refuge once. Now it was something else, a place wounded, but not beyond healing.

A soft tap sounded against the doorframe. Henry stood, leaning lightly on his cane. He tapped the wood again, more out of habit than need, and gave a crooked smile.

Evelyn's face lit up at the sight of him.

Henry smiled back, though there was a shadow behind it, a weight time could not lift. "Almost the way I remember it," he said. "I miss my time here."

Evelyn rose to her feet, her smile softening. "We miss you too, Henry."

He shifted his cane, his expression turning graver. "I'm sorry, Evelyn," he said. "For giving the bookstore to Magnus. It should have been yours from the start."

Evelyn placed a hand on his arm, firm and forgiving. "Thank you, Henry," she said. "We'll make it right again. Together."

Henry nodded, the lines around his eyes deepening.

Iris entered then, a broad wooden sign cradled in her arms, paint still gleamed wet at the edges. She placed the sign carefully atop the desk:

Whispering Pines Books
Reopening Soon!

"Folks are already peering through the windows, wondering what'll rise from the ashes. Best to give them something to hope for," she said. "We're not scrubbing away ghosts, are we?"

Autumn looked down at the cloth in her hand. "Not ghosts. Just the stain of someone who thought he owned everything he touched."

Iris rested a hand on the desk's edge. "Then let's make sure it belongs to the right people again. Stories deserve better than him." Her voice softened. "And so do you."

Henry leaned close to read the sign, a slow smile tugging at his mouth. "I think we're doing the right thing," he said quietly.

He turned to Autumn, his mouth opening, words gathering at the back of his throat. "Autumn, I have something for you. It was at the old house. I took it before it burned down."

The book.

The very one that had set Autumn's path twisting into shadow and flame. Its leather cover, once rich and dark, had faded to the dull hue of worn bone. No title marked its spine. Only the faint ghost of tooling remained.

Henry pressed it into Autumn's hands. The book was heavier than Autumn remembered. It settled in her palm like a living thing, breathing the weight of its secrets into her skin.

A thought took root in her mind, quiet but unshakable; a seed pressed deep into hard soil. She would mend it. Piece by piece, page by page, she would stitch its torn wisdom back together and unravel all the mysteries locked within.

Somehow, she knew: the book's story was not yet done.

And neither was hers.

Aster peered at the worn book. "What's that, Miss Evelyn?" she asked. Evelyn smiled, the kind of smile that bore the weight of all they had endured and all they still hoped to build.

"It's an important old book. It carries pieces of who we are."

"I'd like to mend it," Autumn told them.

"So we can pass it down to those who come after. So the history of Whispering Pines is never lost again."

***

The town was stirring as usual. Autumn stepped outside, seeking a quiet place to take her lunch. Evelyn stood by the door, carefully fastening the new sign in place. She stepped back, tilting her head to better admire the work, while Iris laughed softly with Birdie and Callum near the inn.

Across the way, the candy shopkeeper swept her doorstep with steady strokes, each flick of the broom quick and certain, as though preparing for unseen guests.

The scent of baking bread drifted from the bakery. The baker laid out rows of golden loaves, each one dusted lightly with flour. Autumn could see them through the wide shop window.

Children ran between the market stalls, ribbons streaming from their hands, their laughter as clear as bells.

From the blacksmith's forge, Samuel's hammer sang its steady, rhythmic song: metal striking metal in a voice older than the town itself.

Clara and Thomas worked near the fountain, their hands busy among baskets of earth-scented carrots and apples so bright they seemed lit from within.

The whole square hummed with life, but it was not the usual bustle. There was a waiting to it, a quiet gathering of breath, as if the town itself held still in expectation.

Not for a festival. Not for a feast. But for something smaller, quieter, and far more precious.

The sounds of their work, the sweep of broom against stone, the soft clang of tools, the low murmur of voices—folded together like the preparations for a surprise long in the making.

The townsfolk gathered then.

Autumn stood still, the sunlight warm on her shoulders, the air thick with something unspoken. "What is all this?" she asked.

Iris stepped forward from the gathering. Her hands trembled slightly at her sides. "Autumn," she said, "I know you don't always see it. How much you are needed here. How much you are...appreciated."

Iris swallowed hard, blinking back the tears that welled in her eyes. She glanced over her shoulder at the others—Samuel wiping his hands on his apron, the baker standing with arms crossed, the old men and women, the children peeking shyly from behind their parents.

Their faces told the same story.

"I hate to think," Iris said, "that I, or any of us, ever made you believe you didn't belong. Because you do. You always did."

The crowd stirred. A low murmur rose among them, a hundred small affirmations weaving together into something larger.

Nods. Soft, broken smiles.

The kind of understanding that needed no more words. And for the first time in weeks, Autumn felt the walls she had built around her heart loosen, just a little.

Henry stepped forward. He cleared his throat. "The Autumn I know is somewhat timid," Henry began. "She has always preferred to avoid conflict, finding peace in the quiet corners of our town. But when it mattered most, she overcame that natural inclination. She confronted me—yes, me, the stubborn old fool that I am, and warned me about Magnus."

He turned to Autumn. "I remember the look in your eyes when you came to me on Legends Night," Henry continued, his voice growing softer. "There was fear, yes, but also a fierce determination. You showed me just how strong you truly are."

"You have a heart as big as this entire town and a courage that shines brighter than any candle. You faced your fears for all of us, and for that, I am eternally grateful."

She wanted to tell him he was wrong, that her heart had faltered more than once, that she had been afraid the entire time. That courage had nothing to do with it. But the words wouldn't come.

"Autumn's bravery wasn't just in her actions," Henry said, "It was in her willingness to stand up for what was right, to protect those she loved, even when it meant putting herself in harm's way. She reminded me that true courage is not the absence of fear but the strength to face it head-on."

Henry looked around the square, meeting the eyes of his fellow townspeople. "We owe her more than we can ever repay."

A young man stepped forward, rubbing the back of his neck as he cleared his throat. "You've always been mighty helpful," he said, voice shy but steady. "Any time I stepped into that bookshop, there you'd be—ready with a kind word and that quiet smile of yours."

He gave a soft chuckle, eyes dropping to the cobblestones. "Truth be told, I could see the nerves on you sometimes. Like the words came slower than they wanted to. But it never mattered. Not to me."

He glanced back up, something earnest shining behind his words. "What mattered was that you cared. You wanted folk to feel welcome. And we did. I did."

Three young women stepped forward from the crowd, their hands clasped before them, their faces uncertain but earnest.

The first spoke. "We always see you around town," she said. "You always look...a little lonely sometimes. We talked about asking you to sit with us."

Another woman nodded, twisting her fingers together. "We saw you look our way, now and again," she said. "As if you wanted to come over...but weren't sure you'd be welcome. We always thought you seemed kind. Different. Interesting."

The third woman, a little braver than the others, stepped closer. "We should have asked you," she said. "We should have made you feel you belonged. We thought about it a hundred times. You deserved better from us. You still do. I hope you know...you mean more to this town than you think."

There was no applause, no grand declaration, only the truth, laid bare and offered like an open hand.

Little Aster, holding tightly to Evelyn's hand, stepped forward. Her wide eyes scanned the crowd and looked up at Evelyn for reassurance. Encouraged by a gentle nod, she took a deep breath and began to speak, her voice small but clear.

"Autumn helped me when I was having a bad day," Aster said. "She saw me crying and bought me candy."

Autumn smiled.

Evelyn squeezed Aster's hand gently, her eyes filled with pride. "Autumn, you have a way of making everyone feel special. Even on your own difficult days, you always find a way to bring a smile to someone else's face."

She paused, her gaze sweeping over the gathered townspeople. "It was Autumn who brought me and Aster together," Evelyn continued. "Thanks to her, Roger and I have now adopted Aster."

Before Evelyn could say more, Aster interrupted with glee, "Yeah, and Autumn came from Ashwood, just like me. So does that mean we are sisters?"

A soft sound escaped Autumn, surprising even herself. She pressed a hand to her mouth, but the laughter slipped through her fingers. For the first time in longer than she could remember, she heard herself laugh—and realized she had missed the sound.

The town erupted in laughter, charmed by the adorable and heartfelt comment.

"Let's not forget Papyrus," Evelyn said, her voice carrying gently across the square. "He hasn't been seen since that night. The bookstore won't be the same without him. He's been a part of this place for as long as I can remember."

The crowd nodded, small murmurs rising. A few spoke softly among themselves, trading memories of the cat sleeping in sunlit windows, of him curling around the ankles of the readers who stayed too long, of his quiet, steady presence, as much a part of the store as the shelves and the smell of ink.

"We'll keep looking for him," Iris said.

Autumn said nothing.

Papyrus.

She missed him more than she dared say. But his whereabouts, the where and why of his leaving—that was her secret to keep.

Flora stepped forward. She took a deep breath, her eyes shining with emotion as she addressed the gathered townspeople.

"I'd like to add something," she began, her voice steady with heartfelt sincerity. "I don't know if you remember this, Autumn, but on my tenth nameday, you gave me a book about the properties of rare plants. It was an old, worn book filled with intricate drawings and detailed descriptions. It might have seemed like just another gift to most people, but to me, it was the spark that ignited my curiosity and passion for apothecary. That book opened a world of wonder for me. I spent countless hours poring over its pages, fascinated by its hidden knowledge. It inspired me to explore the forest and to understand the magical properties of the plants around us. That one gift from you set me on a path that has defined my life."

She looked around at the crowd. "I owe it all to her. Without that book, without Autumn's thoughtfulness and generosity, I don't know if I would have found my true calling. She believed in me before I even knew what I was capable of. Autumn has a way of seeing the potential in others, of nurturing and encouraging it. She gave me the gift of knowledge, and with it the confidence to pursue my dreams. She has touched so many lives in so many ways, often without even realizing it. Autumn's kindness, her generosity, her belief in others—these are the things that make her so special. We are all here today because you have touched our lives in some profound way. I know I speak for everyone when I say we should never have doubted you, or thought of you as foolish."

Flora stepped forward and folded Autumn into her arms. It wasn't a delicate embrace. It was the kind that held tight, like someone who'd nearly lost something precious and wasn't ready to let go.

Autumn stood stiff at first, caught off guard. But then her arms rose, slowly, unsure, and wrapped around Flora's back. She pressed her face into the woman's shoulder. Her throat burned with the effort not to cry.

One after another, townsfolk stepped forward to share their stories and feelings. Each voice added to the collective appreciation of Autumn, painting a picture of a young woman who had woven herself into the very fabric of Whispering Pines.

CHAPTER 31:

A CHANGE OF SCENERY

The sound of hooves broke the afternoon's gathering. All eyes turned as a grand horse and carriage approached, its wheels creaking against the cobbles. A tall, regal figure stepped out, his polished boots tapping lightly on the stone.

"Good morning," he said. "I'm looking to meet with someone from the town council."

Evelyn stepped forward. "I can help," she said, motioning to her companions. "This is Clara and Thomas. We're all part of the council."

Clara and Thomas politely nodded. The man looked at each of them thoughtfully before offering a small smile.

Two more carriages arrived.

Evelyn blinked. There was something unmistakable about the man's bearing. It was not merely his fine cloak or the sigil brooch glinting at his shoulder; it was the way he held himself, a refinement in every step.

"Oh... Your Royal Highness," Evelyn stammered, casting a wide-eyed glance toward Clara and Thomas. Without hesitation, the three of them dipped into hurried curtsies and a bow. Autumn, standing a pace behind, mirrored them a heartbeat later, her mind already racing.

"Thank you," he said. He stepped forward, taking Evelyn's hand briefly, a firm yet respectful clasp, before offering the same courtesy to Clara and Thomas.

"I come on behalf of Their Majesties," Prince Dorian declared, "to claim custody of the prisoners Sylas Finch and Magnus Blackthorn, and to extend the aid of the Crown in this time of need." He paused. "Furthermore, I am charged with escorting Miss Autumn Ashwood to the city, at the express request of Their Majesties."

A ripple of gasps stirred the square.

"Summoned?" someone whispered.

"By the Crown?" said another, the words half disbelief.

Evelyn pressed a hand to her chest. Iris's mouth dropped open. Even Clara, never one for courtly things, looked up from beneath her bonnet with wide eyes.

Autumn heard the shift of feet on stone, the rustle of sleeves, the faint intake of breath from somewhere behind her. She didn't need to turn to know they were watching—all of them.

"I am Autumn Ashwood," she said, stepping forward despite the tremor that ran through her limbs. Her heart pounded so fiercely she wondered if those nearest could hear it. "May I ask why I have been summoned?"

The prince's eyes softened, though an iron thread wove through his words. "I am not at liberty to say, my lady, until you are brought before Their Majesties themselves."

The words struck like a bell in her chest.

My lady.

Weeks ago, she might have refused. Might have turned and fled back to her cottage, to her shelves and her quiet places. But that girl was ash now. Burned away in the fire she had survived.

"I accept," she answered.

The prince inclined his head, just so. "Wonderful," he said. "We depart in three days' time."

Iris curtsied. "We can put you up at the inn until you depart. It's beautiful and quaint, though I'm sure it's not quite what you're used to."

Prince Dorian smiled graciously. "That would be lovely. It sounds like a charming place. I enjoy a change of scenery now and then."

***

A knock stirred the quiet of Autumn's cottage. She rose from her chair and crossed the wooden floor barefoot, savoring the cool press of the planks beneath her soles. This simple feeling—earthbound and familiar... She would carry it with her, a memory pressed like a dried flower between pages, when Sylvancrest City's stone corridors replaced the timbers of home.

She opened the door. Flora stood there, framed in evening sun. She was radiant in a simple red gown, and her cheeks were kissed with rose as if the wind had just whispered to her.

"Are you excited?" Flora said gently.

Autumn managed a laugh, breathless and honest. "Yes. And terrified. I've never left Whispering Pines. The furthest I've wandered is the edge of the Northwoods. And now... Two fortnights on the road through cities I've only seen on maps. It sounds lovely, in the way unknown things often do. Please come in."

Flora smiled.

Autumn glanced down at her feet again, still bare. Still home.

A tiny spec of gold darted through the air. Then another. And another. Three golden fairies flew into the room. They circled

Autumn's head like dandelion seeds caught on a breeze, leaving a faint trail of golden dust in their wake.

Autumn smiled, her eyes following their dance. "Flora, I'd like you to meet some friends."

Flora stepped back instinctively, then leaned forward, wonder blooming across her face. "By the stars... They're beautiful. May I sketch them sometime? Just a quick study for my notebook."

"I'm sure that can be arranged. They rather enjoy being admired."

"Are you ready to go?" Flora asked.

"Ready as I'll ever be."

Flora walked beside her to the square. She said little, but her presence spoke what words could not—that Autumn would not face this alone, not until the very last step.

They had gathered: Iris, Birdie, Callum, Flora, Evelyn, and little Aster. Each one stood like a thread she could not bear to cut.

Birdie wiped at her eyes, sniffling. "Now don't go forgettin' us while you're off with princes and crowns," she teased. "You'll be missed, you will."

"Aye," Callum chimed in, straightening his coat. "And if they give you any trouble up there in those gold-plated halls, just send word. We'll storm the gates with pitchforks and sass."

Autumn laughed, but her throat tightened. "I wouldn't expect anything less."

Evelyn stepped forward, folding her hands as if to still their tremble. The calm in her voice was hard-won. "Don't let them sweep you away in titles and silk. Remember who you are, and where you come from. That's your compass."

Iris flung her arms wide, nearly knocking into Callum. "Promise me you'll write! Describe every window, every corridor, every banquet. I want to taste the story in your words!"

Autumn smiled, brushing a strand of hair behind her ear. "I promise."

Flora stepped last. Her eyes held the gravity of the earth. "Even the tallest tree needs roots. The wind may carry you far, but soil remembers." Flora reached into the folds of her dress and drew out a small cloth pouch. She placed it gently in Autumn's hand. "Take a bit of Whispering Pines with you, and leave a bit of yourself behind." Autumn nodded slowly. "I will. Send my love to Henry for me."

The pouch was light in her hand, but it felt heavier than her bags. It carried the weight of everything she couldn't take with her.

Aster darted forward, wrapping small arms around Autumn's waist. "You come back, okay? Books are boring without you."

Autumn crouched, pressing a kiss to the girl's hair. "I'll come back. I promise." That shy little girl had become family. So had they all.

The carriage stood ready, its wheels sugared with pollen and dawn-kissed dew. One gray horse tossed its mane, iron shoes striking sparks from the cobbles. Autumn kept her eyes low, following the play of light across worn stone while the guards urged Magnus first, then Sylas, toward the open coach door.

"Wait!"

The shout cracked across the square like a whip. Autumn's head snapped up, breath caged in her throat, as every villager stilled. Sylas Finch, half-bound, twisted in the grip of two soldiers; regret weighed upon his lined features.

"Autumn, please, listen."

She nodded, but a flush climbed her neck.

"Years ago, I made a terrible mistake. I harmed your mother, an act driven by my greed and desire for magic and power. I placed you in the orphanage, thinking it was the easiest way to rid myself of the evidence of my wrongdoing. It wasn't right or fair, and I let my own corruption guide my actions."

Autumn's fingers tightened around the leather strap of her satchel until her knuckles whitened.

Tears welled up in his eyes as he continued. "But watching you grow up, seeing you become the strong, courageous young woman you are today… It softened me. It made me realize the depth of my mistake and the pain I had caused. I don't know what my life would have been if I had continued down that dark path. You gave me a glimpse of what I could be. What I should be. Autumn, you always listened to my words without interruption; you never turned away."

A tremor rippled through her shoulders. She swallowed hard, tasting copper where she had bitten her lip.

He paused, and a faint smile grew on his lips. "Though it was clear you often didn't fully understand what I was saying, you always gave me the chance to say it. You never dismissed me, never made me feel my words were meaningless."

Memories flickered: quiet evenings in the bookshop, Sylas's rambling philosophies, her own polite nods. She blinked and the vision dissolved in the morning glare.

His voice became softer now. "You made me feel heard in a world that often turned away from my musings."

A single tear threatened the corner of her eye; she inhaled steady air and willed it back.

He looked around at the faces of Whispering Pines, his expression one of deep gratitude. "Autumn's simple act of listening was a lifeline, a reminder of the humanity I had almost lost. I know I can never fully atone for what I did, but I want to make amends for the wrongs I've done. She showed me the way back to my humanity, and I owe it to her to follow that path."

Autumn's throat worked, yet no word rose; her silence felt both shield and confession.

Evelyn stepped forward, her voice gentle. "Thank you for your honesty, Sylas," she said. "But it's time for your departure."

Sylas straightened, gathering the last strands of dignity around him. He spoke then in that measured, winding cadence the folk of Whispering Pines had grown to expect.

"Sorrow is a shadow that clings to the heart, but even in the darkest night, a single spark of hope can light the way."

The guard guided him up the step. The carriage door closed, and only then did Autumn exhale.

Autumn rested her hand on her carriage door, then turned for a final look at the town that had shaped her. The fairies were circling Flora, seemingly taken with their new friend.

The road to Sylvancrest stretched beyond the treeline, a pale ribbon winding north through mountain passes toward names she had known only from ink and parchment.

A breath of pine and farewell steadied her heart. She gathered her cloak, set her boot on the iron step, and climbed into the coach. Leather cushions creaked beneath her, the air inside scented with cedar and lamp-oil. Outside, the driver flicked the reins. Whispering Pines eased behind her at last, its stories pressed into her spine, its roots still curled around her bones.

CHAPTER 32:

THE BROKEN CROWN SHALL FIND ITS THRONE

Autumn pressed her palm to the carriage glass as the last line of pines yielded to the first gardens of Sylvancrest City. Sunlit terraces rolled outward like green seas, their slopes sown with orchids and foxgloves whose colors rivaled a jeweler's trove. Beyond them rose arcades of white stone, bright awnings rippling above grand markets where merchants called in a dozen accents. Perfume-laden air drifted through the shutters; citrus, warm bread, and faint river mist.

So much life in one place. How does anyone breathe beneath it? Yet she refused to turn away. She glimpsed children chasing streamers, a minstrel striking a harp, and—in the distance—the citadel itself: Greenhaven Keep.

The road divided at a bronze fountain, and the coach bearing Magnus and Sylas peeled off toward a postern gate.

Autumn's carriage soon rocked to a halt before a stair of white granite where guards in forest-green cloaks formed a corridor. She smoothed her wrinkled skirt, forced her breath steady, and stepped onto Sylvancrest City soil.

So this is where it begins, she thought.

The air smelled of stone and rosewater, of order and old power. Here, everything stood tall and still.

A doorman and a silver-haired maid swept in, gathering her satchel, her sack, and the small walnut trunk that held what little of Whispering Pines she could carry.

"Welcome, my lady," the woman said with a respectful dip of the head. Autumn managed a nod, still searching for words when a shadow crossed the sun.

Prince Dorian.

Polished leather boots, doublet of deep green trimmed in sable, a signet ring glinting at his finger. Yet his eyes—green, thoughtful—held none of the cool hauteur she feared.

"Lady Autumn Ashwood," he said, offering his hand.

She placed her fingers in his. His grip was sure, warm, nothing like the chill she remembered from Maxwell's hand on the cobbled street. "The road was kinder than the stories claimed, Your Highness."

His mouth curved. "Then let the worst of those tales end today." He carefully guided her up the steps, as though aware that the watching courtiers might carve meaning from a misplaced glance. "All of Sylvancrest owes you a debt for what you endured on our behalf."

Debt? The word surprised her. She had come to save a realm that didn't know her mother's name, yet here was the prince treating her as guest, perhaps ally.

Hospitality can be a noose braided with rose petals.

Vaulted halls opened like the ribs of a great stone beast. Light spilled through high windows set with colored glass, painting the flagstones in ruby and diamond. Servants bowed as they passed beneath banners of green and gold, their silken folds bearing the emblem of Sylvancrest: a great oak, its broad crown of branches adorned with gold, its pale roots flared wide across dark thread, reaching deeper than the eye could follow.

Autumn paused beneath one of the banners, her eyes drawn to the roots. The thread there was finer than the rest, delicate as veins, almost hidden unless one knew to look. A strange pressure gathered behind her ribs, unshaped and unwelcome. She looked away, unsettled.

All around, servants vanished behind carved doors and guards shifted their weight with ease. Somewhere beyond the stone, steel rang against steel in measured rhythm. Rumors stirred in her wake like fallen leaves. Yet it was not the crown that haunted her thoughts as she moved on. It was the roots, and the sense that they had reached for her.

"You will stay in the West Spire," Dorian said, leading her along a gallery where statues of ancient queens stood sentinel. "It overlooks the orchards. Fewer eyes to pry, more quiet to think." His voice lowered. "And to breathe."

"Thank you, Your Highness."

He paused before a carved oaken door. "You will find a meal waiting. Rest if you can; the king and queen will receive you at breakfast. Until then, consider yourself under my protection." A tilt of the head, almost a bow. "If you lack anything, send word. Oh, and call me Dorian."

She saw neither pity nor disdain, only careful sincerity. "You've given me more than I expected already."

"Good day." He turned, cloak whispering against the flagstones, and was gone.

Autumn entered alone. She closed the door and leaned against its cool surface. The chamber was spacious: a canopied bed of dark cherry, hearth laid ready, windows thrown wide to an orchard where apple blossoms stirred in the breeze like pale snow.

So this is the heart of the realm: bright gardens outside, unseen knives within. And she, a bookkeeper from a forgotten town, carried a power neither court nor crown fully grasped.

Autumn's arms now braced upon the stone ledge of her window. A bell tolled the second hour past noon, solemn and deep. She exhaled.

A bumblebee, round and drowsy, found its way through the open pane. It circled her, then hovered just beyond reach. Old habits tugged at her tongue.

"What news have you for me?" she asked softly, as she might have done in Whispering Pines, where creatures had a way of answering back—sometimes with words, sometimes with something deeper.

But the bee offered nothing. No reply, no flicker of knowing in its black eyes. It bobbed in the air a moment longer, then turned toward the orchard, lost to the afternoon sun.

The castle walls, grand though they were, felt colder for it. Here, the old magic fell silent. Here, even bees kept their secrets.

Let me not falter.

She pushed away from the window, squared her shoulders, and crossed to the trunk and undid its buckles with care. Folded linens, a second pair of boots, a satchel of ink and quills. Beneath it all, wrapped in a length of cloth, was the book.

The book that had started it all.

She laid it gently on the table beside the bed. Here, with access to the royal library, perhaps the gaps might finally be filled.

Soon, she thought, *I'll see the library.*

***

Autumn woke with the dawn pressing against the stone walls. Pale light crept across the chamber floor, fingers of gold and gray slipping past the heavy drapes. The bed was softer than any she had ever known. It was so large, she might have vanished into its folds, swallowed whole and granted the kind of peace she feared would never be hers again. Overhead, a painted stag leaped through a sky of midnight blue, crowned in gold, doomed to chase the same scattered stars for all eternity; a Sylvancrest king caught mid-stride, his glory endless and his freedom gone.

Autumn rose from the bed and let her feet find the cold stone. Beyond the window, the gardens spread in careful rows, herbs and flowering trees, paths winding like a serpent's spine toward the distant walls. Everything here obeyed patterns older than memory, held together by rules she barely understood. The apple trees bore fruit in their proper season, as they had for her grandmother, and hers before her. The orchard's sweetness seemed foreign, and though it was lovely, it was almost sharp, a fragrance she did not yet trust.

She told herself to be grateful. Today, she would see the royal library—those vaulted rooms she had conjured so many times in idle daydreams. Knowledge slept in those shadows, waiting for a hand to wake it. She used to believe she might disappear there, slip into other lives, and let her own burdens dissolve among the pages.

She pictured herself wandering beneath chandeliers of crystal and iron, breathing in the scent of old leather and dust, growing drunk on histories of distant realms and queens whose names had been lost to all but the most faithful chroniclers. Books had always been her refuge, the only kingdom where birth held no sway, and a quick mind could make even a forgotten orphan noble.

Autumn had read every book in the library back home. Now she stood ready to lose herself in volumes she had never met, hungry for their stories.

She pressed her palms over her eyes. The promise of the library stirred her heart like wine, but she still longed for the library in Whispering Pines, the familiar dust softening every corner, the quiet broken only by the turn of a page. She missed a life where her silence meant nothing at all. And she missed her dear Papyrus.

Why did I come? The question curled inside her, tight and bitter. Was it hope? Duty? Or because she already knew that running had never changed the end of any story worth telling?

A cautious knock sounded at her door. She sat up, gathering the coverlet to her waist. Before she could grant entry, the door opened, and a young woman slipped inside.

She wore a pale blue gown, her hair the color of ripe wheat, braided with a twist of silver ribbon. Her steps were quiet, more the bearing of a servant than a courtier. There was a wariness to her, as if she were a sparrow urged to settle among hawks.

"Forgive me for intruding, my lady—Miss Ashwood," she began, her voice thin. "I am Lynette. The queen has appointed me to serve as your lady's maid. Only if you wish it, of course."

Autumn fumbled for a reply. "Oh, you're not intruding." The words felt small on her tongue.

If anyone is out of place here, it's me.

Lynette looked down at her shoes, a flush coloring her cheeks. "It is my first real appointment. I am to learn my role, as you are to learn yours. The queen thought we might both be a little out of our depth."

"My role?"

Lynette offered an uncertain smile.

Autumn nodded, not sure if the gesture was encouragement or surrender. Through the window, a bell tolled the hour, a sound unlike the bells of Whispering Pines. It was clearer. Colder.

"I'll need a guide," she said at last. "The castle—" she faltered, searching for words that would not betray how lost she felt. "It's not as easy to map in my head as Whispering Pines."

The young woman's face brightened. "My father serves as the archivist here. I grew up in these halls. I can show you the library and which corridors to avoid if you'd rather not be noticed."

"I would like that very much."

Lynette hesitated, and the next question was almost unwilling. "If I may, my lady, do you mean to stay? Or will you return home?"

Autumn tucked her knees close, watching sunlight carve strange shapes across the floor. "I don't know. I keep thinking I'll wake soon and find none of this was real."

Lynette nodded. "My mother says the library knows more than it tells, but it never lies." She gave a half-curtsy, both formal and uncertain. "Shall we?"

Autumn let Lynette help her into the gown that had been left for her—a deep purple, richer than anything she had ever worn. It reminded her of Iris, that beautiful, free-spirited woman. The sleeves billowed, belled out nearly to her fingertips. She wondered how she would ever manage to sift through books in sleeves made for show, not purpose.

"The seamstress will come by this afternoon," Lynette said, smoothing a wrinkle from the skirt. "She's been gathering materials for your new wardrobe."

Autumn touched the fabric. "A new wardrobe?"

Lynette replied. "If you'd like, I can brush your hair as well."

She ran a hand through her tangled hair, hesitating. "Could I—could I have a bath first?" The thought of it, a small ritual, a piece of home, stirred longing in her.

Lynette shook her head. "Baths are drawn at night, unless there's a special occasion. Only then is it permitted in the morning."

Disappointment curled low in Autumn's belly. Her hand drifted to where her locket should have rested—then stilled, empty. The world felt too large, her place in it far too small.

Lynette then led her through corridors and down ancient staircases. She tried to memorize each turn, but the castle's maze defied reason—one hallway blurred into the next, banners of green and gold flickering at the edge of her vision.

Their silken folds bore the emblem of Sylvancrest: a great oak, its crown of branches stitched in gold, roots flaring wide in pale thread, reaching deeper than sight could follow.

The halls were quiet, and torchlight now danced along the stone, casting the passageways in a soft, wavering gold. She moved in silence, led by a guide whose boots made no sound upon the rugs.

Part of her still drifted in the depths of the feathered bed upstairs, the softest thing she'd ever lain upon, large enough to lose herself in. She hadn't meant to sleep so long, but sleep had taken her just the same.

The doors to the great hall were tall and carved with ancient boughs. Oaks, again, and the ever-reaching roots.

Lynette offered a gentle smile and a promise to return once the meal had ended, then disappeared down the corridor. Heat prickled at Autumn's neck as she stood alone, nerves stirring like embers caught in a sudden draft.

When the doors opened, warmth met her first: the glow of torches, velvet, and the long stretch of green and gold banners that swayed in the morning's breath.

At the far end of the room, beneath a great stained-glass window, sat the King and Queen of Sylvancrest.

King Alden rose first. His crown caught the firelight, simple in design but unmistakably royal. He was a man grown into age with quiet dignity, his hair silvering at the temples, the rest still dark, swept back from a weathered brow. Handsome in an ordinary way, like a farmer whose face had once been sun-kissed but now bore the creases of long seasons and heavier burdens.

There was something honest in his bearing, a steadiness that didn't need to be spoken aloud.

As he stepped forward, the sun struck the edge of his cheek and Autumn thought, just for a breath, that his eyes shone a little too brightly. Tears, perhaps. But if so, he gave no voice to them, and she dared not ask why. Whatever grief lingered there, he carried it in silence, as kings often must.

Beside him stood Queen Seraphina. Her long hair, silver as frost, was braided and pinned in loops that crowned her shoulders like soft armor. The years had not dimmed her beauty. Her cheekbones were still sharp, her eyes like burnished oak behind lashes gone silver. Her crown was finer than the king's, wrought with filigree and emeralds that glinted like deep forest leaves.

Autumn dipped into a curtsy, pulse quickening beneath her ribs. She had crossed mountains and secrets to stand here, and still the weight of their eyes made her feel like a child again, half-formed and far from ready.

"Now that we are all gathered," the queen said, "we may begin."

She descended the marble steps. "Autumn Ashwood, your courage spared Whispering Pines from ruin. The realm owes you more than words."

The queen's perfume, something like cedar after rain, followed her. She paused before Autumn, studying her as though comparing memory to flesh. Then, with surprising gentleness, she brushed Autumn's ginger hair away from her brow. The gesture felt almost...familial.

"Let's take our seats, dear."

The king sat at the table's head, hands folded. The queen sat beside him, straight-backed, her presence filling the space more than the light or the silver. Her expression was stern, but her eyes held a softness that did not quite fit her reputation.

The table stretched almost the width of the chamber, set with gleaming silver and bowls of fruit, flanked by platters of eggs, crisp bacon, pastries stuffed with apple and cinnamon, cherry tarts, biscuits, and steaming pots of tea. The smell was almost enough to make her forget, for a moment, that every eye in the room belonged to someone born to a station she could barely name.

"I trust you slept well?" The king said, inclining his head in greeting.

"Yes, thank you, Your Majesty."

The king offered a quiet smile. "If there is anything you desire, you need only ask."

Autumn thanked him and reached for a cup of tea. Her hands trembled, just a little.

"What are your plans for the day, my dear?" the queen asked.

"I hope to visit the library. I have always wanted to see it."

The king seemed pleased. "You'll find it well worth the time. The library is older than much of the keep. Some say its stones remember every hand that has ever turned a page."

The queen's mouth curled in the faintest smile. "There are smaller libraries scattered throughout the city, if you should wish for solitude. Autumn nodded, uncertain what to say. Their words were generous, but sometimes kindness carried a weight.

"I look forward to seeing it," She managed. "And thank you."

The queen's gaze softened a fraction. "You need not thank us. It is time the castle knew the sound of curious footsteps again."

Autumn sipped her tea. "Where is Prince Dorian this morning?" she asked, looking at the empty chair across the table.

The queen's mouth tightened just slightly. "He is tending to some matters in the lower vaults," she said. "There were disturbances last night—nothing to trouble yourself over. Dorian takes his responsibilities seriously."

Magnus? Weeks ago, his hand found the small of her back, and she felt something shift inside her. Love was too generous a word. Lust was too simple. Desire, perhaps—a yearning as sharp as it was senseless. She told herself she was glad to be rid of him. She wanted to believe it.

Autumn sipped more of her tea, the warmth steadying her hands as she turned to the eggs and bacon. She ate until she was full, but the sight of the pastries: apple, cinnamon, cherry—pulled at her. Callum would have insisted she try them all, and the memory of his laughter coaxed a reluctant smile to her lips. She reached for a pastry, telling herself it was only right to honor old habits, even in a place where nothing else felt familiar.

***

The final bite had been taken, the plates left gleaming and bare. The king patted his full belly with a satisfied sigh, then rose from his seat. The queen followed a moment later. Their movements were almost ceremonial.

Autumn stood then, tucking a loose strand of hair behind her ear. "I am humbled, but I do not yet understand why I was summoned to Sylvancrest City."

"We have searched for you many years," the queen said.

"Searched? Why?"

At last, the king stepped forward with tears he now made no effort to hide.

"Because, child," he said, "you are our granddaughter."

Torches crackled. The grand walls sighed like an old secret finally set free.

Autumn felt the world tilt, memories of orphaned years colliding with this impossible truth. Yet in the king's eyes, she found no deceit, only a plea for belief.

"I... Your granddaughter?" she whispered.

Seraphina's hand came to rest over Autumn's, firm and warm. "By blood and by destiny both."

"Then... My mother was—?"

Queen Seraphina's reply came softly. "Princess Nyssa, our daughter, was your mother." She gathered her composure, though grief flickered in her eyes. "There is a long road of truths between us, child, and we must walk it before this day is done."

Autumn's heart lurched. Blood roared in her ears. She tried to draw breath, to form a question, but the room swam, shadows leaping and shrinking at the edge of her vision. She had spent so many years longing to know where she'd come from, desperate for truth, but the answers, when they finally came, were far heavier than she ever imagined.

Her knees gave out. The last thing she felt was Seraphina's grip tightening on her hand as the world slid away.

EPILOGUE:

THE LAST WATCH BEFORE DAWN

Summer night lay over Whispering Pines like a gentle cloak. The sky stood clear, the moon full and the stars scattered like bright coin on black silk. A mild breeze slipped through the leaves, bearing the forest's breath of night-blooming jasmine.

The town seemed timeless beneath the stars. Its well-worn streets murmured of the years already gone and the mornings yet to come.

Each ivy-clad house held its stories behind shuttered panes, the day's cares folded away till dawn.

Here and there a lamp still glowed, someone reading by the last of the oil, another murmuring goodnight in a quiet room.

Only small lives broke the calm: a rabbit's quick dash over stone, the soft stir of a moth around a lantern, the distant hoot of an owl high in the ancient border oaks.

While the town slept, a thin thread of magic rode the air. The old trees, keepers of secrets older than any house, rustled in low conversation.

From that stillness a small flare of golden light flicked in and out, accompanied by soft, certain footfalls that headed for the square.

A shadow-cloaked creature moved there, graceful enough to leave the peace unbroken. It halted where a statue had once stood tall. The stone figure had fallen during the clash between Magnus and the dragon; only rubble remained. Scaffolding encircled the base, and tools lay in neat rows awaiting morning hands.

Eyes that gleamed faintly in the moonlight regarded the scene in silent tribute. With a slow sweep of its tail, the creature slipped on.

It was a cat, sleek, contemplative, its coat black as wet ink with golden eyes, the color of old parchment. Every step landed without a sound, the tail ticking behind like a measured pendulum.

The cat arrived at the bookstore, bounded up the steps, and grazed the wood with a soft scratch. No answer came. It slid round the side where familiar crates formed a ladder. One silent leap followed another until it reached a window left ajar.

A gentle nudge widened the gap. The cat vanished inside, greeted by the dry perfume of aged pages.

Through dim aisles it padded, weaving past high shelves and battered spines, until a worn burgundy armchair appeared in its corner sanctuary. The cat sprang to the cushion, curled tight, and loosed a quiet, even purr.

Moonlight spilled across its closed eyes, while his steady rumble blended with the bookstore's subtle, ever-present hum, as though the walls themselves recognized an old companion come home to rest.